ed . . .

For Bob and Eleanor

Avenging ANGELS

Mary Stanton

BERKLEY PRIME CRIME, NEW YORK

THE BERKLEY PUBLISHING GROUP
Published by the Penguin Group
Penguin Group (USA) Inc.
375 Hudson Street, New York, New York 10014, USA
Penguin Group (Canada), 90 Eglinton Avenue East, Suite 700, Toronto, Ontario M4P 2Y3, Canada
(a division of Pearson Penguin Canada Inc.)
Penguin Books Ltd., 80 Strand, London WC2R 0RL, England
Penguin Group Ireland, 25 St. Stephen's Green, Dublin 2, Ireland (a division of Penguin Books Ltd.)
Penguin Group (Australia), 250 Camberwell Road, Camberwell, Victoria 3124, Australia
(a division of Pearson Australia Group Pty. Ltd.)
Penguin Books India Pvt. Ltd., 11 Community Centre, Panchsheel Park, New Delhi—110 017, India
Penguin Group (NZ), 67 Apollo Drive, Rosedale, North Shore 0632, New Zealand
(a division of Pearson New Zealand Ltd.)
Penguin Books (South Africa) (Pty.) Ltd., 24 Sturdee Avenue, Rosebank, Johannesburg 2196,
South Africa

Penguin Books Ltd., Registered Offices: 80 Strand, London WC2R 0RL, England

This is a work of fiction. Names, characters, places, and incidents either are the product of the author's imagination or are used fictitiously, and any resemblance to actual persons, living or dead, business establishments, events, or locales is entirely coincidental. The publisher does not have any control over and does not assume any responsibility for author or third-party websites or their content.

AVENGING ANGELS

A Berkley Prime Crime Book / published by arrangement with the author

PRINTING HISTORY
Berkley Prime Crime mass-market edition / February 2010

Copyright © 2010 by Mary Stanton.
Cover illustration by Kimberly Schamber.
Cover design by Rita Frangie.
Interior text design by Laura K. Corless.

ISBN: 978-0-425-23309-2

BERKLEY® PRIME CRIME
Berkley Prime Crime Books are published by The Berkley Publishing Group,
a division of Penguin Group (USA) Inc.,
375 Hudson Street, New York, New York 10014.
BERKLEY® PRIME CRIME and the PRIME CRIME logo are trademarks of Penguin Group (USA) Inc.

PRINTED IN THE UNITED STATES OF AMERICA

10 9 8 7 6 5 4 3 2 1

Cast of Characters

The Winston-Beauforts

Brianna Winston-Beaufort ... attorney at law

Antonia Winston-Beaufort ... Bree's sister, an aspiring actress

Royal Winston-Beaufort ... Bree and Tonia's father, an attorney

Francesca Winston-Beaufort ... Bree and Tonia's mother, a sociable person

Cecilia Carmichael ... Bree's "Aunt Cissy" and Francesca's sister

Franklin Winston-Beaufort ... Bree's great-uncle, deceased

In Savannah

Sam Hunter ... lieutenant, Chatham County Sheriff's Department

Eddie "the Ninja" Chin ... a New York City police detective

Cordelia Eastburn ... the district attorney

Payton McAllister ... attorney, associate at Stubblefield, Marwick LLP

John Stubblefield ... senior partner, Stubblefield, Marwick LLP

Megan Lowry ... a forensic pathologist

Emerald Billingsley ... a secretary

Beaufort & Company

Armand Cianquino . . . chairman
Petru Lucheta . . . Bree's paralegal
Ronald Parchese . . . Bree's secretary
Lavinia Mather . . . Bree's landlady
Gabriel Striker . . . private investigator
Sasha . . . Bree's dog
Miles . . . a guardian
Belli . . . a guardian

Members of the Celestial Court System

Goldstein . . . a recording angel
Beazley . . . an attorney for the Opposition
Caldecott . . . an attorney for the Opposition

Members and Associates of the Savannah Shakespeare Players

Russell O'Rourke . . . former chairman of O'Rourke Investment Bank, deceased
Tully O'Rourke . . . the Players' owner and artistic director and Russell's widow
Russell O'Rourke II ("Fig") . . . Russell and Tully's only son
Danica Billingsley . . . Tully's secretary-companion
Harriet and "Big Buck" Parsall . . . former O'Rourke Investment clients, from Texas
Cullen Jameson . . . former CFO of O'Rourke Investment Bank, currently on parole
Rutger VanHoughton . . . Dutch banker and a backer of the Players
Sir Ciaran Fordham . . . an Australian actor

Lady Barrie Fordham . . . Ciaran's wife and Tully
   O'Rourke's close friend
Anthony Haddad . . . an Egyptian playwright, director
   of the Players
And various stagehands, actors, actresses, and
   supernumeraries

One

Brianna Winston-Beaufort wasn't interested in antiques, particularly, but the desk really was a beautiful old piece. Made of dark, hand-rubbed cherry, it had legs that ended in hand-turned lion's paws. The top was inlaid with fine-grained leather, edged with a hairline of gold leaf. Gold-leaf bees danced in a fanciful design in the desk's center. The auction people had set it on a raised dais, but it was crowded on all sides by the sheer weight of the other stuff due to be auctioned off.

Bree flipped through the auction catalog and found the desk listed on a page all to itself. *(Probable) Empire campaign desk, circa 1789. May have been carried by Napoleon Bonaparte in the Egypt campaign of 1799 .*

An old silver inkstand sat to the right of the golden bees, and a cloisonné jar with a jade lid sat to the left.

"Gorgeous," Antonia said. "I think this is part of the lot that Tully O'Rourke's trying to buy back from her husband's estate." She cocked her head speculatively. "It

1

might even be the desk where he shot himself. Russell O'Rourke, that is."

"Ugh," Bree said. Her sister had a ghoulish side. "So we should make a bid on it when it comes up?"

"Don't be a jerk," Antonia said crossly. "I'm here to . . . well . . . just sort of make contact with the widow."

"No!" Bree said in feigned surprise. "I thought you were here to pick up some inexpensive stuff for your theater group."

Antonia was the stage manager for the Savannah Repertory Theater. It had been her brilliant idea to attend the auction for the ostensible purpose of picking up props for the theater's upcoming winter season. The O'Rourke estate was part of a larger (and much cheaper) sale of various items from the World of Art Auction Mart. Yesterday's sudden announcement that the auction was to be held early Sunday morning had swept through Savannah's gossip mills like brushfire. Bree's aunt Cecilia had called Antonia, Antonia had called Savannah Rep's finance guy and talked him into handing over a modest budget, and here they were.

"You know perfectly well why we're here. Aunt Cissy promised to introduce me if we just happen to run into each other here, and how can I pass up a chance like this? But I'll tell you this! Trying to grab her dead husband's desk out from under her nose isn't going to make the best impression on Tully." Antonia poked fretfully at her hair. "I don't know why you insisted on dragging along with me, anyhow."

"Well, here's a fine thing," Bree said indignantly. "This is the first Sunday I've had off in weeks. I'm only here because you flat-out begged me to come."

"I don't want Tully to think I'm trolling for a job."

"You *are* trolling for a job."

"Hush *up*. Somebody will hear you."

Bree rolled her eyes. She could be jogging along the Savannah River with her dog Sasha. She could be drinking a nice cool glass of white wine at Huey's. She could even be catching up on back copies of the *Law Review*. Instead she was stuck indoors with a couple of hundred gawkers all trying to catch a glimpse of the notorious Tully O'Rourke and maybe grab a piece of the bankrupt estate. And on top of it, she had to put up with the company of her aggravating little sister.

Rumors about Tully O'Rourke had been flying around Savannah for weeks. The widow had recovered both her composure and a pile of insurance money after her late husband's headline-grabbing suicide. The most persistent rumor—and the one most important to Antonia—was that she had decided to bring back the internationally known Shakespeare Players to her hometown of Savannah. But first, Tully was going to recover the contents of her several mansions from the bank that had grabbed them at the conclusion of O'Rourke's bankruptcy.

"And since you did insist on coming along, you might have dressed up a little bit. You've got Sasha's dog hair all over your sweater," Antonia said. "Honestly. Of all the times to look like an unmade bed."

Bree brushed futilely at the golden fuzz spread over her sweatshirt and thought about whacking her sister with the auction catalog. Antonia had changed her outfit three times before they'd set off for the auction house. Then she'd driven Bree to the screaming point about whether to wear her dark red hair up in a topknot or cascading down her back. Then she'd slugged back five cups of coffee, sending her nerves into the stratosphere. She dived into her purse for her mirror and checked her makeup every three minutes. At this point, Bree was beyond affectionate exasperation and into serious annoyance. Her little sister was beautiful, no matter how she wore her hair or what kind of T-shirt she put on, and despite the Bobbi Brown lip gloss smeared over her upper lip. Even someone as used to a celebrity-soaked lifestyle as Tully O'Rourke could see that. And Bree was really tired of telling her so.

Antonia's acting talent was another issue altogether. (Bree loved her sister dearly—but she really wasn't very good on stage.) There was no way to convince Tully of her talent during Aunt Cissy's carefully planned chance meeting, unless Tonia engaged in some highly suspect boasting. So that was Bree's job, should the Great Mrs. O'Rourke actually ask about Antonia's credentials: to brag on her sister. "Just say you're my lawyer," Antonia had said as they set out from their town house on Factor's Walk to the auction house. "Which you would be, actually, if I ever needed one. And when you talk about my reviews in *Oklahoma* it'd be okay if you didn't mention it was a high school thing."

So Bree had spent most of that morning alternating between telling her sister to shut up and threatening to go home.

"You know, Tonia," she said as she bent forward to take a closer look at the cherry desk, "this isn't as much of a waste of time as I thought it'd be. There's some pretty cool stuff here. Just feel this leather. It's like silk." She placed her palm on the desktop and swept her hand past the jar and the inkstand.

Help me!

Bree jumped back, as if burned. The scream was all the more agonizing for being silent.

HELP ME!

The air above the desktop rippled, as if stirred by a witchy hand. Bree took a deep breath and glanced cautiously around. Antonia had drifted on to look at the contents of a glass-fronted cabinet some thirty feet away. Bree caught a glimpse of people clustered at the far end of the narrow aisle that snaked through the clutch of auction stuff. For the moment, though, she was alone.

The eddy of cold air spiraled upward. Bree reached out to touch the desk again. The air thickened to a gray and white soup.

Let me out. Letmeout. LETMEOUT!

A skeletal hand formed in the middle of the gray and white mist and stretched out imploringly. Bree was never quite sure what to do in these circumstances. Should she try to give the ghostly hand her business card? She wished, not for the first time, that her prospective clients had clearer avenues of communication. Barring face-to-corpse conferences, which circumstances didn't allow her to do—a phone call would be nice. E-mail would be even better.

"Mr. O'Rourke?" Bree whispered. Then, feeling an obscure obligation to make certain her client knew how to find her, she said as she placed her card on the desk, "I'm Brianna Winston-Beaufort. I'm an attorney, and I can help you. My staff of angels and I represent dead souls who need to file appeals about their sentencing. Our office is at 666 Angelus Street here in Savannah. Can you tell me what the trouble is?" She thought a moment, remembering Benjamin Skinner. "Or you could call me. The cell number's here, too."

I WANT TO GO HOME!

"Um," Bree said, in a diplomatic way, "that isn't possible, of course. But we can certainly try to get you moved to more comfortable quarters. Can you tell me where you're located right now?" She gritted her teeth. She still wasn't used to this. If it was Mr. O'Rourke—and who else could it be but the dead financier?—he must have a lot on his conscience. He was somewhere in the higher circles of Hell, she would imagine. And it was very hard to hear him. The clarity of her conversations with her clients was directly affected by interference from the Prosecution. The more static, the greater the crime, and the higher the stakes.

"Sir?" Bree said again.

Help me . . . I looked back. I looked back.

The hand clenched into a fist, then rotated suddenly and opened up, palm up, fingers splayed like a beggar pleading for alms.

The black-and-white stutter of light faded away. Bree stood looking at the smooth leather top of the "probable" late eigthteen-nineteenth-century desk of the late Mr. O'Rourke, which held nothing now but the inkstand and the cloisonné jar. She rather liked the jar, which was covered with intricately worked enamel. She didn't like the fact that she had almost nothing to go on except Mr. O'Rourke's agonized desire to go home.

"Bree!" The all-too-human shriek of her little sister startled Bree into awareness. "The auction's starting. We want to get seats up front."

"Mr. O'Rourke?" Bree said again, a little louder. She swept her hand back and forth along the leather top. Her first two cases as an appeals attorney for dead souls had come to her in much this way: a faulty apparition of her client at the site of the client's death, a sighting that resembled film from an old black-and-white movie, and then occasional appearances at the same spot after that. She wondered if she'd have to buy the desk to keep in touch with Mr. O'Rourke. Fake or not, it looked expensive.

Antonia tugged impatiently at her sleeve. "C'mon! Why are you still hanging around this old thing?" She drew her eyebrows together in a frown. "You're not seriously interested in bidding on this desk, are you?"

Bree glanced at the reserve listed in the catalog. Even a (probable) late eighteen-nineteenth-century desk was way out of her price range. On the other hand—if she had a new client—and she was reasonably certain she did—how was she to keep in contact with him if somebody else bought the desk?

"Wait! Of course you have to bid on this desk! You're brilliant!" Antonia grabbed Bree's wrist and pulled her briskly along. "I should have thought of this myself! You buy this desk out from under Mrs. O'Rourke, and then, just as a, like, humanitarian gesture, I present it back to her, on behalf of a grateful public." She shoved her way through the throng of auctiongoers settling into the rows of chairs facing the auction block and sat primly down in the aisle seat in the second row from the front. Bree stepped over Antonia's feet and sat down next to her.

"I don't think I can bid on this desk." Bree showed her the reserve price. "Eight thousand dollars. I'd have to empty my office account to come up with eight thousand dollars."

"You're going to let a small thing like the rent and groceries stand in the way?" Antonia sighed. "And I suppose you think you have some sort of obligation to Ron and Petru. Well, nuts, sister. Just my luck to have a responsible relative."

Bree didn't think Petru, her Russian paralegal, and Ron Parchese, her secretary, relied on paychecks for their temporal existence. She wasn't even sure, apart from their very human appearance when they were with her, that they had a temporal existence at all. As for Lavinia Mather, her landlady, Bree knew for certain that the last time Lavinia required human sustenance was in 1783 when she was sold to the notorious slave owner Burton Melrose. But her Company of angels and its needs wasn't something even her sister knew about. And her immediate problem was what to do about the desk that was the contact point for her newest client.

A burst of singing from the front stage made Bree sit up and take stock of her surroundings. She'd been to auctions before, with her parents, but the auction house here was very different from those near the family's North Carolina home, Plessey. For one thing, the room where the bidding took place was huge, as high as it was long, and stuffed like an Aladdin's cave with ornately carved sofas, tasseled pillows, huge fake ferns, oil paintings in gilt frames, ten-foot-tall mirrors, and a herd of oversized marble statues of Greek goddesses and Egyptian pharaohs. And for another, it was a lot livelier than the auctions Francesca and Royal Winston-Beaufort attended. A group of red-shirted employees formed a line in front of the auctioneer's platform and began a loud, off-key version of "Puttin' on the Ritz" to mild applause. The employees scattered, and one of the auctioneers grabbed a microphone, shouted a welcome, informed the audience that many many *fine* items were here to be auctioned off today, and the bidding on the O'Rourke estate was to begin after an initial round of sales from the many, many *fine* items right up here on the stage. A few of the employees began to circulate with trays of food, juice, tea, and soft drinks. Several more stationed themselves along the rows and chairs and began a rhythmic clapping. The rest of them wheeled platforms of furniture, urns, statues, and boxes onto the stage. Two eight-foot-high stone vases stood to the forefront. Two sturdy guys hefted one up and rotated it around. It was like the first act of *Fiddler on the Roof.*

The lead auctioneer brought the microphone close to his mouth and said in a low, thrilling tone:

"Both of this fine pair of limestone planters are for sale, for one-money, one-money, one-money. Do I hear five hundred and a little bit *more*?"

The auctioneer was generic of his kind, middle-aged, middle-sized, with a bit of a potbelly and a cheerful grin. Like the adult half of the staff at the World of Art Auction Mart, he was dressed like a down-market riverboat gambler: red canvas vest, white shirt, black trousers, and a skinny black tie. The kids that lugged the sale items wore jeans, tennis shoes, and baggy red T-shirts labeled *ONE WORLD* in eight-inch-high iron-on letters.

The verbal cadence was hypnotic. Bree was disoriented by the shouting, the background music, and the bursts of applause from the auctioneer's assistants, meant to jolt the audience into bidding. She sat up a little straighter in the folding chair, to get rid of the feeling she was trapped in a TV game show among people who knew her even though she didn't know them.

"Do I hear four-fifty, four-fifty, four-fifty and a little bit *more*?"

Antonia raised her numbered paddle and called out, "Twenty dollars!" As loud as her sister was—and Antonia had trained with some pretty good coaches in her pursuit of a stage career—nobody noticed until she leaped to her feet and bellowed, "Twenty-*five* dollars," louder than Patti Lupone bellowing "Everything's Comin' Up Roses" in *Gypsy*.

"Thank you very much," said the auctioneer, unflapped at the insult implicit in Antonia's rock-bottom bid. "Do I hear fifty, fifty, fifty and a little bit *more*?"

Antonia stuck her chin out and got down to business. After a spirited exchange of bellows, she nailed the limestone urns for forty-five dollars and settled into her chair with a satisfied grin. "Am I good, or what?"

"Or what," Bree said. "It's because you're louder than God and terrified the poor man into submission. What are you going to do with those urns, anyhow?"

Antonia followed the removal of the urns to the holding area with a watchful eye. "It's for George Bernard Shaw," she said darkly. "Otherwise known as Greatly Boring

Shaw. I told you we're doing *Pygmalion* at the Savannah Rep, didn't I? We were supposed to be doing *My Fair Lady,* right? I would have nailed an audition for the singing Eliza. But no. John Allen Cavendish himself thought we should go back to the original Shaw. So we are. And let me tell you—that old Victorian had a mania for scenes on lawns and terraces. Also a mania for putting anyone under thirty to sleep, which is me, of course, and even you, although just barely." She glowered. "I'll have to kill you if you tell anybody I said that. About Shaw. Not about the fact you're practically thirty. Anyhow, the urns will give the terrace a nice English manor house look even if they were made in China three weeks ago. I'll stuff them full of fake ivy." Suddenly, she clutched her head and groaned. "I've just got to move on from this, Bree. The tech managing part, I mean. I love anything to do with the theater, you know that. But I want to act!"

Bree didn't give her sister a sympathetic pat, although she wanted to. Antonia had spent most of the last week happily memorizing huge chunks of Shavian dialogue for the previous day's audition, and it'd been a bust. She auditioned faithfully for a role in each new production and it looked as if she was going to remain assistant stage manager for quite a while. Unless she could convince Tully O'Rourke she should be part of her newly resurrected Shakespeare Players.

"So," Bree said brightly. "Did you get what you needed? Can we think about bumping into Tully O'Rourke and then going home?"

Antonia rolled her eyes. "Like, hello? Did you hear me mention fake ivy?"

"Right." Bree settled back with a sigh and took a sip of iced tea. The World of Art Auction Mart was still keeping potential bidders happy. Those employees not engaged in clapping and hauling continued to pass around trays of sweet rolls, cold drinks, and fruit salad. The tea was brewed, not powdered, and tasted faintly of lemon, which made it more than palatable, but she hoped the fake ivy was coming up for bid pretty soon so they could get on with the O'Rourke estate.

Up on stage, three burly guys held a brocaded settee over their heads and rotated it in unison so that bidders could see it from all sides. There wasn't a tendril of fake ivy in sight.

Bree drifted into a light doze. She'd settled her last case several days before, but it had required some heavy-duty nights, and she hadn't caught up on her sleep. Beside her, Antonia slumped down in her chair and brooded. She roused when Antonia elbowed her in the side and hissed, "Wake up!"

Bree sat up and suppressed a yawn. "What's the matter?"

"I've been thinking," Antonia said gloomily.

Bree glanced at her. The last time her sister sounded this depressed, she'd gone to work as a pizza delivery person and gained thirteen pounds in three weeks.

Antonia bit her thumbnail and stared unseeingly into the distance. "Maybe I wasn't cut out for the Savannah Rep. Or Tully O'Rourke's Shakespeare company. You're right. Maybe we should just go home and I should go back to delivering pizzas."

Bree set her plastic cup carefully on the floor at her feet. Her sister was volatile—always had been. This self-doubt wasn't new. There was nothing their parents wanted more than to see Antonia settled happily into a secure, rewarding life. The theater was at the bottom of their list, and her mother, especially, would have seen this fit of the glums as an opportunity to get Antonia back into school. Bree herself just wanted to see her sister happy and she didn't think a career of unsuccessful auditions would make anybody happy. If Antonia was serious about giving up the theater, she had to be careful. "You were perfect for the part," Bree said. "John Allen must have been insane to cast somebody else."

"Which part?" Antonia asked skeptically.

"Eliza," Bree said promptly. "And Irene Adler, before that." She waved her arm in a grand gesture. "All of them."

Antonia shook her head. But she smiled.

"You're gorgeous. You're talented. You're superb. But!"

"But?"

"But maybe you want to think about finishing your degree before you commit to the stage full-time." Bree held her hand up. "Just wait. Have you thought about ageism?"

"Ageism?"

"Sure. You know what I think? I think you're a victim of ageism. John Allen Cavendish knows you're twenty-two, and these parts you've been auditioning for are for much older—*Ow!*" Bree rubbed her arm. "I've warned you about pinching. Haven't I warned you about pinching?"

"Look who just walked in!"

"I don't care if it's the pope," Bree said crossly. "Where do you get off pinching me like that?"

"That's Tully O'Rourke! She's here!" Antonia looked

rattled. "Gosh. I didn't actually think she'd show up. And—I don't believe it! Do you see who's with her?!" This time she pinched Bree really hard, just above the elbow. Bree hated being pinched.

"It's Aunt Cissy!"

"Oh?" This was not enough to justify battery, in Bree's opinion. "And my opinion is worth something," she said aloud, "given my law degree and all."

"Hush up." Antonia's fit of depression was gone, melted like snow in July. She quivered with excitement. "Of course Cissy's going to come through for me! She's always smack in the middle of anything that really matters in this town."

Bree left off rubbing her arm—Hell would freeze over before Antonia apologized, and it'd freeze over twice before she promised never to do it again—and turned in her chair and watched Tully O'Rourke pick her way down the aisle to the front row seats.

Like a lot of celebrities, she was smaller in person than on the TV news channels. But she was unmistakable. Her hair had gone completely white in her midtwenties, and it cupped her cheeks in a severe bob in a look that hadn't changed for thirty years. Her eyebrows were dark, her eyes darker, and she wore her signature gold choker close around her throat. She was thin, too, but without the sinewy gym look. She chatted in a languid way to Cecilia Carmichael, who chatted animatedly back. Aunt Cissy, who was blonde, and even thinner than Tully, did look like a gym rat, mainly because she was one. She practically lived at the Athletic Club. She was their mother's

youngest sister and all of the Carmichael charm and soft-
ness had disappeared with Cissy's second husband, who
in turn had disappeared with his much younger secretary
some years ago.

"I just told you that I'm not cut out for the Savannah Rep, didn't I?" Antonia shone in the overstuffed,
overcrowded confines of the warehouse. Her sister was
beautiful—Bree had been truthful about that, if less truthful about her acting talent—and when she was alight with
enthusiasm, she was flat-out gorgeous: blue eyes, auburn
hair, and camellia-petal skin. "What I am cut out for is the
Savannah Shakespeare Players."

"Oh, my," Bree said.

"Even you have to agree it was the best rep theater outside of the Royal Shakespeare Company."

"What do you mean, 'even' me?"

Antonia patted her arm in a kindly way. "You're so
caught up in your cases that I'm amazed you even know
it's November."

Her new career defending the dead *had* been absorb-
ing all of her time lately. This was absolutely true. But
you'd have to be living on the moon not to know about
the Shakespeare Players. Russell O'Rourke and his wife
had been patrons of the usual charities when they lived
in New York—the Met, MoMA, and the New York City
Ballet—but their most famous excursion into the arts
was the subsidy of the Savannah Shakespeare Players.
Under the direction of a very hot, very talented young
Egyptian director named Anthony Haddad, the Players'
productions of *Hamlet*, *Shrew*, and the *Henry*s had gotten

amazing reviews. The Players had collapsed, of course, with the bankruptcy of O'Rourke Investment Bank.

Antonia grabbed Bree's hand. "What was that you just said? About the ageism thing? That I'm too young for those old fogey plays John Allen Cavendish loves to death? Well, whoo-ee, sister, I'm exactly the right age for the kind of plays the Savannah Players are going to stage. Modern. Cutting edge. A marriage of high tech and high drama. Stuff that London and New York have never seen before."

"I thought the Shakespeare Players would put on, well, Shakespeare," Bree said.

"Are you crazy? How old is Juliet? Viola? Portia?"

"Fifteen, twenty-six, and thirty-four," Bree said, who had no idea but was willing to guess.

"Bull," Antonia said inelegantly. "The average life span of a person in Renaissance Europe was twenty-seven. Heck, Bree, I'm practically too old for the parts."

"Well, that's a point."

"I heard she's putting ten million dollars into the Players," Antonia said in an awed undertone. "And I work cheap."

"I wonder where she got the money."

"Her husband was rich."

"Her husband went bankrupt. All the assets of O'Rourke Investment Bank were seized by the feds."

Antonia shrugged. "Insurance?"

"Maybe." Bree wasn't an expert in bankruptcy law, but the feds should have seized the policy along with the furniture.

Bree nudged her sister. "That older guy she's with

looks familiar. I think that's Rutger VanHoughton. Maybe it's his money."

Tully and her entourage had paused at the foot of the auctioneer's stage and turned to survey the audience. She and Cissy were trailed by two men in gray slacks, blue blazers, and cotton shirts and a browbeaten young black woman with the air of a hyperefficient assistant. Bree recognized the taller, older man from coverage in the *Wall Street Journal*. Rutger VanHoughton was Dutch, a banker, and one of the superrich who'd survived the volatilities of the international financial markets. He had white-blond hair, intense blue eyes, and a boxer's body. There was something in the stance of the younger man with him that reminded Bree of Tully herself. She poked Antonia again and whispered, "They had a son, didn't they? The O'Rourkes?"

Antonia shrugged.

"I'm pretty sure they do. Did. Whatever. He's Russell the Second. I think they call him Fig."

"Fig?" Antonia leaned forward a little. "Looks like a spoiled brat."

"Like you can tell," Bree said.

"Actors," Antonia said, "are good at sizing people up instantly. It's part of our craft."

Aunt Cissy caught sight of them and waved wildly. Antonia waved enthusiastically back. Cissy nudged Tully and said something. For a brief moment, Tully's eyes rested on Antonia and Bree. She bent her head sideways and, without directly addressing the young black woman who trailed behind her, spoke briefly.

"Her assistant," Antonia said. "I'm good at sizing up occupations, too."

Bree slouched back in her chair, shoved her feet under the chair in front of her, and sighed. Antonia leaned forward eagerly, her eyes locked on the group as they settled themselves in the front row seats. "So what do you think? I mean, I know her husband went bankrupt and all, but these superrich types are good at squirreling money in the Caymans and places like that. I'll bet she's got the bucks and I'll bet she's going to use them."

"She's raising ten million dollars, from what I heard, not funding the whole thing herself," Bree said in a near whisper. "She hasn't actually said she'd put her own money into the Players. She got whacked by the SEC for lying about her participation in some of her husband's other business schemes, so she's being pretty careful now. I wonder if she thinks Cissy's going to cough up a pile." Like Bree's mother, Cissy had been left a respectable fortune by the grandparents. "But I'll bet you the Dutchman's involved in some way."

VanHoughton's bright blue glance met hers, and he smiled. Then he sat down next to Tully and put his arm casually over the back of her chair.

Tully sat with her straight, tailored back facing them. The auctioneer, with a stiff nod in Tully's direction, signaled the start of bidding again, this time on a huge oil painting of Oglethorpe Square in Old Savannah.

Bree wasn't sure what she should do when the O'Rourke assets came up for bid. She paged through the catalog. The desk was part of a lot that contained almost all of O'Rourke's home office: a fine rosewood credenza, a set of worn leather chairs, a box of odds and ends, and a surprisingly utilitarian gray metal filing cabinet.

The auctioneer disposed of an imitation Louis Quatorze lounge, a ten-foot resin replica of the Sphinx at Giza, and a large silk ficus before he got to the O'Rourke collection. First up was a twenty-six-piece set of Rosenthal china. The reserve was at eight thousand dollars. Tully opened the bidding at five thousand and dropped out at seven. The bidding reached eight and then stalled. The lot went to a quiet, gray-suited man in the last row of seats. The pattern was repeated each time an O'Rourke lot came up for bid. Tully started the bidding, dropped out just before the reserve was reached, and then sat in equable silence as the lot went to the man in the corner.

Antonia nudged her sharply in the side. "What's the matter with you?"

"Nothing," Bree said crossly. "I'm fine. What's the matter with you?"

"You're scowling."

Bree put her hands to her face. "I am?"

"You're scowling and you're muttering under your breath and you look like you're going to jump somebody."

"I'm not going to jump anybody."

Antonia eyed her doubtfully. "You're sure?"

"I'm sure." Bree shook her head impatiently. "I gave all that up, anyway. I told you."

"Thumping people?"

"Yes."

Antonia patted her hand sympathetically. "At least you usually thump people who're in the middle of thumping somebody else." Bree tried not to think about it. She did have a history of letting her temper get the better of her common sense, dating back to Antonia's first day in kindergarten when a fellow sixth grader had smeared playground mud all over her sister's Miss Kitty backpack. In return, Bree had smeared playground mud all over him. At thirteen, she'd coldcocked a shoplifter at Radio Shack who'd pushed over a little old lady on his way out the door. At seventeen, she'd blacked the eye of a guy beating on his seven-year-old son in the plumbing aisle at Home Depot. As a law student dealing with a sexist linebacker in Moot Court—well, everyone in her family preferred not to talk about that. Besides, Bree had paid for all the medical expenses herself, feeling honor-bound not to land the school clinic with the costs of a felony misdemeanor she'd committed voluntarily. Then there was the spectacular tackle of her much-loathed former lover, Payton the Rat—at Huey's restaurant on the River Walk a month ago. The fallout from that particular escapade was so humiliating she'd sworn off losing her temper for the rest of her natural life. "I think she's cheating."

"Who?"

"Tully O'Rourke. She was supposed to come here to retrieve her husband's former possessions, right? Well, she's bidding up to a certain point, and then she drops out. And either that guy"—Bree indicated the gray man in the corner with a sideways movement of her chin—"or that woman over there ends up with whatever's up there."

Antonia half rose in her chair and stared frankly at the woman seated at the opposite end of the room from the man in gray. "Jeez!" Antonia said. "Do you know who that is?"

Bree grabbed her and shoved her back into her seat. "Will you hush up, for heaven's sake?"

"That's Barrie Fordham!"

"Barrie Fordham?" It took Bree a minute, and then the penny dropped. "Ciaran Fordham's wife? Wow." She resisted the temptation to stand up and stare the way Antonia had. Ciaran Fordham was the most famous Shakespearean actor since Laurence Olivier and John Gielgud.

"Oh, my gosh." Antonia gasped, gulped, and went into a coughing fit. Bree pounded her on the back until the coughing subsided and she sat back up in her chair. "Sorry," she whispered, "I just thought of something and I got so excited I swallowed my spit. You don't suppose that Tully O'Rourke is going to get Sir Ciaran Fordham for the Shakespeare Players! Oh. My. God."

Bree shook her head. "You wouldn't think so. But classical theater's fallen on pretty hard times and maybe he needs the money. Ciaran Fordham. Good grief." She'd had a major crush on him since she was twelve years old and saw him in a PBS production about Cleopatra. He'd played Julius Caesar, and Bree hadn't seen anyone that sexy her entire life. He had peculiarly penetrating blue eyes, a tormented brow, and a husky, golden baritone that made music out of a script that forced him to growl lines like, "Cleopatra! My love! My life! Caesar salutes you!" Bree choked back a laugh. "I can't believe it. I'm too intimidated to turn around and look at her now that I know who she is." She paused. "Um . . . *he's* not sitting there with her, is he?"

Antonia looked over her shoulder. "Not a chance." Then, with the insouciance of the true theater professional, she added, "She's a terrific actress in her own right, you know. I saw them in *The Winter's Tale*. She was terrific.

His Leontes wasn't half bad. None of us thought he was anywhere near par, I remember that. But it was awfully soon after his heart attack, so nobody expected too much out of him, but still. He's Ciaran Fordham."

Antonia's theater gossip slid in one ear and out the other. Bree had never really paid attention to Barrie Fordham—she supposed it was actually Lady Fordham, since the great actor had been knighted—but she did now. Fragile. That was the word. The actress was slender, with a ballerina's grace of movement and a mobile, expressive mouth. Her eyes were huge, sunken, and faintly shadowed. She raised her auction paddle, and Bree turned back to the bidding with a start.

The lot containing Russell O'Rourke's desk was up for auction.

Bree nudged her sister. "Give me your paddle."

"What for? You're not going to bid on anyth . . ." Antonia stopped in midsentence, and then her voice rose to a shriek. "You're kidding. You're going to bid on that desk? Why?"

"Will you keep your voice down, please?"

"But, Bree!"

"Hush." Bree grabbed the auction paddle and held it out of reach. She wasn't sure what she was going to do. She doubted she could get the desk for anything close to what she could afford to pay, but she owed her new client an attempt, at least. And besides, she was very interested in how Tully O'Rourke would view the intrusion of a new bidder in the middle of what looked to be a not very expert scam.

She raised the paddle. "One thousand dollars, for the Empire desk and contents."

Barrie Fordham jerked around in her chair and stared at Bree with the wide, startled gaze of a rabbit caught in the headlights. "Seven thousand," she said in her beautifully modulated voice. "Seven thousand dollars. And I'm not going to stop with that."

TWO

La propriete c'est le vol.
(Property is theft.)
—Pierre-Joseph Proudhon,
Qu'est-ce que la Propriete?

"Whatever in the world possessed you to bid on that damn Russell's desk?" Aunt Cissy was a lot shorter than Bree, who was five-nine in flat shoes, and she had to stand on tiptoe to reach her niece's ear.

"I didn't get it," Bree pointed out.

"Well, no, of course you didn't. But Tully ended up paying twenty percent over the reserve for her own furniture. And it isn't even authentic Empire!"

"I thought Barrie Fordham bought that stuff," Bree said. "Or did she?"

"You know very well what I mean, Bree Beaufort."

"It wasn't Tully O'Rourke's furniture," Bree pointed out. "It belonged to the federal government. You're a tax-paying citizen, right?"

"Lord, yes."

"In a sense, Aunt Cissy, then, it was your furniture more than Tully O'Rourke's."

"Don't be absurd."

"Well, there's a little bit of skullduggery going on, don't you think? Mrs. O'Rourke's just purchased all this stuff for a lot less than she should have. And nobody else seems to have had a chance to bid on it at all."

"I hope you're not turning into a little prig, Bree."

Bree thought about this for a second and then made a rueful face. "Ouch. Well, there's little danger of that, with you to remind me, and all. I apologize for sounding like a prig. But not for thinking it's wrong to cheat. And Tully's hardly overpaid for that stuff. The desk is fake, but the credenza that comes with it isn't. The credenza's worth a fair bit."

"Still," Cissy fussed. "Oh, I don't know. This whole thing is just as tacky as can be. And you're just adding another layer to the tackiness, niece."

Bree, half listening, was watching Antonia charm Rutger VanHoughton and Fig O'Rourke. She was also watching Tully O'Rourke watch Antonia charm Mr. VanHoughton and the heir to whatever remained of the O'Rourke fortune. "And that nice cloisonné jar and the inkstand came with the job lot. Those items are worth a fair bit, too. Besides . . ." She glanced sideways at her aunt. "Mrs. O'Rourke made out pretty well on the other stuff, Aunt Cissy. I'm assuming that the successful bidders were putative."

Cissy blinked a little, so Bree clarified. "The gentleman in the gray suit and Lady Fordham were both bidding on behalf of Mrs. O'Rourke, right?"

Cissy pursed her lips and said with some heat, "If Tully's friends want to make up for that absolutely awful time she went through, who's to complain?"

"Well, the auction house, for one, and the federal government, which was expecting to recoup a reasonable amount of the money lost to the O'Rourke bankruptcy, for another." Bree shook her head. "Y'all are skating on some pretty thin ice."

Twenty feet away, Antonia burst into a delightful trill of laughter. Rutger VanHoughton laid a proprietary hand on her arm. Fig, whose features were a watery shadow of his mother's, glared at VanHoughton and laid a hand on Antonia's opposite arm. Tully O'Rourke's pale white skin flushed pink and her eyes narrowed to nasty slits. Bree took an involuntary step forward. "Cissy? We'd better go rescue Antonia."

"Oh, Lord," Cissy said. "I didn't notice. When Tonia puts her mind to vampin', there's not a man in the room that's going to shake loose. Tully's not going to like that at all." She tucked her hand under Bree's elbow and pulled her toward the group clustered at the auction podium.

The O'Rourke estate had been the final items up for bid, and the warehouse had emptied out pretty quickly after the last item had sold. The food and drink had been whisked away and the sold items wheeled out to the loading docks. The only people remaining were Tully and her friends, the head auctioneer, who was looking very unhappy, and a lone cameraman from the local TV station. Cissy approached them with a cheerful "Whoo-ee!" and shoved Bree between Antonia and Rutger VanHoughton, so that the two of them faced Tully O'Rourke and left VanHoughton standing rather awkwardly all by himself.

"This is my other niece, Tully," Cissy said proudly. "This is my sister's oldest girl, Brianna. The best attorney in Savannah, if not the whole state of Georgia. This girl here"—and she shook Bree's arm so energetically Bree lost her balance—"was the one that got that dreadful Chandler child out of trouble just a few days ago. I assume you read about that."

Tully's face showed mild interest. It may have been more than mild interest, but like Cissy, Tully seemed to be a Botox devotee, so it was hard to tell. "Well, I never," she said politely. "I could use a good Georgia lawyer right now. Unless"—she turned to the auctioneer with a consciously charming smile—"you've reconsidered your position, Mr. Finnegan?"

"Bert," Finnegan said. "Y'all call me Bert." He mopped the back of his neck with a large handkerchief. "The thing is, Miz O'Rourke, it's that I've got to account to the feds for the price on all this stuff. And my own bosses, too."

"You made the reserve every time," Tully said. There was an edge to her voice. "And in one case, you made well over the reserve." Her eyes were a deep, almost plum-colored black, and they slid over Bree in cool speculation. "What's your legal opinion, Miss Beaufort?"

"I'm afraid I don't have a clear understanding of the question," Bree said pleasantly. "Not only that, I'm sure your own legal team could provide you with better counsel than I can, at this point."

Tully's coal-black gaze drifted to the man in the gray suit, who, with Barrie Fordham and the oppressed-looking assistant, had somehow segregated the TV cameraman from the main group. Smart move, Bree thought. The last thing Tully O'Rourke needed was more bad press. "You mean Barney? He's headed back to his New York firm on the noon flight. As for Barrie—well, what can I say? I have such wonderful friends." She shook her head in mock wonder. "I had no idea they were going to show up here today to help me get my things back. Besides"—her voice chilled a few degrees—"it isn't as if there were a ton of other bidders." That speculative gaze brushed Bree again. "So I'm afraid I don't quite understand Mr. Finnegan's problem, either, Miss Beaufort."

"We should have cleared fifty k profit on this auction, easy," Finnegan said loudly. "If the right bidders had shown up, we could have made more, maybe."

"Well, Mr. Finnegan," Bree said reluctantly, "speaking strictly as a private citizen and not as counsel to Mrs. O'Rourke, she does seem to have a point. There weren't any other serious bidders."

"Except you," Tully said.

"Except me," Bree agreed.

"There, you see!" Tully squeezed Finnegan's hand.

"This was property of the federal government. They expected to make more than they got, too. It'll be a cold day in Tahiti when they let me handle another government job after this."

"And why should you give a hoorah in hell about some old government busybody?"

"As for the fact that there weren't any other bidders," Finnegan said, with increasing heat, "y'all are right. There weren't any other bidders except you, Miz Beaufort, and that man there in the gray suit, who seems to be a New York lawyer who knows you pretty well, Miz O'Rourke, and that Miz Fordham, who knows you pretty well, too. An auction like this one, we send out special invitations, if you get my drift. To our good customers." He exposed his teeth in a cheerless grin. "Got the invitations printed up at our usual print shop, like always, and you know what?"

Nobody said anything.

"Misprint about the date." Finnegan tapped Bree on the shoulder. "Those special invitations all went out saying the O'Rourke auction was a week from now. So the customers we were counting on are all gonna be here bright and early next Sunday morning, and there's not a thing for any one of them to buy. And you know what else? The second round of notices saying that the auction was this afternoon at two P.M. got changed around to eight in the goddamn morning. Who shows up for an auction at eight o'clock on a Sunday morning?"

"You did," Tully said.

"Yeah, well, word come on down that we had to. I'd sure like to know who you talked to at my headquarters, Miz O'Rourke."

"I'm not sure why you think any of this is my problem," Tully said. "The stuff's sold. I'm not responsible for a screwup at your printer's. My advice to you is to suck it up."

"Right." Finnegan mopped the back of his neck again. "Right. Well. We're looking into it." He nodded to Bree, seemingly unable to meet Tully O'Rourke's triumphant black gaze. "You'll be hearing from us, Miz Beaufort." He turned on his heel and stalked off.

"But I'm not representing Mrs. O'Rourke," Bree called after him.

"Sure you are," Cissy said comfortably. "This is a local problem and you need local representation, Tully. And I can't think of a smarter lawyer than my niece. You just go ahead and write her a check with a nice retainer and she'll take care of that old grouch Finnegan in nothing flat."

"I'm very sorry," Bree said pleasantly. "But I'm not able to take on new clients at the moment. I can offer you a few names, if you're in need of local representation."

"What stuff, Bree," Cissy said. "Tully, talk some sense into my crazy niece."

Tully shrugged. "I could use a friendly face here in Savannah. I'm so excited about starting up the Shakespeare Players again. And there's bound to be all kinds of contracts and such that will crop up. There's the lease of the theater, for one thing, and the contracts for the actors."

"You'd need a specialist in entertainment law for that," Bree said.

"It'll be a wonderful thing for the community," Cissy agreed. "And a marvelous chance for Antonia." She smiled meaningfully at Tully. "You do know that Antonia's a wonderful actress. She's my other favorite niece."

"Absolutely I can arrange an audition," Tully said. Her smile was firmly in place, but her eyes were glacial. "No guarantees, of course. Haddad is a perfect demon about that. Artistic integrity. But the poor thing deserves at least a chance. Now, what do you say to that, Bree?"

No guarantees my foot, Bree thought. She'd sooner have rabies than give Antonia a job. But her sister was glowing like the sun at high noon.

Tully cocked her head and added shrewdly, "I do believe you're in a bit of a state over Mr. Finnegan's little controversy. You realize the man's just after a bigger commission."

Bree's temper stirred, which was not a good thing. Tully's persistence didn't surprise her; she'd met a lot of spoiled rich people in her time, and the best of them hated to be balked. The worst of them believed you could buy anyone, if the price was right, and Tully had that familiar cynical glint to her expression. She would be hell to work for, and worse to represent.

But then there was Antonia, vibrating with hope.

Silently, Bree counted backwards from twenty-five. When she reached eleven, she said, "I can make some recommendations for local counsel, Mrs. O'Rourke."

"As good as you?" Tully switched on her charm as easily as slipping on a pair of shoes. She tucked her arm into Bree's. "Just when Cecelia here is telling me you're the best. I never settle for second best, Miss Beaufort. Never. I tell you what. Cissy, you bring Bree here and her sister on over to my house this afternoon about two o'clock. I'm having a late lunch for some of my friends. Haddad will be there. I'm sure you'd like to meet him."

Antonia's eyes widened.

"And Ciaran, too, of course." She hugged Bree's arm close to her side and said confidingly, "He's promised to become a permanent part of the Savannah Shakespeare Players. Sir Ciaran Fordham. The greatest Shakespearean actor of our day. You're one of the first people to know. So you'll keep it to yourself for the time being, won't you? But it's truly exciting news for Savannah." She stepped back, her expression wistful. "If only my Russ were here to see this. I think you would have been one of the few people who'd really understand my Russell, Bree. If ever a man was unjustly accused, he was. If ever a man deserved better, he did."

Well, she was about to find out about Russell O'Rourke, wasn't she? That—and if Tully O'Rourke was the kind of person who had driven a man to suicide, and to a place in the circles of Hell.

Three

Just a little touch of star quality.
—Tim Rice, "Buenos Aires," *Evita*

"How do I look?" Antonia tugged nervously at her black bustier. She'd been so nervous at the thought of meeting Ciaran Fordham and Anthony Haddad at the same party that she'd only changed once, into an outfit that had brought her luck at three auditions: black leather pants, black bustier, and a pair of long gold mesh earrings that tangled in her red hair when she tossed her head.

"Fabulous," Bree said absently. She parallel parked her little Ford Fiesta into a place not much larger than the length of a shopping cart, in front of a row of clapboard-sided town houses, all painted white. Oglethorpe Square was less than a quarter mile from their town house overlooking the Savannah River, but Antonia had gotten shrill about sweat, so she'd reluctantly agreed to drive. St. James Episcopal Church towered over them at the east end of the square, the carillon clanging out "Abide with Me" at the cadence of a funeral march. A mid-nineteenth-century Carpenter Gothic mansion, painted pink, sat elegantly opposite the church. It had been a restaurant for the past fifty years, named, with a kind of direct and unambiguous naïveté, the Pink House. A clutch of churchgoers came down the steps of the restaurant, looking well fed and contented with the cool and sunny November afternoon.

"You couldn't find anywhere closer to park?" Antonia tugged at her strap.

"We're lucky to find this one! The O'Rourke house is, like, three hundred yards across the middle of the square," Bree said. "And you won't get sweaty if we just sort of stroll along like we're enjoying the gardens on a nice autumn afternoon."

"Stroll," Antonia said. "Right."

When James Oglethorpe founded Savannah, he'd created the bones of an enduring beauty. Twenty-four squares formed the heart of Historic Savannah. And each was anchored by a garden in which flowering bushes, trees, statues, fountains, and benches offered a pleasing refuge to passersby. Oglethorpe had seen a community—not just a city—and he'd mandated that a church, a government building, and fine homes surround each of the squares. Through three hundred years of Revolutionary War, pirates, slave auctions, Civil War, and fires, storms, and tornadoes, the bones of the city endured. Most of the original Georgian homes were replaced by succeeding generations of Federal, Colonial Revival, Country French, and Southern Plantation. With each addition, the beauty of the city grew.

The O'Rourke mansion—one of five houses owned by the couple in more successful days—was a brick Queen Anne, set well back from the one-lane road that ran around the square. The gardens were lush—and carefully landscaped—showcasing late autumn flowering shrubs and plants. Milk-soft camellias shouldered against the blush and lime of flowering hellebore. The orange-yellow honeysuckle poked brave blooms against the November chill. The most direct route was through the gardens in the middle of the square. Bree locked the car and headed across, Antonia trailing behind.

"We're strolling, right?"

Bree caught two dark, familiar shapes out of the corner of her eye and slowed down. Antonia bumped into her.

"You're not strolling. You're ambling." She shoved Bree forward. "And now you're not even ambling."

Miles and Belli sat at the foot of the bronze statue of a forgotten Civil War general. The guardian dogs had vanished at the end of Bree's last case, and here they were, back again. They were huge, fifty-two inches at the shoulder, and so black that they seemed like a hole in the universe as they sat there. Belli's fierce yellow eyes brightened as she caught sight of Bree. She rose to her haunches and stood, ears upright, her short, stubby mastiff's tail wagging back and forth to the doleful chime of "Abide with Me."

"You seriously don't want to meet Ciaran Fordham, right? That's why you're standing there like a booby?" Antonia plowed on straight ahead. She hadn't said a word when Miles and Belli had disappeared, and she walked on past them now. As if she didn't see them. Just like all the other people walking through the square. None of them behaved as if the dogs existed. And surely, the sight of two massive canines would have pulled people up short.

Bree sighed. She didn't know what the dogs meant, or why they were here. But she was pretty sure they hadn't shown up to play a game of fetch.

"Tonia!" she said suddenly.

"What?"

"Look who's back." Bree nodded toward the dogs.

"Oh, my God," Tonia said. She stopped and threw her hands in the air. "General Sherman! Good to see you, buddy."

This was Antonia's idea of humor. General Sherman was the last person Savannah would erect a statute to. Bree still didn't know if she saw Miles and Belli or not.

"That's all you see?" Bree said carefully.

Her sister stared at her. "What do you mean? There's a forty-foot bronze statue in the middle of the park. It's pretty hard to miss. Glad he's back—although I have to say"—her voice dripped with sarcasm—"I hadn't noticed that he was gone. Now, will you come on? We're going to be late."

Bree nodded. She walked past the dogs and they wheeled and fell in step behind her. When the four of them reached the white-painted fence that surrounded the O'Rourke house, the dogs melted into the shade and settled beneath the pair of mullioned windows overlooking the square. As she mounted the brick steps to the oak front door, she could feel Belli's level gaze on her back.

The dominant color inside Tully's house was lemon. The front door entered into a square foyer, a long sweep of staircase leading up to the second floor, and huge parlors off to the left and the right. A twenty-four-foot dining room table ran the length of the parlor on the right.

Expensive yellow velvet drapes hung at the windows facing the square. Egyptian artifacts hung on the yellow-painted walls. The table was loaded with an elaborate English-style tea. Tiered servers held sandwiches, cakes, buns, and a variety of amuse-bouches cupped in pastry shells. A lowboy set against the back wall held crystal decanters of Scotch, bourbon, and what had to be either gin or vodka.

The living room on the left was just as large. It held a grand piano, more velvet drapes, and a quantity of chairs and love seats in lemon-patterned chintz, arranged to accommodate conversation. The very back of the room had a double set of French doors that led to an exquisite garden.

People moved edgily back and forth across the foyer carrying glasses and plates. A young guy in black pants and a white shirt circulated with a tray of filled wine-glasses. Somebody was playing the piano. Mozart, Bree guessed, but she couldn't identify the piece.

"Cooee! Girls! Over here!" Cissy stood near the piano and waved at them. Antonia grabbed Bree's arm. "Ssst! There he is! Right next to Aunt Cissy."

Bree didn't need to ask who. Ciaran Fordham leaned against the wall, a drink in his hand, a look of polite attention on his face. Bree hadn't met many celebrities in her life, and she was surprised (and a little embarrassed) at the wave of excitement that hit her. A small dark man with expressive hands was talking to him.

Antonia poked her in the back. "You go first."

"Sure."

Antonia poked her again. "Are you going?"

"I'm going."

Aunt Cissy met them with an enthusiastic kiss, although they'd parted less than a few hours before. "Sir Ciaran," she said. "I'd like to introduce you to my nieces. Brianna Winston-Beaufort and her sister, Antonia."

"Miss Beaufort, Antonia." Ciaran's hand was cool, dry, and curiously light. There'd been a lot of media comment about Ciaran Fordham's looks. He wasn't conventionally handsome. His nose jutted out at an aggressive angle and was too big for his face. His jaw was massive. His face was broad, with flat cheekbones that gave him the look of a latter-day Genghis Khan. But his eyes were beautiful— a clear, brilliant blue almost too bright to look into. His shoulders were wide, his chest broad, and his posture that of a king or a cardinal.

"Your New York *Hamlet*!" Antonia gurgled. "Definitive! Brilliant! Brilliant."

Bree moved sideways, stepped lightly on Antonia's foot, and moved back.

"Yes," Antonia gasped. "Well. I'm burbling. Sorry. Um."

Ciaran's voice was dry, and a little bored, with only an echo of the famous organlike baritone tones. "It was Haddad's *Hamlet*, to be precise. Ladies? This is Tony Haddad. He directs."

"Directs!" Antonia shrieked. "That's like saying Pavarotti sang! I—Ow!" She reached down suddenly, rubbed her left foot, and glared at Bree.

"I'm glad to meet you, Mr. Haddad," Bree said. She found herself really liking the looks of the guy. He was slim and elegantly dressed in a dark navy shirt and beautifully cut gray trousers. He was also flat-out gorgeous. He smiled at her. "Now here's a bright spot in this dreary afternoon." He touched her hair gently. "I do beg your pardon," he said. "But that silver-blonde color is very rare. And very lovely."

"Thank you," Bree said. "And for the record, I thought the New York *Hamlet* was brilliant, too."

His eyebrows quirked upward. "Hm. And what particularly did you like about it? There was some controversy about our interpretation of Hamlet's affection for Laertes."

"The sword fights," Bree said promptly. "I'm not big on Shakespeare, as such, but I do love a good sword fight." She waited a few beats and said innocently, "Um. There are sword fights in *Hamlet*, right?"

His hand brushed hers. "Sword fights are a specialty of mine."

I'll just bet they are, Bree thought. She had the oddest feeling—that she was suddenly wide awake.

"Oh, my. We're being summoned," Cissy said. "Tully's just come in." She pulled Antonia gently, but firmly, a small distance away from the group and tilted her head questioningly at Bree. "Gentlemen, I know y'all will understand if I drag my two girls here over to say howdy to Tully. She asked Bree here specially to talk about signing her on to handle some contracts, and there she is, beckoning us on over."

"So we may meet again?" Haddad leaned a little closer and she caught his scent: spicy and warm.

Haddad's smile, Bree decided, ought to be registered as a lethal weapon. "We just might," she said.

Cissy propelled the two of them through the crowd and hissed into Bree's ear, "You were flirting with that man, Bree Beaufort."

"I would have been, if you hadn't dragged me off."

"Well, I'm glad to see it. These past few weeks you've been in Savannah, I thought you'd given up on life altogether." Then at full voice: "Well, now, Tully. Here they are."

"I see you've been talking to my favorite Egyptian," Tully said smoothly. She'd exchanged the blazer and slacks she'd worn at the auction for a deceptively simple-looking dress. It was gray, belted at the waist, and flowed around her like a soft wind. "He's agreed to sign on for another year as director of the Players." Something like triumph flickered in her eyes. "And Ciaran, too, of course. We confirmed that as of this morning. But look at this. You don't have anything to drink. Antonia, get your sister a glass of wine. Or a julep? No? Take your time about it, please. And Cissy, go with her. Bree? Come with me."

Her aunt and her sister trotted off obediently. Bree thought about throwing a Nazi salute, but didn't.

"We're over here." Tully sailed briskly through the crowd, like an arrogant sailboat on the Savannah River. And I, Bree thought irritably, am the little rubber dinghy bumping behind. They walked across the foyer and then straight down the hallway leading to the back of the house. "Kitchen's straight ahead," Tully said with a jerk of her thumb. "And I asked Fig and Danica to meet us in here." She opened a mahogany door set in the wall a few feet in front of the foyer leading to the kitchen and stepped aside. "Go in. Both of them will be there. I'll be back in a moment. I need to speak to the kitchen."

"And speak to the kitchen she will," Fig O'Rourke said. "Was she carrying a cleaver?"

"Nope," Bree said. "Just an attitude."

"Heads will roll anyway." Fig got to his feet, reluctantly. "Come in and sit down."

Somebody had banned the color lemon from this room, and Bree was glad of it. It was an ordinary, rather undistinguished home office. A set of barrister bookshelves sat under the windows on the far wall. A small round table with two chairs was tucked into one corner, and a leather recliner and reading lamp sat on the opposite side. Fig O'Rourke sat back down in the recliner. The quiet black woman Bree had seen at the auction sat at the table, an open briefcase on her lap.

The middle of the room was empty. A very good Turkish carpet covered the floor. From the four indentations at the corner of the rug, Bree could tell a large desk or table had sat there.

"Father's desk was supposed to be here already," Fig said. "I guess Mother Dear went to shriek at whoever screwed up."

Bree didn't believe that people's looks reflected their character, or at least, she didn't believe in prejudging character based on the shape of, for example, somebody's mouth. (Fig's was sulky.) Or eyes. (Fig's were the color of muddy coffee—and he squinted at people in a very supercilious way.) Or even fingernails. (Fig's were bitten to the quick.) But she did wonder how well the quick-tempered, intolerant Tully got along with her only son. She already had a good idea of how well Fig got along with Tully.

"It'll be odd to have it back," Danica said from her chair in the corner.

"How do you do, Ms. Billingsley?" Bree said quickly. "I do beg your pardon. I'm Brianna Beaufort. I saw you at the auction this morning, but we haven't really met, have we?"

"And I'm Mrs. O'Rourke's executive assistant, as you seem to have figured out already. Won't you come and sit down?"

Bree crossed the rug and they shook hands. Danica's handshake was firm, her hand warm, and Bree sensed a nice, rather solid composure behind her reserve. "Have you been with Tully long?"

"Three years. I graduated from Moorhouse with a degree in accounting and a lot of student loans. I was on my way to become a CPA, but money got pretty tight. And the job market hasn't been all that hot, so when my mamma got me this chance with Mrs. O'Rourke, I took it. My mamma," she added, "works in the kitchen back there where Mrs. O'Rourke went to pound some heads."

"Is she pretty fair? As fair as employers go?" Bree liked—and respected—Danica's slight hesitation. "I only ask because I offered to refer her to local counsel. Some of my friends are sturdier than others. And it looks as though a sturdy advocate will serve her better than a namby-pamby one."

"Not work for the great Tully O'Rourke?" Fig said. He clutched his chest dramatically. "I thought you were here to take the job."

"You could do worse," Danica said. "I can't say fairer than that." She glanced at her watch. "She ought to be back soon. I'm sure the desk is here—it's just a matter of finding out where they put it."

"My father," Fig interrupted loudly, "killed himself at that desk."

Bree and Danica looked at each other.

"Now, Fig," Danica said.

"I told her we ought to burn the damn thing. And bury the ashes with Father. Not have it here in the house."

"I should think it would be very odd to have it back," Bree said. She hesitated and then sat down across the small table from Danica.

"Well, *Mother*"—the venom in those words would have slaughtered a cockroach or two—"insisted on getting the damn thing back. Can't think why."

"Of course you know why," Danica said gently. She glanced at Bree then away again. "I don't normally betray confidences, Miss Beaufort . . ."

"Bree, if you would."

"Bree, then. But Mrs. O'Rourke will tell you herself, at some point. And if you are going to represent some of the family's concerns, it's as well to know about this ahead of time."

Bree folded her hands on the table and looked expectant. One of the things she'd learned early in her practice was the value of an encouraging silence.

"She thinks he'll come back," Fig said. He sniffed. More of a snuffle than a sniff, as if his nose were clogged.

Whoa, Bree thought. "I'm not sure I understand what you just said."

Using both heels, Fig extended the footrest of the recliner with a thump, then stretched out and locked his hands behind his head. "Father shot himself in front of her. She's got some hairball idea that if she sits there, like he used to do, and works there, like he used to do, he'll come back and tell her what happened. She thinks he was murdered. And that he'll tell her who murdered him. Have you ever heard of anything so goddamn stupid?"

"I don't think it's so stupid," Bree said.

"It's grief," Danica said. "Grief and guilt. I mean, yes, things looked very bad from the outside. If you were reading the newspapers at the time, and believed all the misinformation out there, Mr. O'Rourke's suicide made sense. If suicide ever makes sense." She made a vague gesture toward the contents of her briefcase. "But Mr. VanHoughton had come up with some outside financing that very afternoon. It wasn't going to put everything right, not by a long shot. But it was going to go a fair ways toward rescuing part of the business. And Mr. O'Rourke was a hard man to keep down."

"Murder?" Bree said. "Tully thinks her husband was murdered?"

"And she's pretty sure who did it," Fig shouted. He seemed unable to keep his voice at a normal level.

"She is?"

"Ever heard of a guy named Cullen Jameson?"

The name rang a faint bell. Then Bree said, slowly, "Yes. Wasn't he O'Rourke Investment's CFO? And isn't he . . . ?"

"In the slam," Fig said in satisfaction. "Serving five years for securities fraud."

"And your mother thinks he arranged for the murder of your father?"

46

"It was either Cullen or those stinking Parsalls, Fig." Tully swept into the room and propped the office door open. "Out of the way, Fig. The desk has been here for a couple of hours, for God's sake, and those idiots in the kitchen just let it sit there in the backyard."

Bree heard the shuffle-thump of a large object being moved along the carpeted hallway. The desk was propped upright on a dolly, wrapped in protective burlap. Two of Tully's household staff maneuvered through the door and positioned it in the center of the rug. They removed the cloth and wheeled the dolly away, closing the door behind them.

"Well," Tully said.

The desk dominated the small confines of the room. Tully ran her hands over the leather surface. Bree found herself wondering if there had been any blood.

"You'll have to move those barrister bookshelves if you want the credenza in here, too," Fig said. He slung himself out of the recliner and motioned Danica out of her chair. He placed it behind the desk and, with an exaggerated bow, indicated that his mother should sit.

Tully sat down carefully, arranging her skirts with precision. For a moment, she looked uncertain, and then she slowly raised both hands and held them level. "Russell!" she said, with a familiar kind of authority that gave a little more insight into the nature of her marriage. Then, in a more intimate, questioning tone: "Russell?"

Bree realized she was holding her breath. Maybe. Maybe. Maybe a miracle would happen, and she wouldn't be the only person visited by the dead. And she was amazed at Tully, who seemed to have no inhibitions at all.

"Give it up, Mother," Fig said.

Tully laid her hands flat on the table. Outside the half-open window, the church bells sounded again. "Amazing Grace" this time, but still at the funereal pace.

A sharp knock at the door made them all jump. Barrie Fordham opened it slightly and looked around. "There you are," she said. "And for God's sake, Tully. What do you think you're doing?" She was wearing what she'd worn at the auction: a long, flowing skirt with a simple tee. Her sandals were dusty, and her brown hair floated around her face like soft fog. She was carrying the cloisonné pot and the inkstand and she waved them in a kind of salute before she set them down. "The credenza's here, too. But you're going to have to move those books . . ."

"I know, I know," Tully said crossly. "And you're not needed in here, Barrie. This is a business meeting. Go back to *your* husband." She gave a sharp, nasty twist to the words. Bree felt her scalp prickle.

"Didn't mean to intrude," Barrie said mildly. "Just wanted you to know there's two huge dogs in your garden. Big, mean-looking ones. You know how Ciaran is about dogs."

"Well, chase them off, then!"

"I think your houseman called animal control."

"Actually," Bree began, "I think that's my fault."

Tully raised her eyebrows in supercilious inquiry, and suddenly Bree was seized with irritation. What was she doing here? What were the damn guardian dogs doing here? Why was she in the middle of all this craziness and not somewhere else? The feeling passed her by as quickly as it had come, and she said, "Actually, they belong to me.

48

In a way. I'm taking care of them for a friend. I'll come out and take them on home." She got up and set her purse on the desk.

"It seems very odd that you would have brought them here." Tully's voice was cold.

"Yes. I apologize." Then with more confidence than she felt: "They're quite well trained and wouldn't hurt a soul. I apologize again if they scared anyone."

"They aren't doing anything," Barrie said with a reassuring smile. "But my poor Ciaran is terribly allergic. And anything that affects his voice is just *fatal*. And it's even little dogs. We had the most darling little poodle that we had to get rid of. It came on," she added wistfully, "rather late in life."

"I understand completely," Bree said, although the image of the great Ciaran Fordham sneezing his head off was somewhat at odds with his aristocratic composure, and made her want to laugh. "I'll take care of it right now."

"And you should really come out and see to your guests, Tully," Barrie said. She had a remarkable voice, Bree thought. Light and rather bell-like, but very clear, so that the words carried easily on the air.

"All right, we'll all go." Tully stood up. If she was disappointed at her failure to raise her husband's ghost, it didn't show. Barrie was the first to leave, then Fig, then Danica. Bree followed Tully halfway out the door, then said, "Sorry, forgot my purse," and slipped back inside. She walked over to the desk, reached for her purse, and felt the cold, cold swirl of a fetid wind.

Help me, the voice cried. *Help me! I want to go home.*

Damn, Bree thought. So he is there, after all.

"Bree!" Tully's voice from the hall was sharp and imperative. "You are going to take care of those dogs, aren't you?"

"I'll be right there." Bree slung her purse over her arm. The faint outlines of the desperate hand faded into nothing.

"Damn it all," she said to the empty air. "Can't I get just a little bit of time off?"

Four

Bree made her excuses, turned down an invitation for drinks with Anthony Haddad, apologized again for the dogs, and left Antonia at the party. Miles and Belli sat where she had left them, underneath the mullioned windows on the north side of the house. She realized, as she stood on the brick pathway and waited for them to accompany her home, that the windows were those of the office where Russell O'Rourke's hand—and presumably, the rest of him—waited to snatch at her peace of mind.

Belli took up her position at Bree's right, Miles at her left. "I suppose," she said aloud as she turned to walk back to her town house, "that I should thank you for saving my bacon a few days ago. And Sasha's, too." Her last case had featured a spectacular spray of bullets. Belli's intervention had been quite welcome.

No response. Not a twitch of an ear or a brief wag of a tail, much less a mental message of the Sasha kind. (Most of the time, she knew what her own dog was thinking, or thought she did, which amounted to the same thing.) She didn't have a clue about these two. They just paced along six feet to the rear, golden eyes watchful, the "tick" of their claws a faint distraction in the silence, a pair of animated Fu dogs.

"There's a good fifty pounds of that Iams dog kibble left," she said over her shoulder. She looked both ways across Broughton before she crossed to the park. The street was empty, almost eerily so. All the churchgoers had gone home, and the carillon itself was still. A cold wind swept up from the river, and she shivered a little, wishing she'd thought to bring a light jacket. November weather in Savannah could be tricky. "So at least you'll have something for dinner. I suppose you're both going to stick around. No way I could persuade you to go some-where else? I can't be the only person on the planet you've been sent to guard."

She wasn't, was she? The only person cursed with this awful responsibility.

"Oh, there are others, of course," said a voice at her elbow.

Bree wasn't of a nervous disposition, but she jumped. She stopped and turned around. "Oh, bloody hell," she said. "You two."

"Beazley," said the taller one.

"And Caldecott." He ducked his head in expressionless acknowledgment.

"As if I needed reminding."

Bree looked at the two attorneys for the Opposition with barely concealed distaste. Beazley was tall, and, at a distance, looked like an out-of-shape accountant, or maybe a seedy banker. Until you saw the vertical slits of his pupils. And if you ignored the furnace yellow of his eyes. Caldecott reminded Bree of her shop teacher in high school—slightly potbellied with thick, horn-rimmed glasses. But her shop teacher's fingernails weren't long, pointed talons rimmed with a dark red crusted substance that didn't bear thinking about. They both smelled like burned matches. And both of them hovered several inches off the pavement. Caldecott, prone to sudden fits of fatigue, had a tendency to sit down in midair.

"So what's up?" She glanced back at Miles and Belli. They sat on their haunches, looking bored. She swept her gaze around the square. Still empty, although on York, the next street over, traffic moved at a normal pace.

"Our visit . . ." said Beazley.

"A matter of professional courtesy," said Caldecott.

"And not to be in any way construed as an attempt at undue influence." Beazley grinned, showing pointed teeth stained a repellent brown.

Bree waited them out.

"This latest case of yours . . ." Beazley shook his head.

"Such as it is . . ." Caldecott muttered.

"There have been threats," Beazley concluded with the air of someone disposing of an unpleasant obligation. "Significant threats."

"And you two—with my best welfare at heart, I'm sure—are taking this opportunity to save me from myself? 'Drop the case and no harm will come to you.' That sort of thing?"

Caldecott looked offended. "Not at all."

"We couldn't guarantee no harm would come to you."

"We're in the business of doing harm, so to speak." Caldecott reflected a moment. Then, in a pleased way: "As much as possible."

"So why the concern for my welfare?"

"Oh, we're not at all concerned for your welfare," Beazley assured her. "Your immortal soul—now, that's a different matter altogether. We would very much like to get our hands on *that*. No, no, this is procedural. We caught wind of an intent . . ."

"A stirring," Caldecott mused.

"Regarding a party none of us have heard from for some time."

"Millennia," Caldecott said.

"Not that long, surely," Beazley said. "But it's old, very old. At any rate." His head rotated on his shoulders and he looked at the two dogs. "You'd be advised to keep those two near . . ."

"And your guard up . . ." Caldecott whispered.

"And stay out of the Pendergasts' way."

"He's made a bad bargain . . ."

"A terrible bargain . . ."

Beazley bent close. His breath smelled like a cesspool. "Even for a soul already condemned without hope of redemption of any kind . . ."

They were gone.

The wind picked up and a frigid blast of air nearly knocked her off her feet. Belli pressed close to her side. She buried her hand in the dog's thick ruff and walked on home. "Intimidation," she said several minutes later, when

she let herself in through the kitchen door. "Phooey."
Then: "The Pendergasts again! Double phooey."

But she threw the dead bolt, just the same, and sat down
on the couch to think.

Antonia snapped on the overhead light, flooding the town
house living room with a sudden glare. Bree shaded her
eyes with her hand and said crossly, "For Pete's sake,
Antonia."

"Why are you sitting here in the dark?" Antonia
dropped onto the opposite end of the couch and swung
one leg over the armrest. "I didn't wake you up, did I?"

"No."

"Well, what have you been doing here in the dark?" She
was fretful. She'd planned to leave the party at five, to go on
to handle the Sunday evening show at the Rep, and Bree assumed she'd done just that. "You got something to eat, didn't
you? You haven't been sacked out here for six hours!"

Had she? Maybe she had. Bree dropped her hands in
her lap. "Thinking about my new client."

"That is so *awesome*, that you're going to represent
Tully O'Rourke."

Bree didn't say anything. She hadn't been thinking
about Tully O'Rourke. She'd been thinking about Russell's skeletal hand clutching at her from the depths of
God-knew-where. Hell, probably, given what the media
said about him, and as close to the core of the Dark Sphere
as it was possible to be. Her appeals cases came from all
nine circles of the afterlife; those condemned to the pe-
riphery paid penance for lesser sins in milder ways. Surely

greed, fraud, and outright theft carried grave and terrible punishments. Although, come to think of it, lying to the SEC had been the only provable charge. His death had stalled further investigations.

But the pitiable desperation in those fragile, shadowy bones had pulled at her as surely as chains. And that led to turning over the hundreds of questions she had about her law practice, about the exact nature of her inheritance from her great-uncle. Then there was the unsettling visit from opposing counsel; her difficulty sleeping; the recurring dreams, at night, of death and worse.

With a faint brush of unease, she realized she *had* been sitting here in the dark for six hours.

She got up and walked restlessly to the fireplace. The family town house had been built before the Civil War, when the Savannah River had been a busy port channeling cotton across the Atlantic to Europe and hemp to the mills up North. The lower half of the building had been offices for the warehouses on each side, with living quarters up top, at the street level of Factor's Walk. Winston-Beauforts had always lived here, since 1813, warming themselves at this same fireplace. The bricks, the mantel, the wrought-iron grate of this fireplace had endured through a lot of family history. Bree ran her thumb along the pine mantel and looked into the depths of the elaborately carved mirror that hung above it.

Shadows moved there. She reached up and laid her hands flat against the cold surface. It seemed to pulse, faintly, under her palm, as if it breathed.

Antonia's voice cut into her thoughts. "I said, where's Sasha?"

Bree brought herself back to the present with an effort and turned around. "Sorry. He's curled up asleep right over there."

"No, he's not."

"He most certainly is," Bree said. "Right by the rocking chair."

"Where?" Antonia leaned forward, hands on her knees, and then said, "Oh." Her voice dropped a few decibels. "That's funny. I could have sworn . . ." She rubbed her face with both hands and shook her head violently. "I swear I'm going nuts. He was there all the time? Sasha? Sash?" She patted the sofa. Sasha got up and ambled over to her. He put his head on her lap and sighed as she rubbed his ears. A handsome golden retriever/mastiff mix, he was the only canine member of Beaufort & Company.

"Honestly, Tonia." But Bree looked at her dog reprovingly. He rumbled a little—which she took for an apology. There were times when you could actually see Sasha, and times when you couldn't. It was all part of her Company's way of operating in the temporal world. Generally speaking, Petru, Lavinia, Ron, and even the imperious and irritating Gabriel Striker made the effort to keep an unobtrusive profile. Sometimes they slipped up and the people around Bree asked uncomfortable questions.

Antonia set her jaw in a determined way. "Sit down, Bree. I want to talk to you."

Bree raised one eyebrow. "You sound exactly like Daddy when he wants to have a Serious Talk. Do you want to have a Serious Talk?"

"Don't get lippy with me, Bree. Not now."

Antonia was six years younger. From the time Francesca had brought her little sister home from the hospital, Bree had brushed her hair, read her bedtime stories, and watched over her on the playground. As time went on, she kept an eye on the dozens of dazzled teenage boys that trailed after her sister in high school like hounds after a particularly delectable fox. She'd thrown herself into the breach when their parents went ballistic over her sister's merry distaste for college and took her in when she left home to chase after life on the stage. Not once, in all that time, had Antonia reared up and tried to come over the parent with her. Until now.

"Okay," Bree said, amused.

"And if you keep on smirking at me, I'll pull your hair so hard your scalp'll be pink for a week."

Bree tucked her hair behind her ears. It was long, silver-blonde, and, as Anthony Haddad had seemed to figure out, her one vanity. She wore it in a coronet of braids to keep it out of the way when she was at work, but she hadn't bothered with that this weekend. It fell freely down her back, almost to her waist. "Got it." Then, since her sister looked both worried and cross, she added a real apology. "Sorry. It's usually me talking to you like a Dutch uncle. Not the other way around."

"Yeah. Well. Get used to it. I mean, we're here to take care of each other, right?"

"Right. Sisters forever."

"Right." Antonia took a deep, nervous breath. "So. What's up with you, anyway?"

"What do you mean, what's up with me? Nothing's up with me."

"Something's wrong."

Bree gathered her hair up and twisted it into a long tail. "Got a scrunchie on you?"

"Something's really wrong . . . a what? A scrunchie? We're having the most important talk of your life and all you can think of is your hair?"

Bree held her hair in one hand and extended the other. "Just keeping my hair out of the way of your grabby little fists." Antonia dug a rubber band out of her jeans pocket. Bree sat next to her on the couch and fastened her hair up in a ponytail. "Now," she said kindly, "spill it."

Suddenly Antonia looked much older than twenty-two. "I don't want the kindly big-sister act. I don't want the mother-in-absentia act. I want you to take a good look at yourself and then . . ." She took a deep breath. "I want you to see somebody."

Bree stared at her.

"A doctor, first. You know, like an internist. And then maybe a shrink."

"Don't be ridiculous." Her voice seemed to come from somebody else.

"I'm not ridiculous."

"You think I'm going crazy?"

"I don't know what to think. All I know is, ever since we've moved here you've gotten well and truly weird."

"Maybe you could be a little more specific," Bree said. She could be very sarcastic if she put her mind to it and she was putting her mind to it right this minute.

Antonia flinched, but said, "Sure. You want specific? I'll get specific. I hear you talking to people and when I walk into the room—nobody's there. I hear you screaming at night with bad dreams. And those huge scary dogs? Miles and Belli, you call them?"

"They're Russian mastiffs," Bree said. "I told you: I'm

taking care of them as a favor for Professor Cianquino while he's out of town." This was a good fib. She wished she'd thought of it before. "They're a pair of perfectly normal Russian mastiffs."

"You didn't tell me any such thing. And if you had, I would have said bullshit, bullshit, bullshit! If those are Russian mastiffs, I'm king of the Martians."

"King of the who?" Bree said, bemused.

"Well!" Antonia stood up and placed both hands on her hips. "I know you don't have a lot of respect for me, Bree, being your dumb little sister and all, but I just happened to mention them tonight at the theater, and you know what John Allen Cavendish said?"

Bree chewed on her lower lip. John Allen Cavendish had been a classics undergraduate at Yale before he'd gone on to the drama school.

"He says those names mean 'War' and 'Soldier' in Latin. So what's normal about that? *Nothing!*" Antonia yelled "Aaagh!" for good measure, and then went on, rapidly, "Nobody I know seems to be able to find this office on Angelus you've supposedly rented—and the only actual live employee of yours I met is Ron Parchese, and there's something weird about him, too."

"He's gay," Bree said flippantly. "Maybe that's too weird for you."

"You're a lot of things, Bree Beaufort, but you're not a creep. At least, not until now."

Bree flushed with embarrassment and said, firmly, "Cut out the drama queen crap, will you? I don't have time for it."

"And there's something else." Antonia had the brave,

rather hopeless air of someone walking defenseless into an ugly storm. "Which is why I want you to get, like, a complete physical or something. You're getting harder looking, Bree."

Bree stared at her in exasperation. "What?!"

"Maybe it's because you've lost weight. Don't think I haven't noticed those size six jeans of mine are, like, hanging off you."

"Those aren't your jeans."

"They absolutely are! Who picked them out?"

"Who paid for them?" Bree shot back.

"Fine!" Antonia, prone to fits of temperament which were very satisfying to her, if to nobody else, made a visible effort to get herself under control. "Let's not talk about jeans, okay? Let's talk about this weirdness I'm seeing."

"Okay, let's." Bree was good at keeping a poker face. Even a lawyer specializing in corporate tax law—actually, now that she thought about it, especially a lawyer specializing in corporate tax law these days—needed to 'keep her head when all about her were losing theirs.' "What's weird, exactly?"

Antonia squinted at her. "It's hard to say out loud. It's like part of you is being pruned away."

Despite Antonia's out-of-control imagination and fondness for melodrama, she was an acute observer. Most actors had to be, if they had any hope of a career, as Antonia frequently pointed out. Bree patted her sides and admitted, "I have lost a couple of pounds. But who doesn't need to lose a couple of pounds?"

"You remember that ceramics class Mom dragged us to when you were in Girl Scouts? It's like you went into the kiln a person and came back out something else. Harder. Tougher. Glossier." She leaned forward and said, with an urgency that made Bree's flesh creep: "It's like you're turning into something else. Tell me something. When's the last time you had a date?"

"A date?"

"You know. A date. A normal sex life. I thought maybe you were coming back to normal when you were flirting with Tony Haddad this afternoon, but after you came out of that meeting with Tully, and he asked you out for a drink, you, like, totally ignored him. Tony Haddad! I mean, even if you can ignore what a fabulous, fabulous brain he's got, he's absolutely gorgeous!"

"I don't have time for this. I've got to go to work in the morning."

"You'd better have time for this. You're, like, consumed with this career thing. It's not normal. It's unhealthy."

Bree got up. "I'm going to get something to eat. Did you have dinner at the theater or do you want something, too?"

Antonia grabbed her elbow.

Bree shook it off and said tightly, "It's not a good idea to piss me off, Antonia."

"Oh, yeah? Like, you're the Incredible Hulk or something?"

Or something. Bree had to smile. "Okay. You made your point. I hear you. I said I'm not in the mood for this right now, and I meant it." She wheeled around and drove herself into the kitchen. Sasha got to his feet and followed her, and then, after a long moment, so did her sister.

Bree opened the refrigerator door and began to pull

containers and packages out one by one and stack them on the blue-tiled countertop. Genoa salami. Yogurt. The last few slices of a seven-grain bread from the bakery on Bull Street. A jar of sweet pickles. She hated sweet pickles.

"Here." Antonia pushed her into a kitchen chair and worked a jar of pesto free from her clutching fingers. "First, I'm making us both a cup of chai. Then I'm making us both a sandwich. I picked up some watercress from Parker's Market yesterday and it's going to be fabulous with the salami. You just watch." She kept up the stream of aimless chatter as she plugged in the electric tea kettle, took down plates and cups from the cupboard, and brewed the tea. Bree listened and reminded herself to be patient, and when, finally, their impromptu supper was laid out in front of her, she said, "What's this really all about?"

Antonia poked at the sandwich she made and set it aside. "I'm scared of you."

Then:

"It's like those pod people in the movies."

And finally:

"I don't know who you are anymore."

Bree stared at her sandwich. She wasn't hungry. She hadn't really been hungry for a long time. And she couldn't remember the last time she'd had a good night's sleep.

———∞———

Bree took a good look at herself in her bathroom mirror before she went to bed. She was thinner; there wasn't much doubt about that. Her cheekbones stuck out. The skin around her eyes had a silver-gray cast to it. She glanced down at Sasha, a warm and reassuring presence at her side.

There is a price. Nothing occurs without cost.

And Antonia, who just wouldn't shut up: *How long since you've had, like, a regular date? Gone out like normal people? Had a normal life? You want me to lay off? Fine. Then start living like a person.*

"This case will take a few weeks," Bree said to the mirror. "I can think about it then."

At her feet, Sasha sighed and looked away.

Five

You've got to ask yourself one question: "Do I feel lucky?" Well, do you, punk?
—H. J. Fink, R. M. Fink, and D. Riesner,
Dirty Harry

"We're going to have to open a satellite office sooner or later," Bree said to her office staff early Monday morning, "and this may be the best time to do it." She moved restlessly in her chair. She hadn't slept well again. She felt like she hadn't slept well for weeks.

"They'll want a pot of money for the rent, those folks," Lavinia said. "If you're talking about Franklin's old place. Nowhere near as good a bargain as this."

"Yes," Bree said. "But it's a normal office, isn't it? I mean, my friends and family will be able to come and visit me there? They'll be able to find it? Walk in? Sit down? Have a cup of coffee? And I'll have a semblance of a normal life?"

"Ah," Petru said.

"Oh, dear," Ron said. "It's getting to you, isn't it? This life. Beaufort & Company."

Her landlady clucked disapprovingly—Bree hoped at

65

the prospective cost of the new office space, and not at her bid for a little freedom—and moved the cream pitcher within Bree's reach.

The five of them sat around the long oak table that served the little conference room in the office on Angelus Street. Bree rented the first floor of the two-hundred-year-old house, and, as Lavinia had just pointed out, the rent was indeed cheap. The house sat smack in the middle of Georgia's only all-murderers cemetery. Despite the fact that they were a mere three blocks from the Savannah River in the highly desirable Historic District, the weedy graves and pallid oaks surrounding the house were distinctly off-putting. Bree sometimes wondered why she had to pay rent at all, since the office location served only the dead, but she didn't have the nerve to address Lavinia about this directly. She went ahead and paid Ron's and Petru's salaries, too, even though she wasn't at all sure what the two other angels did with the money. Ron was exceptionally well dressed, so she suspected he spent a lot of his salary on custom pima cotton shirts and elegant ties, but Petru wore the same dingy black suit to work day after day. And if the state of his thick black beard was any indication, he did all his own barbering. As for Sasha . . . her dog lay curled next to her chair, and she bent down and scratched behind his ears. He yawned happily, rolled one golden eye up to her, and went back to sleep. Sasha didn't have any expenses at all, since she bought his dog food herself.

"Uncle Franklin's old lease was voided by his death," Bree said. "And what with the brouhaha over the Benjamin Skinner case, I never did get around to talking to the owners about a new one. If you could check on that, Ron, I'd appreciate it." Great-Uncle Franklin, who had left Bree her unusual law practice and her even more unusual set of employees, had a small one-room office in a refurbished brick warehouse six blocks from Angelus Street. Like many of the great old brick buildings lining the Savannah River, it was in constant need of updating. The latest remodeling had been lengthy and expensive. The entire brick façade had been pointed, the terrazzo floors ground and waxed, and the elegant basswood moldings and balustrades stripped and refinished. But the renovation was almost complete, and she needed to address the issue of moving in.

Ron entered a brief note into his BlackBerry and looked at her expectantly. "Office furnishings?" he said hopefully. "Do we have a budget for that?"

Franklin had died in a fierce fire, which had been contained within his office on the sixth floor. The only things that remained were his desk, which Bree used in her Angelus office, and an old leather chair. So the new space would have to be furnished from scratch. "A small one," she said. "Maybe you can find a few things at Second Hand Rows off Whitaker. Not too much—a little conference table for the corner window and a desk and a chair for me. We'll keep most of the files here."

"The widow O'Rourke?" Petru rumbled. "She has offered a retainer? This should help the finances."

Bree set her coffee cup down, and then crumbled the remains of her piece of Lavinia's cinnamon cake into even littler bits. "I'm still not sure we should take her on as a client."

"A conflict of interest, perhaps? If we are to represent the husband it would be against the widow's interest?" Petru tapped his cane on the floor with a thoughtful air.

"Well, he's dead and she's not," Ron said crossly. "We're not filing an appeal for her. We'll be reviewing contracts and setting up leases. Two different areas of law entirely. You're the paralegal. You should know that."

"I am ke-vite well aware of the areas of law in question," Petru said. When he was upset, his Russian accent became more pronounced. "And as you are merely a secretary, I doubt that you should be offering an opinion at all."

"Stop," Bree said. She had no idea what had started the two angels sparring with one another this time, but she wasn't about to let it affect affairs in the office. "I'm not concerned with conflict of interest. I just don't like the woman or the way she operates." She held up a hand to forestall any protests. "I know. An advocate's role is just that. We stand up for the client's interests and we have no business passing judgment on personalities. But honestly, the way she stiffed that poor auctioneer was brutal. A client like that will try and stiff us, too. You can bet on it." Bree rubbed her face briskly. "Anyhow. Let's finish up the coffee and get started. Petru, I'm going to need all of the background material you can find on Russell O'Rourke, especially the circumstances surrounding his suicide. He died in New York, at their penthouse. It was somewhere near Central Park, I think, but I don't remember much more than that. So if you can get onto the Internet and start creating a file, I'd be grateful. Ron? The two of us better get over to the records department at the courthouse and see Goldstein. We're going to need a copy of the appeal that's been filed."

"Anything I can do for you this morning?" Lavinia asked hopefully. Her landlady was tiny. Bree was willing to bet she was no more than ninety pounds soaking wet, and her bones were as fragile as a bird's. She was dressed in her usual droopy skirt, worn woolen cardigan, and soft print blouse. Her cloud of white hair drifted around her mahogany face like a halo. "I was thinking that maybe Sasha could use a good bath."

Bree looked down at her dog. After the auction yesterday, Bree had taken him for a nice long run by the river. He could, in fact, use a good wash and a brush. "Good idea."

Sasha lifted his head and looked reproachfully at Bree.

"That's settled, then," Lavinia said with a contented sigh. "I'm givin' some of my littlies a scrub this morning, too. He'll come out smellin' just as sweet."

Bree wasn't sure about the exact nature of Lavinia's littlies, but Sasha's expression seemed to indicate they were beneath his dignity as a noble mastiff-retriever cross. But he got to his feet with a good-natured grunt and padded to Lavinia's side.

Bree collected her briefcase and followed Ron out to the tiny foyer that fronted Angelus Street without looking at the grim painting that hung over the fireplace in the living room. It showed a ship plunging in the midst of a stormy sea, surrounded by the dead and dying. The painting was both a reminder and a statement of the mission she and her Company were on, but she loathed the sight of the thing. She did pause on her way out the door to look at the painted frieze of angels that marched up the wall of the staircase to the second floor. Where the *Rise of the Cormorant* terrified her, the parade of brightly colored Renaissance angels lifted her heart. The figures had wings the color of beaten gold and were robed in scarlet, royal purple, vibrant turquoise, and rich velvety browns. Bronze halos shone about their heads. The angel at the very foot of the stairs, dressed in brocaded robes of sapphire and cardinal red, was crowned with braids of white-blonde hair the color of Bree's own. A small whippetlike creature danced at its side.

"Looks like rain," Ron said from the front stoop. "Do you want to walk or drive?"

Bree peered around his shoulder. The records for the Celestial Courts were on the seventh floor of the six-floor Chatham County Courthouse on Montgomery, which was about ten blocks straight down Bay Street. Bree liked to walk, especially on cool November days. The Historic District was one of the most beautiful neighborhoods in the world, in her opinion, and a walk down Bay, with its pockets of emerald grass shaded by live oaks, was endlessly interesting. But the sky over the nearby river was clouded over and the air held the scent of rain.

"We'd better drive." Her car was parked curbside at the end of the brick path that led from the porch to the street. Despite herself, she kept her gaze firmly ahead as she followed Ron to the car. The Pendergast graves gaped open underneath the dying oak that stood in the middle of the cemetery, and she was never sure what was going to beckon to her from its depths.

She settled into the driver's seat next to Ron and grumbled, "One of these days, we're going to have to do something about those Pendergasts. I can't scuttle down the path to my own office like a scared rat every time I go in and out."

Ron looked at her with interest. His blond hair feathered over his forehead and his light blue eyes were guileless. "Why not? At the moment, the Pendergasts are nothing to fool with. I don't know if you noticed, but I was scuttling faster than you."

Bree started the engine. "It's not dignified."

"You know what they say about pride," Ron said, rather primly. "You may choose dignity over getting dragged somewhere awful by a rotting corpse, but I vote scuttle every time."

"You're pretty smug, for an angel," Bree said. "Do you suppose that's why you and Petru snipe at each other?"

Ron shrugged and then smiled. "Possibly," he said. His smile, like all angels', was impossible to resist. The smile sent warmth from the top of your head to your feet.

"Don't smile at me," Bree warned. "I'm getting wise to your ways, Ron Parchese."

But she arrived at the Chatham County Courthouse in a much improved mood.

Bree had been at the courthouse at all hours during the day, and it was always filled with a cross section of citizens of the state of Georgia. Young kids swaggered through in baggy pants and oversized T-shirts. Blue-uniformed policemen of the Town of Savannah rubbed shoulders with the brown-uniformed officers of Chatham County. Couples with children wandered the lower floors, peering at the office listings on the notice boards. Guys with straw hats and saggy coveralls ambled up to the coffee cart.

And the lawyers were everywhere.

Bree and Ron passed through the metal detector and got into the middle elevator. They rode to the sixth floor and then, after the last fellow passenger, a tired-looking cleaning lady, got off, headed up to the seventh. The doors swooshed open, and Bree faced the familiar gold medallion on the opposite wall that read:

CELESTIAL COURT OF APPEALS

The Scales of Justice, cupped by a pair of feathery wings, were embossed in the center.

She led the way down to the door marked RECORDS and pushed her way inside.

The Hall of Records was an exact replica of an old monastery—although for all Bree knew it *was* a section of a monastery—with flagstone floors, torch sconces, and stained-glass windows topped by Gothic arches. Massive oak beams buttressed the soaring ceilings. Angels robed like monks stood in front of waist-high oak podiums, scratching on vellum with quill pens. There was a faint, winged rustling as Bree and Ron walked down the aisle to the big oak counter at the back. Hundreds of cubbyholes filled with rolls of parchment lined the far wall. Goldstein, his bald head glinting in the torchlight, twiddled his fingers in greeting as they approached.

"Still resisting the computer age, I see," Ron said. He leaned on the waist-high counter and shook his head.

"I like it," Goldstein said. "And you think I'd get any

kind of productivity out of these guys under fluorescent lights? Phooey." He rubbed the back of his neck, and a silvery feather floated upward. "So, what can I do for the two of you this fine morning?"

"Russell O'Rourke," Bree said. "I'd like a copy of the Request for Appeal."

"O'Rourke." Goldstein frowned and then tugged at his ear. "O'Rourke. Doesn't ring a bell, I'm afraid, but let me check." He bent down, rummaged under the counter, and emerged with a leather-bound book. He flipped the pages over with a thoughtful air. "Russell O'Rourke," he said, with a slight emphasis on the cognomen. "I don't see a Russell O'Rourke. Nope." He slammed the book shut.

"But he contacted me yesterday," Bree said.

Goldstein raised one eyebrow. What was time, to an angel?

"He did get in touch," Bree said firmly. "He killed himself several months ago at his desk, at his place in New York. The desk ended up in a job lot at an auction house here in Savannah. I ended up at the auction. I put my hands on the desk and bingo, there he was, or part of him, asking for help. Just like all the others."

Goldstein reopened the ledger and paged through it again. "Benjamin Skinner. Check. Probert Chandler, check. Both cases pleaded and disposed, quite professionally, I might add, dear Bree. But no Request for Appeal has been filed for Russell O'Rourke."

"There must have been an initial disposition of his soul," Ron said. "You've got that cross-reference somewhere in this mass of paper, I hope."

Goldstein scowled, moved to the farthest point of the

wall, and plucked a roll from one of the cubbyholes. He trundled back—he really was a chubby little angel—and slapped the document in front of Ron. "Russell O'Rourke. Consigned to Purgatory. Eternal Life sentence."

"Purgatory? Not a higher circle of Hell?" Bree said. "Good grief. The man's list of crimes is as long as your arm."

"Divine Justice has little in common with the temporal," Goldstein said with an air of reproof. "And it is not for us to question."

"It most certainly is," Bree said, in some indignation. "Purgatory. My word. Do you have any idea how many widows and orphans the man left behind after the crash of his company? On the other hand," she added hastily, suddenly reminded that she was close to violating the canon of ethics by speaking ill of her client, "as Mr. O'Rourke's attorney, I should point out that a sentence of Eternal Life in Purgatory is undoubtedly a miscarriage of justice and should be looked into as soon as possible." She brought herself to a halt and then said, "But how?"

"You can file a Request for Appeal on his behalf," Goldstein said. "Your mother, bless her soul, was prone to do that later in her career."

"Shut *up*, Goldstein," Ron said.

Bree stared at him. Ron covered Bree's hands with his own. "It's the start of a very slippery slope, this kind of advocacy," he said. "We're not ready."

Bree backed away from the two of them. The recent discovery that Francesca was not her biological mother had been painful. The mystery surrounding the death of her birth mother, Leah, was the stuff of her nightmares.

"Tell me what you know, please," she said as courteously as she could. "I deserve to know about this, I think."

Behind her, the soft rustlings in the cavernous room stilled to an absolute quiet.

Goldstein, avoiding Ron's furious gaze, folded his hands on the counter and said, "Leah felt she could save more souls if she went out looking for them." He cocked his head to one side, as if listening, then patted the sides of his habit. "I may even have an old card of hers around somewhere. Yes! I do! Here it is." He pulled a small piece of pasteboard out from the swathe of brown wool and handed it to Bree.

Leah Winston-Beaufort, Esquire
ACLU

"ACLU?" Bree stared at the card in confusion. Other than the gold medallion she wore on a chain around her neck, this was the only artifact she had of Leah's. She rubbed the heavy stock between her thumb and forefinger.

"Angelus Celestial Liberties Union," Ron said. "But truly, Bree, we want to wait on this a bit. You've only been in practice a few weeks, after all."

"Two months," Bree said. "And if Leah could file appeals on behalf of clients, so can I."

"Perhaps we should discuss this with Armand," Ron said. "I don't think he's going to be happy about this turn of events at all."

"Any reason in particular?" Bree kept her voice level and struggled to look polite and not furious enough to spit nails. She hated being balked more than anything. No, she hated being lied to more than that. But a dislike of being stymied was right up there with her pet peeves. She'd learned early on, in her days at the family law firm in Raleigh, that losing her temper was the quickest way to professional suicide, so she said, with deceptive calm, "Why should Professor Cianquino object to my carrying on the tradition of the family firm?"

"Please don't be mad," Ron said.

"I'm not angry," Bree said sweetly. "Truly. I just can't see why we shouldn't proceed with a tactic that's in the best interests of my client. And I see no reason why we need to drag Professor Cianquino into this."

"You're furious enough to spit nails," Ron said. She'd forgotten, for the moment, that she was dealing with angels. "And Armand is Company director, and ultimately Petru, Lavinia, Sasha, and I are answerable to him for your welfare."

This bit of information was new to Bree—the Company was notoriously stingy with information—and it diverted her irritated focus enough to ask, "What about Striker?"

"Gabriel Striker? The private investigator?" Goldstein said. "Hoo. He answers to another set of obligations altogether."

Bree could believe that. Striker was the most militant of the Company, and he only showed up when there was a lot of physical trouble in the offing. She'd met with Striker in his office on Chippewa Square once, and the wall behind his desk was stacked with lethal-looking swords. She couldn't imagine either Ron or Petru picking up a weapon, much less the fragile Lavinia. "Fine," Bree said. "If it makes you feel better, Ron, we'll call on Professor Cianquino this afternoon." She smiled and turned to Goldstein. "But right now, I'd like to go ahead and file a Request for Appeal on behalf of Russell O'Rourke. *Unfairly and prejudicially sentenced,* or maybe make that: *Erroneously sentenced to a punitive term in Purgatory.* How's that?"

Goldstein nodded. "I've heard better, but it'll do. You need the transcript of the trial?"

"Oh, dear, yes," Bree said, flustered. "Sorry. Of course you'll need a brief. I'll get right on it."

"The transcript," Goldstein said, dropping a thick roll of parchment on the counter in front of Ron. "And a list of Facts Stipulated in Evidence." He dropped another. "And a Motion for Dismissal." He dropped a third.

"A Motion for Dismissal?" Bree said. "The guy gets sentenced to Purgatory and he has the nerve to ask for a dismissal?"

"That's pretty standard with people like O'Rourke. Can't live without their lawyers and can't die without them, either. The motion was tossed out, as you might imagine." He gathered the rolls together and tied them into a neat pile with a piece of twine. "Here you go, my dear. And good luck."

Bree tucked the files into her briefcase. She and Ron left the records room for the elevator. She was silent all the way down to the first floor. For one thing, she was never sure when Ron was visible to temporals like herself, and she didn't want to chance anyone seeing her talking to an invisible friend. The professional community in Savannah was small, and word got around fast. For another, she was still steamed, and she made it a rule not to lose her temper with employees. As they lined up to file out of the building through the security kiosk, her irritation got the better of her. She turned to Ron. "Would it just kill you guys to let a little light into things now and then? I mean, why do I always have to find out things about Leah and Uncle Franklin in the wrong place, at the wrong time, and with the wrong people? I mean, finding out just now that my own mother was a prominent legal aid lawyer? And I'm supposed to be running the law firm she and Franklin left to me? You realize I looked seven kinds of a fool in front of Goldstein."

Ron patted her sympathetically. "You're working yourself up into a snit."

"I am *not* working myself up into a snit," Bree began furiously.

"Hey! Bree! Working yourself up into another snit, I see."

Bree turned to see Cordelia Eastburn, briefcase in hand. Cordelia was the DA and made no bones about the fact that she was bound and determined to become the first black female governor of Georgia. Everyone in the legal community in Savannah was sure she was going to make it.

"Hey, Cordy," she said.

"Hey, yourself." Cordy looked at Ron with an inquiring lift of her eyebrow.

"Oh, good, you've seen Ron," Bree said, "Cordy? This is Ron Parchese, who works for me, and Ron, this is Ms. Eastburn."

The two shook hands. "I've been wondering if I was ever going to meet some of your staff," Cordy said. "I hope she's treating you well, Mr. Parchese."

"Ron," said Bree, "is a perfect angel to work with. As a matter of fact, my office staff is stuffed full of angels."

Cordy made a noise that sounded like "Ah-hum." Then: "You bet. Say, Bree, I was hoping to have a word. You got a minute to come on up to my office?"

"Sure."

Ron eased her briefcase from her hand. "I'll just get this back to the office. Would you like me to read over the transcript and check out some case citations?"

"Yes," Bree said, "fine," and then apologetically: "You might give Professor Cianquino a call and set up an appointment for this afternoon. You're right. We should check that, um . . . precedent out with him."

Ron smiled. "Will do."

"My," Cordy said, as they watched him swing out the glass doors to the street, "that man's got the sunniest smile. Must be good to have him around the office." She walked over to the elevator and punched the Up button. "Nice job on that Chandler case, by the way."

"Thanks, Cordy."

The conversation remained desultory until they settled themselves in Cordy's office. A picture of her with the current governor of Georgia held pride of place over the credenza, next to her diploma from Stanford Law School, and to the right of a series of photos of Cordy with street kids from her best-known charity. She was a small woman with a large presence, not as tall as Bree, but much more full-figured. Like most professional women in Savannah, including Bree herself, she favored dark suits with silk tops. Her one concession to a little glamour was her earrings. The pair she had on today was made of turquoise beads that hung almost to her shoulders. Bree leaned closer for a good look. "Haven't I seen those before?"

"Picked them up at the auction yesterday."

"The O'Rourke auction? I didn't see you there."

"Came late and didn't stay too long. Had a big to-do at the Help Center. But I did stay long enough to have a chat with Bert Finnegan. You know Bert? Decent sort of fellow for a red-necked, money-grubbing white boy."

Bree pursed her lips so she wouldn't laugh.

"He's got some kind of beef with this Mrs. O'Rourke."

"Over his commission, I expect," Bree said cautiously.

"Says she rigged the bidding. Seems to think he was robbed. Next thing I hear is you've signed on as this woman's local counsel."

"This sure is a small town. And word sure gets around fast."

"That it does. And thank the good Lord that the first person people think to talk to is me." Cordy leaned across her desk. "Now, my office isn't about to get involved in some pissant little wrestling match over a salesman's commission. But Bert's claiming bribery—of the poor souls at the printer's office who changed the dates on the invitations; conspiracy to defraud—on account of all the bidders on this O'Rourke's estate were buddies; and I don't know what all." Cordy leaned back in her chair and abruptly dropped her good-old-girl persona. "You sure you want to take this woman as a client, Bree? I'm asking this as a friend of yours, you understand, not in my capacity as head of this office." She waved a hand in the direction of the law books in her bookcase.

Bree folded her hands, sat back in her chair, and didn't say anything.

"Fine," Cordy said after a long moment. "Your client's going to be hearing from this office. Just thought I'd give you a heads-up. There's another thing. We've got us a visitor."

Since this didn't seem to require a response, Bree didn't give her one.

"Name's Eddie Chin. He's on leave of absence from his home base, which just happens to be the New York PD. Says he hasn't seen his good buddy Sam Hunter for ages and got to missing him something awful."

"He's a friend of Hunter's?" The Chatham County police lieutenant had been involved in both of Bree's cases. And he'd been making some mild overtures to Bree herself.

"And, oddly enough, Eddie's from the Manhattan precinct, which, oddly enough, includes 380 Central Park West. Odder still, that's the very place where Mr. Russell Clarence O'Rourke shot himself in the head with a twelve-gauge shotgun not more than three months ago."

"You're kidding." Bree was very interested now. "Why is he here, this Eddie Chin?"

"Well, now, no one's said a word to me, officially. But what's your best guess?" Cordy waited a moment and then said, "They call him 'Ninja.'"

"Ninja?"

"That's what I hear."

Bree thought about this for a minute and then said, "Men. Good grief. Ninja, huh."

"Apparently they always get their man. Or woman, as the case might be. Yeah. Well." Cordy got to her feet and opened her office door. "You hear anything about this Ninja, you call me, hear? Or Mrs. O'Rourke."

Bree nodded in a noncommittal way.

"Just a word in my ear, privatelike." Cordy could be a bulldog when she wanted.

"I have absolutely no idea what Tully O'Rourke expects of me, Cordy. If something comes up that I should pass along to you, I'll do the right thing."

"Uh-huh." Cordy looked at her without expression for a long moment. Then she leaned across the desk. "Thanks for dropping by, Bree. My door's always open."

"Yes. It's been a very interesting little chat, Cordy." Bree slung her purse over her shoulder and went out into the corridor. "Ninja?" she said over her shoulder.

Cordy's laugh followed her all the way to the elevator.

Six

Once more on my adventure brave and new.
—Robert Browning, "Rabbi ben Ezra"

"It's such a pleasure seeing you for lunch, Lieutenant. We'll have to do this more often." Bree smiled at his companion. "And it's a real pleasure to meet you, Sergeant Chin."

Eddie Chin was a little less than medium height, and solidly built. Sam Hunter sat at ease next to him, opposite her in the booth. Neither man needed a uniform to look like a cop; there was a skeptical alertness about the two of them that shouted "police" from yards away. But where Hunter had a watchful stillness, Eddie was jumpy with badly suppressed energy.

Bree handed the menu back to the waitress. She liked having lunch at Huey's; it was only a few steps away from her town house on Factor's Walk, and the thin-crust pizza was terrific. A few hundred feet away, across the brick road and beyond the pier, the Savannah River rolled past, its waters a steely blue. "Y'all are going to love this pizza."

"Anchovy pizza's not your traditional Southern food," Eddie Chin said. "I like to eat local when I travel. But Sam told me to pass on the hominy grits and the fried pie."

"I'll order us some pecan rolls for dessert," Bree said. "They're a Southern specialty. You try our pecan rolls, Mr. Chin, and you aren't going to want to go back to New York for weeks."

"Call me Eddie." He gave her a little salute with his left hand. His nails were bitten down to the quick.

"And I'm Bree. Well, then, Eddie. Is this your first visit to Savannah?"

He seemed startled. "Uh, yeah."

"I hope Hunter here's been showing you the prettiest parts of our city."

Eddie looked at her earnestly. For a bare moment, he seemed to relax, and she caught a glimpse of a different man altogether—flirtatious and confident. A quick, cheeky grin flitted across his face. "So far, Bree, the prettiest part of this city is you."

"Why, thank you, sir."

Hunter rolled his eyes. "She's going Southern on us, Ninja. Next thing you know, she'll be batting her eyelashes. We'll both feel a little safer when she reverts to tough-guy mode. Bree, you want something. What is it?"

Eddie's tension returned like the snap of a rubber band. Hunter's eyes rested on him for a thoughtful moment, but he said to Bree, "Out with it, woman."

"Now, Sam. Can't I call up two good-looking men and invite them for lunch without having an ulterior motive?"

"I doubt it sincerely."

That made Bree laugh. "So now I know what you really think of me."

"I doubt that, too."

She met his eyes with a little prickle of excitement. There was electricity between them, she was sure of that. Just how strong the current was—and how much she wanted to explore it—well, she wasn't sure of that at all. Bree took a sip of her white wine. There'd been two major relationships in her life up until now. One, with a lawyer who practiced here in the city, had been a total disaster. The other was with a man who was married to someone else. Her track record, as Antonia frequently reminded her, sucked scissors. She set her wine down and looked at Hunter. Really looked at him, not in a flirtatious way, or even with speculation, but just as a guy she was meeting for lunch. He was an inch or two over her own five-nine. He had broad shoulders, tapering to strong legs. His hands were nice, too, large, well formed, with calluses on the palms. She liked men with calluses; it meant they were doing something physical with their days. He looked older than he was, but then many cops did. That faintly cynical set to his jaw, the lines around his coin-colored eyes, were hazards of the profession.

He flushed a little under her steady regard and then cleared his throat. "Is there something on your mind, Bree? Or was this an impulse you couldn't control?"

"We haven't had much of a chance to catch up once the Chandler case got wrapped up."

"You're right," he said in mock amazement. "It's been what—a week, maybe more."

"I wanted to thank you for jumping in at the last bit,"

she said. "It could have gotten ugly." She turned to Eddie. "Hunter caught a murderer for me. Just in time, too."

"The man justifies his salary once in a while," Eddie said.

"We're lucky to have him here."

Hunter looked genuinely surprised at that. "Is that a 'my hero' squeal? From you, of all people? You're the last woman I'd expect to appreciate an . . ." He paused, searching for the least provocative word. ". . . intervention," he said, finally.

"Yes. Um. Well, I did. Appreciate it a lot. So the pizza's on me, and the pecan rolls, too."

Bree realized she was leaning halfway across the table—practically in Hunter's lap—as the waitress tried to set their lunch on the table. She drew back a bit and waited until both men had loaded their plates. "So, Eddie. Do you plan to stay in Savannah long? Taking a little time off?"

"Got a little business to follow up on."

"Police-type business? Here." She moved the red pepper flakes to within his reach. "You and Sam were on the force in New York together?"

The two men exchanged looks. Hunter said, abruptly, "Now, how did you know that?"

"Cordy Eastburn mentioned it, is all."

"Cordy—who?"

Hunter raised one eyebrow." "She's the district attorney. Tough. A little too political for my taste, but she's honest, at least. Interesting that she already knows you rolled into town." He looked at Bree. "Care to tell me how Eddie's name came up?"

"Cordy knows everything that happens in this town *before* it happens," she said to Eddie. "I took on a new client yesterday afternoon. A Sunday, mind you, and a chance meeting at that, and first thing I know Cordy's got me up against the wall."

"O'Rourke," Eddie said. His left knee jigged up and down like a jackhammer. Bree resisted the impulse to put her hand on it to make him stop. "It's gotta be O'Rourke."

"Tully O'Rourke," Bree said. "That's right."

Hunter exhaled. "Why don't you tell us straight out what's on your mind?"

Was that disappointment in his eyes? It was. Bree sighed. Maybe she had lousy relationships with men because she was lame at the whole business of romance.

"I'd heard that Eddie might have some background information about a client of mine. To be precise, the deceased husband of a client of mine."

Hunter scowled at her. "You shouldn't be getting mixed up with the O'Rourkes, Bree."

"I wouldn't say mixed up, exactly," she said. "And aren't you making some mighty big guesses? Although maybe I'm making an assumption I shouldn't. You *are* here to follow up on the O'Rourke case, aren't you, Sergeant?"

Eddie started to reply, but Hunter got there first. "More to the point, what do you have to do with Tully O'Rourke?"

"She's offered me a retainer to handle some leases and contracts. All civil stuff."

"You actually got a check?" Eddie said.

"Well, not yet. But I plan on setting up a preliminary client interview a little later this week."

"Get a check up front," Eddie advised. "And then wait until the sucker clears before you do diddly."

"Now you see," Bree said, "this is exactly why it's so useful to have friends in the know. She's not the sort of person to pay her bills, Sergeant?"

Eddie set his half-eaten slice of pizza down. "She's a freakin' murderer," he said bluntly. "She shot that poor slob of a husband in the head, set it up to look like a suicide, and skipped town with a couple million in insurance money."

Bree wasn't sure which was the more interesting comment to follow up on first—the fact that Eddie Chin was convinced Tully O'Rourke had murdered her husband, or Eddie's description of the victim as a poor slob. "Four and a half billion dollars disappeared from O'Rourke Investment in the space of three days," she said. "A lot of it was because the stocks were so overvalued it wasn't funny—but a fair amount of it was due to out-and-out fraud. That's why the CFO, Cullen Jameson, went to jail. If O'Rourke weren't dead, odds are he'd be serving ten to fifteen months at Schuyler along with his buddy Jameson. As it is, two of his top men are out on bail, and it's a sure thing that Cullen Jameson, at least, is guilty. I'm not sure about the other guy."

"Barney Gottschmidt," Eddie said. "He was of counsel."

The name rang a bell. Bree remembered the quiet gray man at the auction. "A lawyer? Medium height, balding, midforties?"

"That's the one."

"He was here yesterday, at this auction where I met Mrs. O'Rourke. He seemed very interested in helping Mrs. O'Rourke get her belongings back."

"Gottschmidt's out of it," Eddie said dismissively. "Still has his license to practice law and he seems to be clean for the fraud charges."

"But O'Rourke's a poor slob, and not a crook, you said? That's a switch. It's a bad thing that O'Rourke was driven to suicide, but nobody I know felt sorry for him."

Eddie hunched his shoulders and swallowed pizza. "Whatever," he muttered.

"No, I'm interested. Mostly because I'd like to know about Tully before going in, but your perception of the husband is important, I think."

"You know much about him? O'Rourke?"

"A little," Bree said. "He was from somewhere in the Midwest, wasn't he? Had a full scholarship to Harvard and then a pretty impressive record at the Wharton School of Business. A self-made man."

"You know about Asperger's syndrome?" Eddie demanded.

Bree blinked at him. "I'm sorry, did you say Asperger's?"

"It's, like, related to autism."

Bree looked at Hunter. He grinned suddenly. "Just relax," he said, in an undertone. "Once Ninja's at the wheel, there's no getting out of the tank unless you jump."

"Okay—it's related to autism."

"People like that—they're brilliant in some things, see. But they have no empathy. Like O'Rourke was this financial genius, but he was clueless about human beings. You get some poor fifteen-year-old runaway from Idaho fresh off the bus in Grand Central Station—she'll know more about depravity than Russell O'Rourke. The guy was a walking sucker when it came to his 'loved ones.' " Eddie put the maximum amount of contempt in the phrase. "Well, his loved one screwed him over royally when he was alive, and then murdered his ass to boot. And I'm going to see that she doesn't get away with it." He set his hands flat on the table and stared at Bree. It was a very unsettling look, she thought. The man seemed obsessed with the chase.

"There wasn't much in the media about the suicide itself, was there?" Bree hazarded. "I mean, I didn't pay much more attention to his death than the average reader, but I would have remembered any speculation about murder. Anyone would. Wasn't she out at some big charity dinner? And didn't she come home to find him at his desk? She walks in the door with a few of her friends and he chooses that moment to pull the trigger." She shuddered. "Ugh."

"Yeah. Well. That's what it looked like. But that's not what happened. The widow is smart. Very smart. But not smart enough."

Bree glanced at Hunter. The lieutenant had absolutely no expression on his face. "So," she said, after a lengthy silence, "what tipped you off that this was murder and not suicide?"

Eddie's leg started going up and down again, like a manic elevator. "I've got three things that should have been enough for the grand jury—but we've got this punk prosecutor up north that doesn't take a step out of his office without rock-solid guarantees."

Prosecutorial diffidence, Bree knew, was a very real phenomenon, especially in cases with as high a profile as O'Rourke's. "Three things," she repeated. She kept her voice calm and soothing. Eddie looked like he might fly out of the booth at any minute.

"Yes." He gave Hunter a defiant glare. "You take them one at a time, they don't add up to much, I admit. But you put them altogether and you got Murder One. Murder with intent. Premeditated." Chin slammed his fist onto the table. The glasses rattled. Behind the bar up front, Maureen, the manager, glanced sharply at them. Bree ate at Huey's a lot—and on one memorable occasion, she'd been in the middle of a fracas that upended most of the tables, smashed almost all of the glassware, and left Maureen with permanent skepticism about Bree's potential for disruptive behavior. The only good consequence of that particular skirmish was that Bree always got superb service. They couldn't keep her out of the restaurant, but they could encourage a speedy departure.

Bree smiled and waved reassuringly in Maureen's direction. Then she turned back to Eddie. "There are three things that make this murder and not suicide, you said," she said. "I'd surely like to know what they are, if I might."

Eddie swept the remains of the pizza aside and cleared a space on the tabletop. "It's about seven o'clock the evening of the twelfth of August. O'Rourke's at his desk. He writes a suicide note. 'I very much regret the collapse of the O'Rourke Investment Bank, a regret that I will carry to my grave. My apologies to you all. Good-bye.' He writes that in ink, see? With this Italian pen only he uses, that he got from his wife for his sixty-fifth birthday. Then he rigs his twelve-gauge onto the desk chair, attaches a wire to the trigger, sits on his desk, and waits until his wife walks in with a couple of friend of hers. Then, *blam!*" Eddie pointed his forefinger at Bree and jerked it up with a second *blam!* louder than the first. "Miss Tully's with this Dutchman . . ."

"Rutger VanHoughton?" Bree asked.

"That's the guy. You know him?"

Bree remembered the cool blue gaze from the day before. "I've met him."

"And another friend of hers is there, too. Barrie. So. O'Rourke's brains are scattered six ways from Sunday, VanHoughton calls 911, and by the time we catch the call, she's boo-hooing away in the corner."

Bree exchanged a look with Hunter. "Seems pretty straightforward to me."

Eddie leaned forward, his eyes intense. "She did it. I don't know how. But I'm gonna find out."

Bree frowned. "Do you have photos of the crime scene?"

"I've got a freakin' *movie* of the crime scene. The vic's slumped sideways onto the floor, scuff marks on the front of the desk where his heels whacked into it—yeah, it looks good to go."

"But . . ." Bree said.

"But we got three things that don't add up. First, the top half of the suicide note's been torn off . . . and where's the other half? Second, the security system to the penthouse has been turned off and we don't have a video of the scene—we just got these people swearing that's what happened. And third, we find a fragment of a bullet from a .22 a couple of feet from the corpse."

Eddie leaned back. "Like I say, those things independent of one another, it doesn't sound like much. Adding them up—that's another story."

"Did you question Mrs. O'Rourke about any of these discrepancies?"

"Sure I did. And she's got an answer for each one of them. O'Rourke was the tenth richest man in the world at one point in his career—but he saves scrap paper. Tears the top third of a page that only has, say, a paragraph on it. Saves the paper for notes and such. Two, flipping penthouse is so secure, they don't need an alarm. So half the time, the system's off. And finally, she has no idea—*no idea*—where the bullet fragment came from."

"But it was a shot from the twelve-gauge that killed him. I don't understand what the .22 has to do with it."

"You will," Eddie said confidently.

"Do you?" Bree asked.

"Not yet. But I'm working on it." He ran his hands over the top of his head. "Yeah. I'm working on it."

Bree kept her skepticism to herself. Hunter, on the other hand, shook his head a little. "I don't know, Ninja. I know you have this gut feeling. I respect it. But there's a big difference between what you know and what you can prove. I know you're sure about this. But even so." He didn't say anything more and an uncomfortable silence fell over the table.

Bree kept her cell phone in her jacket pocket, and it vibrated against her hip. She excused herself and walked away from the table to take the call. It was a text message from Ron:

PROF MEET 2 pm SOONEST

She checked the time. Professor Cianquino lived several miles away, on the ground floor of an old plantation that had been converted to apartments. If she cut her lunch short, she'd have twenty minutes to get there. Meetings with her retired professor were command performances, more or less. She texted Ron, OK, and went back to the table to make her farewells.

"I've got to get a move on myself," Eddie said. "Thank you for the pizza."

"I promised you pecan rolls," Bree said, "and Hunter knows I'm not one to forget my word. Are you in town for a while?"

"For as long as it takes."

Bree nodded. "Yes. Well. Maybe in the next couple of days we can sit down and talk again, Eddie." She glanced at Hunter, who could be a stickler about these things. "Maybe even take a look at the file?"

"Sure thing. Be glad of another take on the case."

"You're still insisting on taking Tully O'Rourke on as a client?" Hunter broke in.

"I'm not insisting on anything," Bree said pleasantly. "But I feel obliged to, at this point."

"Obliged?" Eddie asked. "I don't get it."

Bree thought of that pitiable cry for help: *I want to go home.*

"My guess is, Mrs. O'Rourke thinks that Bree has something unique to offer," Hunter said. "And perhaps she's right."

"Perhaps she is." Bree checked the amount on the bill

(she always received the bill with her food, at Huey's) and left the cash on the table. She drove out to Melrose in a thoughtful mood, turning Hunter's parting comment over in her mind.

Bree has something unique to offer.

She'd have to ask him what he meant by that.

Seven

**Tell me before you get onto your high horse
Just what you expect me to do.**
—Tim Rice, "Waltz for Eva and Che," *Evita*

Melrose sat, gracious and aloof, brooding over the river. This late in the year, the gardens surrounding the big old house were subdued to a silvery green. Thick hydrangea blossoms had faded to the color of coffee clotted with thick cream. The rosebushes were trimmed back and tied up with twine. The camellias were soft patches of cloud among the bushes, the scent of the flowers drifting through the air like perfume at a premiere. The lawn was green under drifting piles of Spanish moss. The remnants of silvery branches broken off the live oaks littered the paths like elegant bones.

Melrose was three stories high, each story fronted by a broad verandah supported by Doric pillars. Double French doors led from the verandahs to the house itself. Sometimes Bree thought that what she loved most about Savannah was the immense variety of architecture at the heart of the Historic District. French Provencal sat next to Georgian, which in turn shouldered against Queen Anne,

Federal, and Southern Gothic. But each time she visited Melrose, which reminded her of Plessey, her own family home back in the Carolinas, she knew it was the distinctive style of the Old South, with broad porches and sturdy pillars, that lay nearest her heart. Professor Cianquino must have thought so, too. He'd retired from Bree's former law school the year she'd gotten her JD and bought the ground-floor apartment nearest the river and had lived here quietly ever since.

Bree paused on her way up the brick path to the double front doors. The card with Leah's name embossed upon it was still in her purse. Perhaps, these days, his retirement wasn't as quiet as he'd hoped it would be.

The familiar scent of lemon wax, hothouse flowers, and the musty, welcoming odor of old house greeted her when she went through the front door into the foyer. The flowers in the big jade vases on the Sheraton lowboy against the wall were fresh.

Before Bree could knock at the professor's front door, it swung open and the professor himself greeted her from his wheelchair. He was elegantly thin. At some point in the past year, his hair had turned completely white, and he reminded her now of old silk paintings of Chinese philosophers. Slender, but not frail, and old and weary with what he knew about this world. And, Bree thought, the next.

"How are you, dear Bree?"

"Quite well," she said. "And I didn't think to stop at the Park Avenue Market on my way out here. I was going to pick up some of that shrimp salad you're so fond of, and it completely went out of my head."

"Perhaps next time you visit." He rolled his chair backwards and gestured her inside.

His living room reflected his ascetic habit. A plain leather couch sat at one end of the room facing the windows overlooking the water. The polished pine floors were free of rugs and anything else that would impede his wheelchair. A comfortable chair with a reading lamp occupied one corner of the large room. Except for a small cabinet containing a TV set, that was it. When the Company met, however, it wasn't in this room, but in the Cianquino library.

Bree followed him across the smooth floors to the curiously carved wooden door that led to it. The door was made of rosewood, and the spheres carved into it were the same shape and size of the spheres that composed the wrought-iron fence that surrounded the house at 666 Angelus Street.

Inside, the contrast to the restraint of the living room could hardly have been greater. Bookshelves covered the walls from floor to ceiling, and they were crammed with volumes from everywhere—and as nearly as Bree could figure out, all ages. Fat, leather-bound books with illuminated manuscript pages jostled science texts, law books, poetry, and archeology. From where she stood just inside the door, Bree counted three versions of the Koran, at least six different versions of the Christian Bible, and two editions of the Torah. Works by Confucius, Lao-Tse, and the Buddha lay open on the long refractory table that ran almost the whole length of the room.

In the middle of the heaped volumes was a large birdcage. Bree had never seen the door to the birdcage closed, yet she'd also never seen its occupant out of it.

"Hello, Archie," she said.

The bird shifted on his perch, lifted one leg, and pecked irritably at his claw. He was the size of an African gray parrot, but his feathers were the soft black, dusty browns, and cream of a snowy owl. "You're late, you're late, you're late," Archie complained.

"Five minutes, at most," Bree said. She took her accustomed seat at the far end of the table. Professor Cianquino rolled his chair so that he sat opposite her. Four chairs sat between them, two on each side. Then, one by one, the chairs were filled with man-high columns of softly glowing light.

"Rashiel," said Ron.

"I, Dara," said Petru.

"Mercy me," said a soft voice in a perplexed way. Then Lavinia's faded lavender colors whirled into being and she said her name, "Matriel."

There was a soundless explosion of bright fire, and Gabriel was slouched in his chair, his powerful warrior's body clothed in a leather jacket and a faded T-shirt with a Harley-Davidson logo on the front. He nodded to Bree, his silvery eyes remote.

Finally, Sasha himself was a warm presence under her hand. "Sensiel."

She stroked the dog's ears and waited politely for Cianquino to speak.

"We are assembled, then," the professor said. "And it is to discuss this newest case of yours, dear Bree."

"The client's name is Russell O'Rourke." She placed her briefcase on the table. "I've made a few notes on the file."

"There are a few things we need to discuss first." Professor Cianquino passed his hand over his mouth. He seemed tired. Bree was worried about him. In their temporal forms, her angels were heir to all the vulnerabilities of the flesh. How long had it been since the professor had seen a doctor? What were the practical realities of his existence? As far as she knew, he lived alone. Did he need help? Would he accept it from her if she offered? There was so much about this job she'd inherited that she didn't know. Not to mention the beings that came with it.

At her feet, Sasha stirred and thrust his head under her hand. She passed her thumb gently over the ridged wound under his ear. "Okay," she said. "What's on?"

"You didn't take Sasha with you today." Gabriel's tone of voice was mild, but the reproof was clear. "Or yesterday, to the auction house."

"Lots of places don't allow dogs," Bree said. "Even here in Savannah, which is about as dog-friendly a place as you can get. And I hate to leave him in the car. He's a part of the Company, I know, and more resilient than a normal dog, but he's still recovering from the gunshot wound. And the vet said he should be taking it easy for a while." She blinked. "I guess I thought that's why Miles and Belli are back. Because Sasha's not up to speed right now."

"Guesses," Archie said. He clicked his beak with a sound like spears being sharpened. "Speculation. Not good, not good. She is moving ahead too fast."

"Miles and Belli are the muscle," Ron said. "Sasha's an early warning system. Two separate functions entirely."

"The *canes belli* are much further up the Path," Petru added. "You must have both protections, my dear Bree."

Bree pressed the heels of both hands into her forehead.

"I need you all to give me more information than you have up until now," she said firmly. "I'm confused. I don't know enough. It isn't fair."

Lavinia sighed. "Fair," she said, rather wistfully. "Not much about this life is fair." Then, with a somewhat challenging look directed at the professor, she said, "You just go ahead and ask us your questions, child."

"And you'll answer them?" Bree said.

"If we can," Archie snapped. "How much is an airline ticket? Answer me that one, Matriel. What is the sound of one hand clapping? What about that one?"

"You hush up," Lavinia said. "My goodness, you're an annoying body."

"Archie does have a point," Ron said. "But so does Bree." The column of spring green light that was her secretary spun faster, took shape, and Ron's familiar figure sat upright in the chair. "I vote we tell her what we know."

Gabriel shook his head. "We've always been ready to tell her what we know. Answers aren't going to help."

"Probably not," Ron said. He smiled at Bree. "But we'll do the best we can, boss. Ask away."

Professor Cianquino nodded his agreement. "If we have an answer, you shall have it."

Bree looked up and down the table, struggling with her surprise. "You'll tell me everything?"

"She has been feeling excluded," Petru rumbled. "I told you all this before. We are failing her."

"*You* were the one who said it was too soon," Ron said tartly. "If she's ready, she'll understand the mission and all that goes with it. If she's not, she won't. That's what I've said all along."

"I'm ready," Bree said firmly. She dug her yellow pad out of her briefcase, put it on the table, and uncapped her pen. A warm, very gentle laughter sighed briefly in the room, and someone thought at her: *Notes? You're going to take notes?*

Bree thought it might be Lavinia, but she wasn't sure. She looked ruefully at the pen. "I always take notes." She looked at the faces of her Company again. "Habit," she said. "Pretty useless, I guess." She put the pen away. "Okay. First question."

There was an expectant silence.

"My mother," Bree said. "Leah. Who was she? How did she die? *Why* did she die?"

"Leah is one of a long line of temporal advocates for the damned," Professor Cianquino said.

"I figured that much out for myself," Bree said before she could bite back her rudeness. "Sorry." She glanced at Striker. She'd thrown a barrage of questions at him on her first case, and he'd told her then that he could only respond to specifics. She was beginning to understand, a little. Archie was right: You couldn't buy an airline ticket unless you knew where you were going—and where you were coming from. An answer of two hundred dollars made no sense at all.

Striker watched her think this through. His gaze was almost sympathetic.

"You said she *is*. That she *is* one of these advocates." Bree leaned forward. "Is she still alive?"

Archie screeched and rattled his wings. "Wasting time, wasting time."

Cianquino raised one pale hand and Archie subsided

with a mutter. "We will begin with the Path," he said calmly. He passed his hand over the tabletop and a spinning globe of light appeared under his palm. "We are all members of the Sphere, dear Bree. And we all begin here, at the bottom, and wind our way up the Path." His forefinger traced a continuous line around the globe from the base around and around toward the top. "If you see the Sphere as Knowledge—and many do—you increase your understanding as you go."

"What's at the top?" Bree asked.

The peace that passes all understanding. Eternity.

"And the bottom?"

Nothing. The absence of all that makes existence worthwhile. Eternity.

"And my mother?"

Cianquino passed his hand over the top of the sphere.

"And me?"

Cianquino just smiled at her.

"The Pendergasts," Bree said. Her deadly enemies. One of these days she was going to figure out what had pissed them off.

Cianquino passed his hand under the sphere.

"Each of us makes this trip alone," he said. "The very nature of enlightenment is that one person's journey is unique. Each is like none other's. We can answer you, Bree, but our replies can only be the truth: that you will know truth when *you* come upon it."

The light winked out.

The sphere disappeared.

Bree felt the loss of its beauty like a little death.

"The journey is life. The struggle is life. You only truly

understand at the end," Ron said helpfully. "When you have all the answers, there isn't any more to it."

"We're all walking up the Path as fast as we can," Lavinia said. "We angels move a bit more quickly, but not all that much. There's a lot we don't know, either. Not yet. Not until we get there. One thing at a time. That's the only way."

Bree felt the beginnings of a monster headache. "Okay," she said, although it wasn't, really. "You know what, though? I hate ambiguity. I hate mushy answers. I always have. I want yes or no. I want right or wrong. I want black or white, win or lose, on or off."

"You don't want to choose without some kind of guarantee," Petru said. "Very understandable."

"But not possible," Cianquino said with an air of finality. "And now, Bree. Your next question, if you please."

Bree had a small bottle of ibuprofen in her briefcase. She took it out and dry-swallowed three tablets. "Russell O'Rourke," she said. "My newest case. You wanted to see me about it."

"We did," Striker said. "It's a little early for you to be soliciting cases."

"I didn't," Bree said. "He solicited me."

"True," Ron said. "He showed up where he died. At his desk. That's what Bree said."

"But no Request for Appeal has been filed?" Professor Cianquino asked.

Ron shook his head. "Nope. Not according to Goldstein."

"Hm." Cianquino didn't say anything for a moment. "Well. It's within our jurisdiction. To file on his behalf. I suppose I could check with another firm and we could pass it along to them, but there's very little precedent to do so. And we are obligated to take on pro bono cases, so to speak. So perhaps you will agree to take it on, Bree."

"Wait, wait, wait," Bree said. "There's more people like me? More companies like this one?"

"There's only one in each temporal's lifetime," Striker said.

So she was alone.

Striker's eyes flickered and Bree felt a second wave of rather detached sympathy from him. "So the case would be passed to a firm in another place and time."

"Would it be soon?" Bree asked. "I mean, he's not my client yet, not officially. But you know the saying: 'Justice delayed is justice denied.'"

There was an amused, although kindly, silence, then Lavinia said. "Time makes no never mind to him, Bree, honey. He's dead."

"I see," Bree said. She felt rather dismal. Only one in each temporal's lifetime. And she was it. "Okay. So I'll take the case on. You know, by the way, that I had a visit from Beazley and Caldecott."

"*Did* you," Ron said. "I must say I'm not surprised. Those two are going to get hauled in front of the ethics committee one of these days. We're not even officially on the case. Were they looking for some kind of deal? Trying to warn you off?"

"No. There's been some kind of death threat. Opposing counsel's obligated to let the other guys know if there's been a death threat. At least in the State of Georgia." Bree thought a minute. "And it's part of the federal process, too. I hope the celestial system's the same."

"Indeed it is." Cianquino frowned. "Did they give you specifics?"

"I assumed it was the Pendergasts up to their tricks," Bree said. "So I guess I'm glad Miles and Belli are back for a bit." She paused. Something had been bothering her about Beazley and Caldecott, and she brought it up now. "Beaufort & Company is basically defense oriented, right? I mean, I'm sort of a heavenly public defender."

"Heavenly," Ron mused. There was a pile of books in front of him, and he patted the topmost volume. It was a copy of the Torah. Underneath was a King James version of the Christian Bible, and underneath that, a copy of the Koran.

"I understand that Beaufort & Company is ecumenical," Bree said. "I guess I'm wondering how come the Prosecution doesn't have a temporal advocate, too."

"Oh, my goodness," Ron said. "Of course they do. Beazley and Caldecott are human, Bree."

Petru grinned at her, his teeth very white in his black beard. "Or, at least, they started out that way."

"Started out that way?" Bree said. The room had grown chilly, she thought. She rubbed her arms. "What does that mean? They started out human. I'm human. Is something going to happen to me?"

Archie shrieked, *"Bibamus, moriendum est."*

"You hush up," Lavinia scolded.

"Biba-what?" Bree said. She'd scraped through Latin with gentleman's C's, and promptly forgot everything but how to decline *erro*, "I err."

" 'Death's unavoidable, let's have a drink,' " Professor

Cianquino said. He smiled. "A little early in the day for that, I suppose."

Bree's cell phone buzzed with a text message. She flipped it open:

Drs. Appt. Lowry 7am Tues STAT Tonia

Bree shut the cell phone. "Too early for a drink? I don't know about that." The professor always kept a bottle of wine handy in a little bar at the bottom of his bookshelves. "I think I'd like a small glass of wine before I go." Started out human? What the hell? "Maybe a big glass of wine before I go."

Eight

What is the good of the strongest heart
In a body that's falling apart?
A serious flaw—I hope you know that.
—Tim Rice, "Waltz for Eva and Che," *Evita*

"You're down about five pounds from your former weight,"
Dr. Lowry said. It was early Tuesday morning. It was good
of Antonia to wangle an appointment so fast, but it was
freakishly early. Not even seven thirty yet. "But everything else looks just fine."

"I feel really stupid," Bree said. "About coming in like
this, I mean. I feel perfectly fine."

Dr. Lowry didn't say anything. She just tapped away at the
keyboard in front of her and gazed intently at the screen, which
held a document labeled NEW PATIENT QUESTIONNAIRE.

"The thing is, my little sister got on my case about the
weight loss and my not sleeping so well, and she and my
aunt Cissy basically strong-armed me."

"Any anxiety?" Dr. Lowry interrupted in an absent way.
She was a little older than Bree herself and very thin. She
wore large horn-rimmed glasses that gave her a slightly
owlish look. "Any depression?"

"No," Bree said rather crossly.

Dr. Lowry tapped the "no" response into the computer and sat back. "You are in excellent shape. What's your workout schedule?"

"My workout schedule?" Bree made a guilty face. "I run along the river a couple of times a week. Jog, really. But that's about it."

"Amazing." Dr. Lowry shook her head. "Your blood pressure is ninety over eighty. Your resting heart rate's sixty-five, and your exercise heart rate's eighty after twenty minutes on the treadmill." She peered at Bree with considerable interest. "I know professional basketball players who don't have stats like that."

"Well," Bree said. "Well."

"You've always been this fit?"

"I never paid much attention before," Bree said frankly.

"We got your records in from your family doctor in Raleigh." Dr. Lowry tapped the computer with affection. "Your last physical was three years ago and your stats weren't nearly this good. So whatever you're doing, keep it up." There was a plastic replica of an eyeball on Dr. Lowry's desk. She picked it up, then suddenly pitched it straight at Bree. Bree picked it out of the air before she had time to think about reacting.

"Wonderful reflexes, too." Dr. Lowry extended her hand. Bewildered, Bree dropped the eyeball into it.

Dr. Lowry reached over and shook Bree's hand. "Congratulations on being so fit."

"My sister will be delighted to hear it. And again, sorry to take up your time."

"Makes a change, treating live people," Dr. Lowry said. "I kind of enjoyed it."

"I beg your pardon?"

"I'm assisting at the coroner's office. Hoping to be full-time there as soon as a position opens up. It should happen soon. Dr. Falwell's sixty-five and a smoker. He'll either retire or," she added cheerfully, "drop dead. In the meantime . . ." She waved her hand around her little examining room. "This keeps the bills paid. My older brother heads the practice here," she confided. "This is just until Dr. Falwell . . ."

". . . retires or drops dead," Bree said. "Right."

Dr. Lowry swung back to the computer. "I don't really anticipate any anomalies in your blood work. But the office will mail out the results in a couple of days. If there's any kind of a problem, my nurse will call and ask you to come back in." She rotated in her swivel chair and faced Bree with a smile. "Any other concerns?"

Well, let's see. I'm basically worried about losing my humanity. What kind of tests do you have for that?

"No," Bree said. "Nothing. As I said, I'm just fulfilling a promise I made to my little sister. And I appreciate getting in to see you so fast."

Dr. Lowry nodded. "I owe your aunt Cissy a few favors. And I'm always glad to sit down with a new patient, especially the live ones. Ha ha!"

"Ha ha," Bree said.

"Call me if you have any concerns."

Bree dropped fifteen dollars for the co-pay at checkout and stamped out into a damp, rainy morning in a mood as glum as the gray skies overhead.

She'd spent the night before drawing up the steps for an investigation into Russell O'Rourke's murder/suicide/ whatever. Part of the evening, at any rate. She'd lost a fair amount of time in fruitless speculation about her future. At the very best, it appeared she was doomed to be abnormally fit and sleepless as long as she was part of Beaufort & Company. At worst? What?

She decided not to think about it. Not right now.

"One thing, though," she said to Sasha as she folded herself into the driver's seat of her car, "the next guy that asks me out on a date is going to be in for a surprise. Got that, Sash? I may be doomed to end up a messy victim of the Pendergasts, or blasted away by some grisly spirit from who-knows-where, or turn into some ceramic version of myself, if Antonia's to be believed, but I'm not resigning from the human race just yet. What did Archie say? Biba-whatsis? Death's unavoidable, let's have a drink? Well, there you are. Maybe I'll take up vodka." She thrust the car into gear and drove the short distance back to Angelus Street, stifling the impulse to racket down through the streets at seventy miles an hour.

Once inside the office, it didn't take angelic prescience on the part of her employees to sense she was in a dangerous mood. Ron deposited a carafe of French press coffee at her desk in tactful silence. Petru dropped a warm and sympathetic hand on her shoulder before he stumped off to collect the downloads Bree had requested on the background of her preliminary list of suspects. By the time she assembled everyone for a staff meeting in the little conference room at eleven, she felt less like a candidate for the booby hatch and more like a lawyer in charge of her own life. She faced her totally normal-looking employees with an air of professional competence honed by practice sessions in her bathroom mirror. The celestial questions could take care of themselves. She had a case to solve.

"As you all know by now, we're facing some issues about Russell O'Rourke's death. The NYPD lieutenant initially assigned to the suicide is convinced O'Rourke was murdered by his wife. And Tully is convinced her husband was murdered by either a disaffected employee or a disgruntled investor. Our client himself"—Bree took a deep breath—"is, as you know, somewhat hampered in his ability to communicate with us, but we are operating on the assumption that he believes he's been wrongly sentenced . . ."

"A reasonable assumption," Petru rumbled.

"I never thought Purgatory was all that awful," Ron said. "I mean, considering the alternatives . . ."

"T'cha," Petru said disapprovingly. "Compromise is not to be tolerated. We must consider the best interests of the client."

"Are you inferring I don't care about our clients?" Ron said frostily.

"I am not inferring a thing, except that you are, as usual, not well-informed."

"Yes, well, first things first," Bree said. She was in no mood for a swatting match between the two. "Petru, how did you do on the background checks?"

"Very interesting," Petru said with a pleased air. "Perhaps the most interesting information I shall save for the last. First, you must know that Cullen Jameson is out on parole."

"Already?" Bree said. She had a vague recollection that the chief financial officer of O'Rourke Investment Bank had been sentenced to at least five years and that he had begun to serve time just before O'Rourke's death three months ago.

"Time off for time served while in custody," Petru said. "And, of course, more germane is the fact that without Mr. O'Rourke to testify against him, the case is not so strong."

"And O'Rourke was planning to do that?" Bree rubbed the back of her neck thoughtfully.

"Oh, yes. He made quite a business of it. His belief that Jameson was behind the fraudulent activity was un-equivocal." He laid the Jameson file in front of her. A neat summary of Jameson's background in Petru's elegant calligraphy was attached to the outside of the file. Jameson was fifty-three, divorced, and he had three children in their twenties; he was a bad to medium-poor golfer, if his handicap was any indication. He held an MBA from Wharton and an undergrad degree in economics from Brandeis. He'd been posted overseas for part of his career. He had a short rap sheet, to Bree's mild surprise: two DUIs and a physical assault charge (dismissed), filed by his ex-wife thirteen years ago.

Bree hadn't paid a great deal of attention to the scandal when it hit the media, but she recognized Jameson from the photo Petru had downloaded from the *Wall Street Journal* archives. He was a heavyset, self-satisfied-looking man in his early fifties. Dark hair was slicked back from a balding forehead. A pair of wire-rimmed spectacles perched on his fleshy nose.

"Kind of a belligerent-looking lower lip," Ron observed. "Actually, a scary-looking guy altogether."

The next few photos showed Jameson, in handcuffs, being shoved into a police car by a poker-faced plainclothesman. The expression on his face wasn't self-satisfied at that point; it was murderous. Bree skimmed the newspaper articles detailing the charges: fraud; illegal conversion of a securities instrument; that old standby, insider trading; and illegal transfer of funds.

"Was he in jail when O'Rourke died?" Bree asked.

"As a matter of fact, no," Petru said. "He bounced in and out, as new sets of charges were brought by various jurisdictions. The FBI investigation into securities fraud was perhaps the final blow to this man. That carried the heaviest sentence. The picture here"—he tapped the arrest photo—"was taken the day after the client's demise."

Bree set the Jameson file on the right-hand side of her desk.

"And here is a collection of information about the Parsalls." The file Petru handed her was several inches thick. "They are heavily involved in society matters, you understand, so there is much written gossip about them."

Harriet and Freddy "Big Buck" Parsall were third-generation oil, from Texas. Harriet was a familiar type to Bree, who was a born and bred Southerner herself. Many of her mother's friends still went in for big hair, lots of red lipstick, and toothy, prosthetics-enhanced smiles. Harriet favored expensive print dresses with full skirts, and in each of the photos Bree rifled through (in *People*, *USA Today*, *Redbook*, and *Ladies' Home Journal*) she wore uncomfortable-looking spike heels. She looked good-natured, in that genial Southern way, despite the fact that her feet had to be killing her. A half dozen women Bree's mother Francesca entertained to tea every six months or so looked just like Harriet. She played bridge, drank old-fashioneds, and must have visited a very good plastic surgeon more than once.

"Big Buck" was big and broad and looked like a shouter. A good six inches taller than his wife, he favored string ties, cowboy boots, and deer hunting. He was a Texas Aggie, a member of the university's second-string football team in his undergraduate days.

And he was flat broke after a lifetime of trust fund money.

"Wow," Bree said. "He lost everything?"

"So it seems," Petru said. "He has been petitioning his brothers to support him and Madame Parsall, to no good effect, as yet. But that very large house in River Oaks?"

Bree paged down to a photograph of a sprawling mansion.

"It is up for sale at a distress price." Petru leaned across the table and tapped his summary with a blunt forefinger. "You will note the bar brawls in the gentleman's background."

Bree skimmed the charges in Parsall's arrest records. Menacing with a deadly weapon. Assault with a deadly weapon. Battery. Some of it dated back more than twenty years. "A Texan with a temper," she said. "Any of these charges actually turn into recorded felonies?" (Bree had discovered that Petru's investigations were not limited to institutions that existed in the here and now. But they were accurate, nonetheless.)

"None," Petru said. "And the menacing with a deadly weapon—a twelve-gauge shotgun, by the way—occurred in a very public place."

Bree raised her eyebrows in inquiry.

"Outside Mr. O'Rourke's arraignment."

"And official charges were never filed?"

Petru shook his head solemnly.

"So he called in a few favors, our Mr. Parsall."

"Which may not be as forthcoming, now that he has lost his patrimony."

A cynical view, especially from an angel. But probably true. Bree stacked the Parsall file on top of the Jameson file. "We've got two great motives so far. Next?"

"Mr. Russell O'Rourke, Junior."

This file was slim, and depressing. "Fig" O'Rourke was nineteen, going on twelve. He'd graduated at the bottom of his prep school and flunked out of his freshman year at NYU, and his employment was listed as Administrative Manager, Transitional Services. It looked like he mainly booked air tickets and cruises for his mother. He belonged to a country club, but his chief activities seemed to be drinking and playing poker. He seemed to have no friends, no skills, and very little interest in the world around him, except for a minority share in a movie production company located in California. "A college acquaintance," Petru said, when he saw that Bree paused to take a second look at that. "Who appears to be interested in only the checks that support her experimental movies."

"Oh, my."

"An angry young man, however. His prep school recommended a course of psychotherapy. I will add the records to the file if you like. It is a classic case. Hates his poor mother, and was resentful of his father." Petru looked at her over his wire-rimmed spectacles. "It is fashionable now to decry the insights of my friend Sigmund into the behaviors of such as Fig O'Rourke. But it is clear to me that he was right in many of his comments about temporal behavior."

Bree didn't ask which Sigmund Petru referred to. She was pretty sure already.

"Yes. Well. The poor kid."

"All that money growin' up." Lavinia shook her head and went "tsk." "You'd think he'd be a happy boy."

"But a patricide?" Bree said. "That's pretty extreme. He sounds pathetic, not homicidal. Still . . ." She hesitated, then dropped Fig's file on top of the other suspects.

"And now!" Petru said. "An extremely interesting report, indeed." With an air of quiet triumph, he dropped the last file in front of her.

"Oh, my gosh," she said. "This is Eddie Chin's file."

"A disgraced and dismissed policeman," Petru said. "He is on disciplinary suspension for inappropriate investigatory techniques in the case of Russell O'Rourke."

And so he was. The union was filing to have him reinstated, but for the moment, the Ninja was badgeless, gunless, and free to stay in Savannah as long as his credit cards held out. Bree paged through the file and set it aside.

"And this"—Petru's air of quiet triumph was well deserved—"the complete dossier on the suicide and subsequent investigation."

Bree looked at her assembled staff. "I'm going to read through this, guys. I'll need about half an hour."

"We shall wait," Petru said comfortably.

Bree nodded. What was time, to an angel?

It took more than half an hour because she read through the NYPD file twice. Then she read Eddie's. Petru appeared to doze. Ron messed around with his laptop. Lavinia buzzed around the room dusting, and humming a small song under her breath. Finally, Bree squared the pages, closed the file cover, and placed it neatly on the left side of her desk.

"We don't seem to have a case," she said flatly.

"No murder?" Lavinia said. "The poor soul just shot his own self?"

"First," Bree said, "the New York City Police Department is one of the best in the world. I mean, every system has flaws, and stupid people, and botched investigations, and corruption, but I'll be darned if I can see how the investigation fell prey to any of those things. Russell O'Rourke was a suicide."

"And Lieutenant Chin?" Ron said. "Is he crazy, or what?"

"Well, that's the second problem. Eddie Chin. And I vote for crazy," Bree sighed. "Now, maybe I'm jumping the gun. I don't know. Maybe he's an 'or what.' That is, there's something he knows that no one else does and for some reason he can't tell anybody yet. But these"—she tapped the relevant papers—"are his psychiatric interviews, and the diagnosis isn't real reassuring." She shot a stern glance at Petru. "I get a little nervous once in a while about the legality of the ways you all get this kind of information."

"Any data that will end up in the public domain is ours

for the asking," Ron said. "The rules of procedure are
quite clear. We are able, I admit, to get it released to us a
little earlier than the State of Georgia would like, but it's
all in a good cause, isn't it?"

"Some of this stuff is really confidential. We're invad-
ing this man's privacy big-time. On the other hand . . ."
She sat up. "The poor guy does seem to be a few light-
bulbs short of a full chandelier. Ron? Could you find Sam
Hunter for me? I want to take him to lunch again. And
Petru? If we could get the complete NYPD case notes on
the O'Rourke"—she hesitated—"incident, I guess we'll
call it—I want a complete timeline of the hours leading up
to the death. I'd also like as complete a record as possible
of the whereabouts of the suspects here. The investigating
officers must have put them in with this other stuff." She
tapped the files at her right hand. "Let me know about
gaps in any of the suspects' interviews, and I'll set up interviews with whomever I need to see. And really, Petru.
This was excellent work, thank you."

It was Ron's turn to make the noise "t'cha," so Bree
said, "And there's something you'll be able to handle better than any of us, Ron."

"Well, I'm sure," he said crossly.

"Goldstein."

"Goldstein?"

"We've got the original disposition of O'Rourke's case,
don't we?"

"You mean his Judgment Day file?"

"That's the one."

"We do. We picked it up at the Hall of Records. You
were with me."

"Yes, yes, I remember all that. But do you recall what he was sentenced for?"

"Misdemeanor simony."

"Profiteering, then. In a small way. Hm." Bree thought about this for a moment. In its heyday, the O'Rourke Investment Bank controlled twenty billion dollars, globally, and that was a conservative estimate. Of course, what was money, to an angel? Perhaps in the long run, celestially speaking, twenty billion was a mere bagatelle. Which would be a good thing, since his appeal would rest on proving that the misdemeanor hadn't occurred at all. Or if it did, that it was insignificant when stacked against the good that O'Rourke had done during life. "I'd like the regulations regarding sentencing."

Ron's eyes were large, and blue, and they got even larger and bluer. "All of them?"

Bree had a brief vision of a Mount Ararat–sized pile of parchment. "No, no. Just those bits that are relevant to O'Rourke's sentencing. It's puzzling me some. O'Rourke appears to be guilty of robbing widows and orphans and then some. But he's spending eternity in the same way as Benjamin Skinner, who never had so much as a traffic ticket as far as criminal behavior was concerned."

"Goldstein's just going to get all condescending over the differences in law between the celestial and the profane," Ron said. "But I'll come right back at him about getting a decent electronic database. I mean, there's more than a few of those clerks with parchment allergies, and what kind of work environment makes you sneeze? Not a very nice one." He looked quite smug at the prospect.

"Thank you. And before we go much further, I'll need

to have a heart-to-heart with Mrs. O'Rourke. I'd like to see her as soon as I can. Her assistant . . ."

"Danica Billingsley." Ron nodded. "I've got her number, of course. I'll set up an appointment right away."

Bree pointed to the door. "Find Hunter for me. Set up an appointment with Mrs. O'Rourke, this afternoon, if possible. Then go tackle Goldstein."

Ron was first out, followed by Petru.

"Anything *I* can do for us?" Lavinia asked, hopefully.

Bree looked at her landlady with affection. She wore her usual droopy print skirt, with a woolly cardigan wrapped around her skinny frame. Her hair was a soft, wispy white halo around her wrinkled face. Her eyes were bright with intelligence. She hated not having anything to do. Bree looked down at Sasha, who had been sitting at her feet. He got up and wagged his tail in an anxious way.

No baths.

"I think," Bree said, "that we'll all be ready for some shortbread late this afternoon. And Sasha, you can come with me. With any luck, Mr. Sam Hunter will be free for lunch."

"Nice fellow," Lavinia said. "Been thinkin' you might take him on a date, like."

Bree blinked. "A date? Sam? Maybe. But first, I need to get a better handle on what's going on with Eddie Chin."

"Hm," Lavinia said, with a faint air of disapproval. "You be fair with the man, chile."

"Good grief," Bree said. "He's as interested in this case as I am."

"For goodness' sakes, Bree. The man's also interested in you!"

Nine

**Men have died from time to time,
and worms have eaten them—but not for love.**
—Shakespeare, *As You Like It*

"Not you, too." Hunter balled up the paper bag that had
held his chicken salad sandwich and tossed it into the trash
bin that stood at the base of Oglethorpe memorial in the
Bay Street park. "I'm just getting Eddie to see some sense
about this bloody O'Rourke case, and here you bungle in
with another crackpot theory."

"Bungle!" Bree said indignantly. "Crackpot? I had
lunch with you and Eddie, remember? Yesterday. And you
said—do you mind if I quote you? I didn't think so. You
said: 'Bree has something unique to offer.' That's what
you said." She was so irritated she turned her back to him,
folded her arms, and glared down the high bank at the
river. Her view was partially obscured by the top two stories of the River Front Inn. The old brick building had
been around for close to two hundred years and seen a lot:
pirate raids and slave auctions, not to mention skirmishes
in two wars—1812, and Civil. A little disagreement between friends was a piffle compared to all that history. She

dropped her arms and turned around. "Sorry," she said. "I didn't mean to jump out at you like that. And that's really the reason why I asked you to stop by for some lunch. That the case doesn't seem to have much value, I mean. So I don't know why I ripped up at you like that."

"Guilt," Hunter said.

"I beg your pardon?"

"You're feeling guilty. You pulled that Southern charm on me . . . and, Bree, I told myself I wasn't going to fall for it one more time—and it turns out you're after Eddie."

"I am not after Eddie." She'd been holding her own sandwich bag so tightly it was a crumpled mess in her fist, so she, too, tossed it into the garbage can. And she hadn't finished her sandwich. "And if you're inferring—even in the most sideways sort of manner—that I was leading you on, you're flat wrong."

"I am, am I?"

"You most certainly are."

He stepped closer. Bree liked the way he smelled and the warmth of his body next to hers. "So how do you feel about basketball?"

"Okay, I guess," Bree said cautiously. "I played some at Duke, as a matter of fact. Not since they got good," she said hastily. "I was on the house team. The A team used to whale on us before they went out to really compete. But basketball's okay. More than okay."

"The department's sponsoring a local high school team Thursday night. You want to go? Maybe grab something to eat?"

Hunter's face was calm, his posture casual. But there was a slightly higher pitch to his voice than usual. Then he gulped. It was a quiet, almost unnoticeable gulp. He was nervous. He was afraid she'd turn him down. Bree found it completely endearing. "Sure."

"About six, then. Thursday? I think we'll have a good time." His face darkened. "I say something funny?"

"Sorry." Bree bit her lip, but it didn't help her giggles much. "I haven't had a date in a possum's age. So I promised Sasha . . ."

"Sasha?" Hunter said, a little warily. He looked down at the dog, who wagged his tail cheerfully.

"He's the only friend I've got these days, and that includes my little sister. Anyhow, I told him that the next date I had . . . never mind. Yes, I think we will have a good time." She touched his hand, lightly. "I'm looking forward to it."

He smiled, which made the corners of his eyes wrinkle in a really attractive way. Bree was suddenly conscious of the breadth of Hunter's chest, and the way his hair curled a little on the nape of his neck. She tilted her head.

He leaned forward and kissed her.

He smelled of soap and clean sweat. Bree liked that, and she liked the kiss. *You be fair with the man,* Lavinia had said, so Bree backed away some and said, "Let's make a deal. Let's agree to a clear division between work and play, okay? I've just taken on a new case and right now, I'm wearing my lawyer's hat. Thursday night, I leave my lawyer's hat at home." She looked down at her suit, which was gray summer-weight wool with a hemline just below the knee. "And my lawyer's suit, too, for that matter." He looked delighted and she burst into laughter. "I just mean I'll wear something that doesn't make me look like I'm about to present a defense in superior court." She stuck out her hand. Hunter shook it. Then he said, flatly, "About this business of Eddie's, Bree. Russell O'Rourke killed himself."

"You're sure."

Hunter threw one hand up in a "hold it" gesture. "I've been *fairly* certain twice in my life as a cop, Bree. Both times, we caught the crime on a surveillance tape, we got a confession, and the forensics were solid. But have I ever been one hundred percent *sure* in any case I've ever handled? No."

Bree herself had been fairly certain Hunter was a good cop. Now, she was sure.

Hunter moved restlessly down the sidewalk and then back again. "All cases are about what you can prove. Eddie can't prove murder. Not unless some kind of miracle occurs. And every cop has cases where you know who did it, how they did, but there's no proof. You let those cases go. Eddie's been a cop, a good cop, way too long to get hung out like this." He rubbed the back of his neck in clear frustration. "He just can't let it go. I told him he doesn't need my help, he needs a . . ."

"Shrink," Bree supplied helpfully.

Hunter sighed, an explosion of resignation. "Yeah. Yeah."

Bree had seen the psychiatric summaries in Eddie's file. One of the less attractive diagnoses had been "Obsessive-compulsive personality disorder with long-standing paranoid psychosis/ideation." She wasn't exactly sure what that meant but it didn't sound promising.

"Is there any lead at all? Anything real that he's following up on?"

Hunter shook his head. "It's about time I asked you about your interest, isn't it? Why are you poking into this?"

"Well," Bree said cautiously, "Mrs. O'Rourke seems to feel it's murder, too."

"Smoke screen," Hunter said dismissively. "She's pointing the finger at somebody else, right? Classic move on the part of a perp." Then, in a complete U-turn: "And if she does think it's murder why bring the harassment suit against Chin in the first place? She dropped it almost immediately," he said in response to Bree's raised eyebrows, "but that's what tipped off the suspension."

Bree had a theory about that. But she'd agreed to represent Tully in civil matters, and she couldn't speculate about criminal behavior on the part of a client. But she did say, "I don't think I've met a more arrogant person in my life."

"Vigilante justice?" he said sharply. "Is she expecting you to give her a hand?"

Hunter was quick. She'd have to remember that.

He scowled at her. "Don't get mixed up in this, Bree. Eddie's got enough trouble. The last thing he needs is somebody else feeding this . . . fixation he's got." He looked at his watch. A sudden, boyish smile lit his face. "I've got to be getting back to the precinct. But I'll see you Thursday?"

"Did he tell you why?" Bree asked abruptly.

"Why? We're back to Eddie, now? You heard why. He's got a couple of unresolved questions—the bullet fragment of the .22, the dead surveillance camera, the scrap of the suicide note. Every case has them. If things fit perfectly together in a case, you have to start wondering if you've been set up. Why Eddie can't see that is something that's been driving *me* nuts." Hunter balled his fists in frustration. "I've pressed him on it. But what he tells me doesn't make any sense. Not common sense, anyway. And he won't tell it to the shrinks."

Bree raised her eyebrows in an encouraging way.

"Dreams. He says he has bad dreams." He passed his hand over his mouth, shook his head, and said, "Claims O'Rourke's begging him to solve the case from beyond the grave." Hunter glanced at his watch. "Shoot! Got to run. See you Thursday, then." He hesitated, bent and kissed her on the cheek, then took off for his car at a jog trot.

Bree waited until he was out of earshot, then speed-dialed the professor on her cell.

"Yes, indeed," Professor Cianquino said after she explained Eddie Chin's problem with O'Rourke's ghost. "I wouldn't say it's uncommon."

"I know that. It may even been routine for someone directly involved with a case. Liz Overshaw came to me for just that reason. But she worked with Ben Skinner every day of her life. Eddie Chin never even met Russell O'Rourke."

"I don't have all the answers, Bree. There's certainly precedent for the dead to appear in the dreams of the living. A violent death and a desire for justice can bring the strong-willed back for short periods of time. But no, I would not be frank in my discussions with Mr. Chin. I would say Mr. Chin is a perfectly normal temporal with no connection whatever to the work that we do. An attempt to reveal the scope of Beaufort & Company's activities would certainly alarm him.

"One thing seems to be clear, dear Bree. Mr. O'Rourke was murdered."

Bree clicked her cell phone shut and waved at Hunter's car as he pulled away from the curb and headed back down Bay to Montgomery.

It was past time to sit down with Tully O'Rourke.

Ten

Who profits from this? (Cui bono?)
—Cicero, "Pro Milone"

"The place off Bull Street," Tully snapped into her cell phone. "It's perfect and I don't care if there's an existing lease. I want it. Break it, Barney. That's what I pay you the big bucks for." She snapped the cover shut and slipped the phone back into her purse and addressed the air over Bree's head. "It's a gorgeous building. Just perfect for a theater in the round. Some events company has a long-term lease. Screw that. Built in the 1920s and it was a Chevrolet dealership, if you can believe it. Fabulous tin ceilings." She still didn't look at Bree directly as she talked, but over Bree's shoulder, at the crowd milling in her living room. She wore another one of her filmy, swirling dresses. This one was in shades of navy blue. With her severe cap of white hair, dark eyebrows, and plum-colored eyes, she looked like a product so expensive, an ad writer would only need one word to promote it. The Tully, Bree thought, and suppressed a sigh.

Tully switched into Southern belle mode with a flutter

of coal black eyelashes. "Thank God *you're* here, though, Bree. Barney went back to his New York law firm after the auction and it's a lot harder to intimidate people over the phone. Much better in person. So you can take care of that for me?" She paused in her restless review of the people behind Bree and gave her an appraising look. "I hear you're pretty good at intimidation when you need to be."

"It doesn't seem to be working too well with you," Bree said dryly.

Tully burst into startled laughter. It was more of a bark than a laugh, really, but at least Bree had her full attention.

"It was good of you to see me on such short notice, Mrs. O'Rourke," Bree added hastily, since she'd felt she'd been a little abrupt.

"Please." She fluttered her fingers. "I've said it before. Call me Tully. Mrs. O'Rourke is for the staff. Besides, I like your aunt Cissy and any relative of Cissy's has just got to be a friend of mine."

Bree could do the Southern charm thing with the best of them, and at this point, she should have responded with a "Why, thank you, Tully. And Cissy is just a caution, isn't she . . ." blabber blabber blabber. (Her mother, Francesca, had been a careful tutor.) But she didn't want to. She wanted to solve this case and she didn't give a hoot about the usual civilities. "I'd like to talk with you about your husband. Is there somewhere we can be a little quieter, where we can sit and talk frankly?"

"And I need to give you copies of the Players' stock contracts. It *is* a bit of a zoo around here," Tully admitted. "Even more than usual. But everyone's just so excited about Ciaran signing on with us that they can't help getting together and making plans. Anthony's beside himself, aren't you, darling?"

Anthony Haddad, who was even better looking than Bree's lively libido remembered, wound his way through the crowd and gave Tully an absentminded kiss on the cheek. "Yes, darling, of course." Bree could never figure out why so many creative people wore black. But the black jeans and black shirt suited Haddad nicely. His eyes warmed as he looked at Bree. "And you, Miss Beaufort, are even more striking than I recall. Is it too much to hope that you're here to audition?"

"She's my lawyer, Tony. It's the little redhead who's going to audition."

"Are you holding auditions right now?" Bree asked. Her hand went to her cell phone. Poor Tonia would have a genuine hissy fit if she missed out on this chance.

Haddad surveyed the lively crowd. Bree decided the people in jeans, T-shirts, and flip-flops were the tech crew. The men and women in leotards, leggings, and white shirts tied at the midriff were the artists. "Well, it looks like it, doesn't it? Half of the actors are here and the tech managers, too, but no, this is just Tully's regular afternoon madness. Cocktails, little bits of things to eat, and talk, talk, talk."

"I *hate* silence." Tully pouted. "But my lawyer says I need a bit of silence at the moment, Tony, so I'm hauling counsel away to my little den." She tucked her arm into Bree's. "Come along, darling, and we'll figure out how to break that silly lease on the Bull Street building."

Mindful of her sisterly duties, Bree removed Tully's

arm from her own with a polite smile and said, "Just a second, if you wouldn't mind. Mr. Haddad?"

"Tony, please. Only the bill collectors call me Mr. Haddad."

"My sister is very anxious to audition, as I'm sure you know."

Boredom closed his face. "They all are, Bree. She's sent you as her advance man, is that it?"

Bree felt herself blushing. She was going to kill Antonia when she saw her next. But she was going to get her an audition if she had to embarrass herself six ways from Sunday. "Something like that. But she's truly talented. I don't think you'll be sorry." She pressed on, "Is there a best time for you?"

"A 'best time'?" His eyebrows twitched cynically. "There's never a best time to deal with aspiring actresses. I should tell you, Miss Beaufort, that she's not got a suitable look for anything that I'm casting right now."

"She's very talented," Bree repeated loyally. "Very."

"I'm sure she is." Then he shook himself, like a dog coming out of water. "Sorry. There's no excuse for rudeness. I apologize. Have her call my people, will you? I'll be setting something up tomorrow. I honestly can't think of a place to put a delicious-looking redhead—at least, not for now. But we'll see."

At least his tone was kind, Bree thought. Maybe the audition wouldn't be too awful.

"Now, if only she had some experience with tech, I might be able to use her."

"You mean stage management?"

"Yes. As a matter of fact, I lost Rebecca to a musical

production of *Moonstruck* just a few days ago, and there doesn't seem to be a tech director in the entire state of Georgia that's free to begin work right now." Whoever Rebecca was, he looked extremely sorry to have lost her.

"My sister is a superb tech manager," Bree said with complete sincerity. It was true. Confounding all expectations, Antonia handled the enormously complicated business of staging shows with a great deal of expertise.

"You're kidding."

"Are you familiar with this new play, *The Return of Sherlock Holmes*? The one with the onstage version of the Reichenbach Falls?"

Haddad looked seriously impressed. "You're kidding. Your sister pulled that off?"

"Every last drop of fake water," Bree said proudly.

"Then I'll have somebody talk to her right now. No, no"—he waved his hand as Bree rummaged in her purse for Antonia's card—"I know how to reach her."

"I suppose she's called you a couple of times," Bree said ruefully. "I suppose a lot of actors and actresses call you all the time."

"More than a couple. But don't worry about it." His easy, but detached, professional manner slipped a bit and he quirked one eyebrow at her. "Anytime you want to discuss my directorial woes over a glass of wine? Thursday evening, maybe?"

"For heaven's sake, Tony. Do your seducing on your own time, will you?" Tully's face was sharp with irritation. "Come along. Bree. Danica's set up in that little office at the end of the hall. We'll talk there."

The barrister bookshelves under the windows were

gone, replaced by the rosewood credenza. The gray filing cabinet was tucked behind the recliner. Danica sat at the small conference table, her laptop open in front of her. A vase of roses sat at one corner of the desk. A phone and the jar and inkstand sat at the other. A sleek desk top computer sat in the middle. The room was spotless, comfortable, and, despite the lack of paper files, very businesslike. Tully sat behind the desk. Bree sat opposite Danica.

"Would you like tea or coffee, Bree? Or maybe a drink?" Tully looked at her watch, a Patek Philippe with a diamond-encrusted band. She'd moved her wedding and engagement rings—the one a very large marquise-cut diamond, the other a band set with as many diamonds as the watch—to her right hand. It was an old custom—the only other widows Bree knew who'd adopted it were well in their nineties—and it surprised her a little.

"I'd welcome a cup of coffee."

Tully jerked her chin at Danica. "And the usual for me, Dani. Then you can go out for a bit. Not too far. I won't need you until dinner."

Danica quirked an eyebrow at Bree and left the room without having said a word.

"Well," Tully said, with a brisk air, "I've done some checking up on you." She tapped at the laptop keyboard. "Graduated in the lower third of your class at Duke. Worked at Daddy's law firm for a number of years. Inherited your great-uncle Franklin's practice and moved here to Savannah a couple of months ago. Current residence: the family town house over on Factor's Walk." She frowned. "There doesn't seem to be a current address for your offices."

"It's the warehouse building on East Bay and Drayton," Bree said. "The building's being rehabbed. I'll be taking over Judge Beaufort's office there directly." She emphasized the "Judge" slightly. Tully's dismissive air stung. Between this and Anthony Haddad's casual assessment of Antonia's talents, the Winston-Beauforts were taking a slight hammering. Bree stuck her chin out.

"You do have a competent staff?" Tully said sharply.

"I do indeed," Bree said pleasantly. "Each and every one of them on the side of the angels."

There was a tap at the office door, and Danica came in, a tray balanced on one hand. She set it on the conference table, poured a cup of black coffee for Bree, and handed Tully a tall glass filled with ice and what looked to be straight Scotch. Tully took it with a faint, unconscious sigh, and then lifted it up. "To you, Russ," and took a sip and frowned up at Danica. "This is the Glenlivet. What happened to the good stuff?"

"We've had to reorder the Laphroaig," Danica said. She hesitated, glanced at Bree, and added, "The liquor people wanted a word before they sent the order for this week."

"They want to be paid, I expect. Rutger must have overlooked it." Tully waved her out. "Give him a call. He's in Venice today, at the Intercontinental."

"Rutger is Mr. VanHoughton?" Bree asked as the door closed behind Danica. Then, to prod things along, she said, "Is it Mr. VanHoughton that will be paying my retainer?"

"Retainer," Tully said. She leaned back in her chair, the Scotch held between both her hands. "There are a lot of lawyers who'd jumped at the chance to represent the O'Rourkes just for the PR value, you know."

"That wouldn't be me," Bree said.

"And just how much do you think you're worth?"

"My usual retainer's ten thousand. But for you . . ." Bree paused, for effect, and then said, "More along the lines of fifteen."

Tully laughed, that short sharp bark that was such a startling disruption of her bitchy elegance. "Because you're worth it? Fine. Fifteen it is."

Bree added, pleasantly, "Lieutenant Chin suggested I get the retainer up front."

Tully's black eyes flickered. "How in the world did you get connected with that miserable little bastard?"

"He thinks your husband was murdered, too."

"But he thinks *I* did it." Tully drained half of the Scotch. "There's a restraining order out against him, you know. He's not supposed to come within two hundred yards of me, or something like that. You know the musical *Les Miz*? That one guy that won't let the other guy alone?"

"Inspector Javert," Bree said.

"That's the one. Well, Lieutenant Chin is my Javert. And me? I'm Russell's Javert. I won't stop until I find my husband's murderer. And when I do . . ." Her black eyes glittered. She tapped the laptop. "There's more interesting information about you in here. The first two cases you took on here in Savannah? You solved two murders. One each. And that, Miss Brianna Winston-Beaufort, is what I want you to do for me."

There was a clock somewhere in the room, perhaps hidden in the credenza. Its soft tick-tick-tick filled the silence.

Bree wondered if she really needed this woman as a

client. It was iffy, anyway, since her first responsibility was to her dead husband, and the possibilities for a conflict of interest were too many to ignore. And Bree was an orderly person. The woman in front of her was a mass of conflicting impulses and behaviors, and Bree didn't like her much. Tully veered from imperious to arrogant to rude like a billiard ball. Of course, if a lawyer's affection for a client were a career requirement, three-quarters of the attorneys in the state of Georgia would be out of a job.

But just when Bree was sure she couldn't stand another minute of Tully's willful and careless cruelty, there was that unexpected sense of humor.

And to be fair, Tully had been through a lot in the past year.

"I'll need a retainer," Bree said firmly.

Tully tightened her lips. She got up, went to the gray filing cabinet, unlocked the top drawer, and pulled out a ledger. She scribbled in it for a moment, tore off a check, and tossed it onto the desktop. Then she sat down again. Bree picked the check up. It was drawn on a Cayman bank and it was for fifteen thousand dollars. It'd probably bounce. On the other hand—it could be an offshore account that had escaped the clutches of the SEC.

Bree tucked it into her briefcase. "All right," she said. "I'll do my best. I'm going to ask you some questions. Some of them might seem a little off the wall, but you'll bear with me, please."

Any questions would have to be narrowly phrased. Bree didn't want to spend the rest of the afternoon sorting through a barrage of irrelevant hoorah, so she thought for a long moment before she spoke.

"Tully—you must have one, single, compelling reason to believe your husband was murdered." Tully drew a deep breath and Bree held her hand up. "Hang on. I'm not finished. The police investigation into his death was careful and complete. The NYPD is one of the best equipped in the world. Why are they wrong?" Bree smiled at her. "One sentence. That's all I want."

"You'll think I'm crazy," Tully said sullenly.

"So what? You don't really care about my opinion, do you?"

"That's true enough." She shrugged. "Okay. The truth. Russell is haunting me."

"Okay."

Tully's eyebrows rose. "You believe me?"

"Sure." Benjamin Skinner had haunted his CFO in her first case; Eddie Chin was being haunted in this one.

Tully's shoulders sagged a little. "Well, thank God somebody does."

Bree glanced at the desk and away again. "Is there any particular spot where he shows up?"

"It's when I fall asleep. He shows up in my sleep. He just says, 'They did for me, T. They did for me. I never would have left you that way.'" Her voice wavered, but her eyes were dry. "That's how I know. Russ never lied to me in life. He wouldn't lie to me in death."

"When I was last in this room, you tried to . . ." Bree tried to think of a word that wouldn't sound too hokey, but couldn't. "Summon him, is the best way I can put it."

"I've been trying that several different places. Barrie says you can summon the dead at the place where they died."

"Barrie? You mean Lady Fordham?"

"Yes." Tully shrugged. "Theater people. You know how superstitious they are. Barrie's heavily into some sort of Egyptian crap at the moment. Last year it was the Kabbalah. Next year, who knows? It's all rot." She laughed suddenly. "And look at me! The original skeptic. I believe in money, basically, which is about as real-world as you can get, but here I am, talking to you about ghosts." She shivered.

"Have you been successful? In raising Mr. O'Rourke."

"No. Barrie's sweet, but she's about as bright as a box of rocks. We've tried a couple of goofy rituals. Nothing worked. Just the dreams. It's as I told you. I sleep, and I dream of him." She blinked hard, twice. "And it's him for sure. Asking for help."

"Then we'll see what we can do," Bree said. "Can we talk about suspects?"

"Of course." Tully didn't have any fidgety habits. She didn't bite her lip or tug at her hair or drum her fingers impatiently. She walked tall, sat straight, and gave orders like a five-star general. So when she clasped her hands together, as she did now, it made her seem vulnerable. "He doesn't say *who*," she said fretfully. "You'd think if the dead had the will to come back, they would tell you *who*."

"Frustrating," Bree agreed. "It'd sure make my life easier. But they never do."

"Haunted clients just run-of-the-mill for you, huh?" Tully said ironically. "I appreciate the lip service, Bree, but you don't need to buy into this, too. On my saner days, I wonder just how crazy I really am. But you know what? I

don't give a good goddamn. I just want results." She let her
breath out in an explosive "Pah!" "So. Suspects."

"Cui bono is a good place to start," Bree suggested.
"Who benefits? It's one of the principal rules of any criminal investigation."

"You mean who inherits? I do, obviously."

Bree thought of the check drawn on the Cayman bank.

"But I would have benefited a lot more if Russ were
still alive. You do know that Rutger had stepped in with a
last-minute loan. If Russ had stuck with it, we could have
pulled it out."

"Money seems to be the most powerful benefit," Bree
agreed. "Right up there with love and revenge. Were you,
for example, having an affair with Mr. VanHoughton?"

Tully's laughter had a malicious edge. "We both were,
Russ and I. Does that shock you, Miss Winston-Beaufort?
Rutger didn't need to kill Russ to get to me. He had both
of us right where he wanted us."

Bree didn't think of herself as particularly shockable.
But yes, she was. And jealousy was a powerful force. She
scribbled *VanH* on her yellow pad and went on, doggedly,
"And you mentioned the Parsalls."

"Those people," Tully said scornfully, "and while you're
at it, that little creep Jameson can be added to the list."

"Anyone else?"

Tully shook her head. "I've thought about it a lot. Whoever planned this thing had brains, and a hard-on for Russ
and for me. I know a lot of people who hated us, and a fair
number of people with brains. But the list you've got there
is the only one that combines the two. The Parsalls and
Jameson. One or all of them. They hated Russ."

Motive, Bree knew, offered no kind of proof when stacked up against means, opportunity, and good hard evidence. But she had a start.

"You'll want to look into these people, right?" Tully drained the last of her Scotch. "I'm making it easy for you. I'm giving a party to launch the Players here in Savannah on Friday. Everybody on that list?" She pointed at Bree's yellow pad. "Each of them received an invitation. And each of them is going to be at the party. They're all flying in this week. You want to see each of them in turn, right? I'll make sure they stop by your office. If you've actually got one," She set the glass on the desk with a thump. "So get me some results, Bree. Soon."

Eleven

Where Alph, the sacred river, ran
Through caverns measureless to man
Down to a sunless sea.
—Coleridge, "Kubla Khan"

"Tech director?" Antonia said. "No! No! What about my audition?"

Bree put her head down on the kitchen table and sighed. "Let's see. You've got to run before you can walk?"

"What the heck is that supposed to mean?"

"Just that everybody needs to pay dues. You can't jump into starring roles at any theater company, much less one with the reputation of the Savannah Shakespeare Players, without having worked your way up from the . . ." Bree suddenly realized she had talked herself into a corner. She looked over at Sasha, who was sitting by his food bowl with an expectant face.

". . . bottom," Antonia finished, bitterly. "That's where I am, and that's where I'm doomed to stay. The bottom."

"Sasha's starving," Bree said. "There's some chicken and rice in the fridge. Why don't you mix it with some of the Iams under the counter."

145

"I don't know why I have to do it," Antonia grumbled. "Half the time he gets his food out of the bag himself." She crouched next to the dog and cuddled his head. "You smart puppy, you." She pulled the Iams bag out and shook some into Sasha's blue plastic bowl. "What about those guys?" She nodded toward the living room. When they were in residence, Miles and Belli sat on each side of the fireplace like a pair of giant temple dogs.

"They're back at the office," Bree improvised. "Ron's working late tonight, and he feels more comfortable with them around." Actually, she wasn't sure what had happened to Miles and Belli. When she'd left Tully's house, they weren't at their accustomed spot under her office window. Sasha didn't seem to know where they were, either.

Antonia dumped the chicken and rice from the fridge into the dog food bowl, mixed the whole of it up with a spoon, and then sat down on the floor next to Sasha as he ate his dinner. "Tell me exactly what Anthony said," she ordered. "From the top."

"At the moment, he doesn't have a spot in mind for you. He does need an assistant stage manager."

"What plays are they staging this season?"

"I have no idea."

"If *he* has no idea, then how come he knows he doesn't have a role for me?"

"If," Bree said, a dangerous note in her voice, "you don't shut up about this right now, you are going to be really, really sorry. I said I had no idea about the plays and I don't. The ball's in your court. Call him up. Again. Ask to see him. Again. And tell him you're willing to handle the tech part. Or don't. I don't care."

The silence in the kitchen stretched on a bit. Antonia got to her feet and then sat across the table from Bree. "Sorry," she said.

"It's okay."

"It's just so frustrating! No one will give me a chance!"

Bree sighed. "Now I'm the one that's sorry. You've chosen a tough life for yourself, sister. I'm helping the best I can."

"And I'm being an ungrateful witch, as usual." Antonia stared into space for a moment then sighed from the bottom of her heart. "Thank you for talking to him, though. It's better than nothing."

"It's way better than nothing," Bree said stoutly. "It's a definite maybe."

Antonia grinned. "True. And a bird in the hand, blah, blah, blah. I'll call him. So Tully's hired you to look into her husband's murder?"

"Yep."

"Do you think he was murdered? It's going to be like those other two cases, where the dead guys turned out to be victims after all?"

"I think so," Bree said cautiously.

"And you saw Dr. Lowry this morning."

"I did." Bree sat up. The morning seemed very far away. Then, with some indignation, she said, "And what's with getting me an appointment with the county coroner, anyway?"

"She's the county coroner?"

"One of the assistants," Bree amended. "Part-time. She said she likes that a lot better than live patients."

"She did not." Antonia started to giggle.

"She did so."

"I wonder where Aunt Cissy dug her up." Antonia's giggles turned into whoops of laughter. "Get it?"

"I get it," Bree said. Her little sister could always cheer her up. When she wasn't driving her absolutely crazy. "As for Cissy? Who knows? But I'm fine. Better than fine. Apparently I'm in better shape than I've ever been." Bree flexed her biceps. "Superb reaction times, extra-low blood pressure, which is good. An athlete, that's me."

"No kidding?" Antonia put her hand out and squeezed Bree's wrist. "I'm glad, sister. I guess I got the wind up over nothing."

"And," Bree said, rather smugly, "I've got a date."

"Get out! With who?" Antonia's eyes sparkled. "Tony Haddad?"

"Uh-oh," Bree said. "I guess I've got two dates. Hunter asked me to a basketball game and Tony asked me out for a glass of wine. I'd better cancel Tony."

"Wrong! You start sleeping with Tony, it'll help get me a part."

"I'm not going to start sleeping with anybody, just yet," Bree said. "And anyhow, the way this case is shaping up, I'm not going to have time to breathe, much less cavort."

"Oh, well, work," Antonia said dismissively. "By the way, there were a couple of messages for you. Ron said he checked into the leasing arrangements for Uncle Franklin's office, and they look good. Two thousand a month, furnished, and you can move in right away. And how come your cell phone was off? Petru wanted to know that, not me."

"Two thousand a month," Bree said. "Ouch." She hoped

Tully's retainer check was good. "And my cell battery's dead. I think it's time to get a new cell phone."

Antonia, her mouth full of the remaining chicken and rice, wandered out of the kitchen and back again. "Are you going to have two offices? Don't you have a lease with what's-her-name—Mrs. Mather?"

"Uncle Franklin's office is more convenient for clients," Bree said evasively.

"I'll say. Nobody I know seems to be able to find Angelus Street." The carton was empty of chicken and rice. Antonia dumped it in the sink and started on a banana from the bowl of fruit on the counter.

As things were right now, no clients walked into the office on Angelus Street, which was fine with Bree, since the only clients who could were dead. A fact, Petru had once said, that was all part of the routine at Beaufort & Company. The suspects in Russell O'Rourke's murder were all alive, well, and kicking, though, and Tully was going to send them to see Bree, one by one. So she needed the second office for her live clients.

Bree looked at the kitchen clock. Nine o'clock. She'd left Tully's, gone for a workout at the gym, and then eaten a salad at B. Matthew's across the street. It'd be hours before she was sleepy enough to go to bed.

"I think I'm going to take a look at the place now. Want to come along?"

"To look at office space?" Antonia made a face. "Yuck. I'm going to memorize lines. Don't be too late, okay? When you come back I want you to run them with me. You said the final scene from *The Winter's Tale*? That's what everyone has to prepare?"

"I spoke to the stage manager before I left Tully's house. That what she said."

"Phooey. I suppose I should prepare both Paulina and Hermione."

"I suppose."

"You haven't got a clue about either part, do you?"

"Nope," Bree said cheerfully. "But you'll be brilliant as either one. Or as tech director. Come on, Sash. Let's take a walk." Bree slung her raincoat over her arm, grabbed her purse, and let Sasha precede her out the kitchen door. The huge old brick building was four city blocks away on Bay, and it was a fine November night. Sasha kept the panhandlers that had plagued Savannah in recent years from begging for handouts, so Bree didn't have to make sure she had dollar bills at hand. She snapped the lead on her dog, in case any city patrolmen decided to enforce the leash law, and walked out into the night.

The air was pleasantly cool and the sidewalks were filled with other people: office workers headed for home after restaurant dinner, students from the nearby Savannah College of Arts and Design, city dwellers out with their dogs for an evening's walk.

Uncle Franklin's former office stood at Bay and Drayton, close to Johnson Square. The main entrance faced Drayton and the Bank of America on the opposite side of the street. From her vantage point on the sidewalk, Bree could see that a dozen or so windows were lit up. People were working late.

It'd been a warehouse for the Cotton Exchange in 1820, and the brick walls had weathered the nearly two hundred years since then pretty well. The recent renovation had been thorough: many of the rotten floor joists had been replaced, the brick had been sandblasted and then pointed, and the terrazzo tile floors in the foyer sanded down and refinished. Bree buzzed the security guard seated at the kiosk just inside the double glass doors and he let her in with an amiable smile.

"I'm not a tenant," she said, "not yet. I'm here to see 616. Someone from my office was in earlier today to take a look. Ronald Parchese?"

The guard flipped open the registry, and Bree placed her finger on Ron's signature. "There he is."

"Building manager's gone home," the guard said. "And I'm supposed to sit here all the while. You mind going up on your own?" He smiled over the edge of the counter at Sasha. "No one going to bother you with that fine fellow along, anyways."

"It'll be no trouble at all, thank you." Bree took the ornate brass key—the Historical Society must have insisted that the owners keep the old-fashioned Yale locks—and headed over to the elevators. A directory hung between the two elevators, and she scanned the addresses to get a better idea of her neighbors. An architect or two. A couple of physicians. A few county offices. And lawyers, lots of lawyers, including a small office division of Stubblefield, Marwick. Bree made a sound like "Bleaagh."

"You okay over there?" The guard called out.

"Just saw a familiar name on the board. Payton McAllister?"

"Oh," said the guard discouragingly. "Him. Yeah. He's here two days a week from his big fancy offices over on Abercorn and Park. You know him?"

Wish I didn't, Bree thought. *And it sounds like you don't like him much, either.* The guard was clearly a man of taste and discretion if he didn't like Payton McAllister. She'd gotten over being dumped by the good-looking weasel with the ethics of Joseph Goebbels. "I know him just to say good-bye to," Bree said cheerily. "Ah-ha! Here's my elevator car. Thank you!"

The elevator doors slid open with a whoosh. Bree peered in cautiously. It would be just her luck that Payton the Rat would be working late and decide to leave just as she was headed up to her new offices.

"Not here," Bree said. "Good." She looked down at Sasha and indicated the empty car with a sweep of her hand. "After you."

The sixth floor was dark, except for the night-lights placed at intervals along the hallway. Number 616 was halfway down. Bree had been in the office many times when her great-uncle Franklin was alive, and only once since his death. She'd been on the trail of a murderer then, too. The place smelled of fresh Sheetrock, new paint, and floor polish. Bree was wearing a pair of Borgs, and the faint sounds of her footsteps were swallowed up by the dense silence. The office doors were all alike: mahogany with a pebbled glass upper half. The names of the firms were painted in black Gothic-style lettering on the glass: J. P. WRIGHT, COURT STENOGRAPHER; ALLAN QUANTICO, INC.

The upper half of the door to 616 was blank.

Bree inserted the key into the lock. Suddenly Sasha growled, low in his throat. He nudged himself between Bree and the door.

She stepped back. "What is it, Sash?"

Stranger. Stranger.

"Something bad?" Bree ventured. She'd never been a fan of those Gothic novels where the clueless heroine clatters down to the basement dressed in a nightgown and without a cell phone.

Stranger.

Bree waited a long moment. She looked up and down the hallway. It was still deserted. But nothing lurked in the shadows. And outside on the street were cheerful night sounds: people talking, the sound of cars moving along Bay Street, a siren or two in the distance. She realized she didn't have her cell phone because the battery was dead. On the other hand, she was dressed in sweats and her Borgs, and she could run like hell if she needed to.

"Okay?" she said to her dog.

We don't know.

Bree pushed the door open and stepped inside.

She was in absolute darkness.

And wherever she was, it was huge. Miles and miles of nothing. Space soared above her. She could sense nothing but vast emptiness on either side. The ground was damp and gave slightly beneath her feet. Then, a faint white smudge at the farthest edge of the horizon.

And it was moving toward her.

Sasha panted into the eerie silence. He was confused. Uncertain. Bree cast a look over her shoulder.

There was blackness behind her, too.

The white mass slowed, whirling like a top, and then floated in midair. Bree couldn't say for certain how far it was from her, but the shape was close enough for her to make sense of it.

"Franklin?" Bree said. Her voice dropped into the stillness like a stone. She was aware of stretching out her hand, aware of taking a step forward.

Bree.

The voice was no more than a whisper. But she was sure it was his. Wasn't it?

Breeee.

To her left, something immense slid forward then stopped. Waited. The dark and quiet pressed down, pulling all the air from her lungs.

She heard the sound of wings. A slow, ominous flapping.

Something circled overhead. Then plunged at her. She ducked and fell back.

Bree groped in the dark for Sasha's head, needing the reassurance.

Bree.

A second voice, heavy as iron, cold as the grave, and huge, tremendous with power. And nothing human about it. The handful of white mist shrank to nothing. Then a pustulant yellow-green river of light formed at Bree's feet and curled upward, looking for her. The air was rank with the smell of corpses. There was a snarl (not Sasha!), a monstrous roar, and hell broke loose around her. Something slashed at her arm—and Bree leaped back . . .

And fell, spiraling down, down, down while the blackness and the roaring and the stench filled her head and she stopped thinking altogether.

—◦∞◦—

She woke to a light in her eyes, and an unfamiliar voice. "Ma-am?" the voice said. "Ma'am? You all right, ma'am?"

Bree blinked awake. She was seated in a swivel chair at a utilitarian steel desk. A gray filing cabinet sat against the wall in front of her. She sat up, halfway supported by the guard from downstairs. There was one window in this room, and it looked out over Bay Street.

It was dark outside, and the moon was high.

Franklin's office.

Sasha put his paw on her knee.

"Man," the guard said. "You was some asleep."

"Sorry." Bree took a deep breath and got up.

"You always sleep like that?" the guard asked. He backed away, worry in his face. "Like the dead? It took some doing, waking you up. You didn't come down for some time, ma'am, so when the third shift come on, I told him, 'You wait on me,' I said. 'I gotta go up to the sixth floor and check on Miss Beauford.' And here." He took her arm gently. "You done hurt yourself on something."

Bree looked at her arm. Something had grabbed at her and missed. Blood beaded her wrist.

"Beaufort," Bree said. "It's Beaufort. And I'm so sorry." She faked a yawn. "You're right. I just sat down for a minute . . . and I've been putting in some long hours lately. I'm truly sorry for your trouble, sir. I appreciate the time you took to come and wake me."

"Yeah, well. You'd best get along home, now. You got someone to call? You want me to get you a cab?"

"No, no. I live just down the street." She reached out and shook his hand. "And again, I thank you."

"You go on out ahead of me. I'll just turn out these here lights and I'll be right along."

Bree looked around carefully. The floor was carpeted in that utilitarian gray indoor-outdoor stuff that was a favorite of car dealers everywhere. The walls were a prim beige. The furniture was standard office-issue steel and Formica-topped. No place for monstrous shapes here.

Sasha nudged her out into the hall. She waited for the guard and trailed him to the elevators, not speaking as the car sped them down to the ground floor. She thanked him one final time as he ushered her out onto the street.

Miles and Belli sat under the streetlamp, their eyes glowing red-yellow in the half-light.

"I thought I recognized that bellow up there," Bree said. "I think you two showed up just in time. Thank you."

"Whuff," Miles said. He put his great head against her hip and gently nudged her toward home.

Twelve

Oh, Threats of Hell and Hopes of Paradise!
—Edward FitzGerald,
The Rubaiyat of Omar Khayyam

"I don't know what it was," Bree admitted. "It started out as Uncle Franklin and then something else showed up."

"Them Pendergasts," Lavinia said glumly.

"No," Bree said, "it wasn't the Pendergasts. It was something—I don't know. Older, I guess."

Five of the seven members of Beaufort & Company sat in the small living room of the house on Angelus Street: Ron, Lavinia, Sasha, Petru, and of course Bree herself. Bree didn't know if Miles and Belli could be counted as employees; she rather thought not. They sat on either side of the small fireplace, massive and stolid. She was very glad they were there.

The painting of the slave ship hung above them all. When she'd arrived that morning, Bree had been unsettled to discover a change in the seascape. The waters of the ocean were redder, and the sun a more sullen yellow. The faint outlines of a hook now loomed behind the billowing sails of the ship. Bree squinted at it.

Maybe it was a beak. The thing that had dived at her had a beak.

"Older, you say," Petru said. "You can perhaps be more descriptive?"

"No. I can't. I wish I could." She moved restlessly in her chair. Sasha sat on the floor next to her. Ron and Lavinia crowded together on the small leather couch. Petru stood behind the couch, hands folded over his cane. Bree dabbed at the wound on her wrist. It was shallow, a mere bird scratch, but the blood wouldn't clot. The small, steady seepage had soaked through the Band-Aid she'd placed over it the night before. Her bedsheets had been lightly freckled with bright damp spots when she'd wakened.

"I got something else I want to try on that cut on your arm," Lavinia said. "You sit right there, child." She got up with a small grunt of effort and stumped out of the room and up the stairs. There had been another change in the old house that morning. The first angel at the bottom of the richly colored frieze on the stair wall that led to the second floor had changed direction. She? he? it? (Ron had informed her some time ago that angels were non-gender-specific) wore a rich purple robe and had silver gilt hair the color of Bree's own. The angel didn't look up, now. It had turned halfway, to look back.

As if something were chasing it?

"An anomaly, then," Petru observed. "I have no knowledge of what this might be."

Lavinia came back, a clump of sweet-smelling moss in one hand. "This here's direct from home, from the banks of my river." She took Bree's hand and gently patted the fungus over the cut. "And look there, chile. I do believe it's stopped right up."

"Thank goodness for that," Ron said. "Funny. I was reading about pollution on the Nile just the other day. It just," he added obscurely, "goes to show you."

Bree, who'd been wondering at the elderly Lavinia scouting the banks of the Savannah for medicinal herbs, suddenly remembered that "home" was Africa. "Whatever it was, whoever it was, I don't think it was looking for me. It picked me up and dropped me before Miles and Belli jumped to the rescue. Not," she added, addressing both dogs, "that I wasn't completely grateful for your help. I am."

Belli yawned.

"Well, I don' like to see you move into Franklin's old place, that's for certain sure," Lavinia fussed. "Who knows what all can walk right in that door?"

"It's getting awkward, not having a temporal facility," Bree said. "My family asks questions. My friends think it's odd that they can't come to my office."

"There is that," Ron said. "So what do you want to do?"

"I wondered if any of you had any idea what attacked me last night."

"A mystery," Lavinia murmured. "A disturbing mystery."

"I shall talk to Armand," Petru said. "But I would think, perhaps, that this is outside of his experience, as well as mine."

"And the changes in the painting? And the angel on the stairs? What do you think this all means?"

"Something approaches," Petru said. "But what it is, I cannot say."

"Ron, do you think Goldstein might have a clue?"

"Only if there's a case precedent," Ron said. "He's a recording angel, not a prophet. But I'll put out some feelers. Some of the clerks might know something. They scribble away on all kinds of documents throughout Time."

"Beazley and Caldecott," Bree said. "What about asking them? They showed up to warn me about this. I'll bet they know more about this than they're telling. How do I get in touch with them?"

"I'll ask them to call on us," Ron said. "But those two—they'll only cough up what's absolutely required. And they'll want something in trade, Bree."

"Like what?"

"Your firstborn son. Who knows?" Ron rolled his eyes. "Depends. But it's never something you want to give up. I can guarantee it."

"Striker," Lavinia said suddenly. "He's been a warrior since the Word, I reckon. He ought to know something about all this."

"Maybe," Ron said. "But there was a lot of Dark stuff before the Word."

"Dark stuff?" Bree asked. "What do you mean, 'Dark stuff?'"

"Pre-Sphere," Ron said, as if this explained everything. "I've never paid much attention to it myself. You'd need an Historian for that."

Bree made a mental note. An Historian sounded just the ticket. Maybe Goldstein could point her in the right direction.

Petru tugged at his beard. "It is interesting to consider the lack of Striker. He was nowhere in the vicinity last night?"

Bree shook her head.

Petru nodded decisively. "Then the threat is over."

Ron's eyebrows rose. "That's absolutely true." He leaned across the chest they used as a coffee table and patted her hand reassuringly. "Whatever grabbed you, Bree, isn't likely to grab you again. If Striker wasn't there, it wasn't after you."

"You think so?" Bree said. "But Miles and Belli were there."

"They're the muscle. Striker's got the Power. Big difference," Ron said.

Bree decided to let the distinction between the two drop for the moment. There'd be time after this case was over. She was more interested in what had grabbed at her and why.

"It's Striker's job to see you safe, chile. And he's always up to it."

"Up until now," Petru said sourly.

"What do you mean by that?" Ron demanded.

Petru shrugged.

Lavinia sank back against the couch with a relieved sigh. "You two hush up. Striker's good. It's not a worrisome thing, except for that scratch on her wrist and I took care of that. We should have thought of Gabriel in the first place."

"You're all sure about this?"

"Positive," Ron said with confidence. "Whatever it was—it doesn't seem to be after you. It picked you up and dropped you back down again, right?"

Bree thought of that long, long fall and shuddered. "Right."

"Right."

"Like it was searching for something and thought it was you. Picked you up. Then said: 'Bah! Wrong person. Next!'"

"I suppose so," Bree said dryly. "But if it wasn't looking for me, who was it looking for?"

"Hm," Ron said. Then, to the others: "This is why she gets the big bucks."

"I will talk to Armand," Petru said. "But I, too, believe there to be no danger."

Ron smiled happily. "So we can consider renting the Bay Street office after all."

Bree ran her fingers over the wound on her wrist. Lavinia's Nile poultice worked. The blood had dried. And the scratch was healing fast. "Okay, then. About the Bay Street office. My biggest concern is the expense."

"We have a fair amount in the checking account," Ron said. "I deposited Mrs. O'Rourke's check early this morning."

"It didn't bounce?"

"Don't think it will. Bank seemed impressed with the Cayman address." Ron's desk sat in the far corner of the living room, and he got up to go over and rummage in the top drawer. "Here we go. I make it a total of forty-five thousand dollars deposited since we opened up three months ago. Our monthly expenses, including payroll, utilities, insurance, and the like, run to about eight thousand." He shrugged. "Up to you, boss. Actually, I think we're doing pretty well. And with the opening of the Bay Street office, you're sure to get more temporal clients."

Bree's draw on the Company account had been just to keep up her personal expenses. She wasn't taking a salary. Her angels were. She took a breath. "Do you all . . . I mean . . . Do you actually need . . ." She stopped, momentarily flummoxed.

"You're going to cut our paychecks?" Ron said.

"You goin' to stop payin' rent?" Lavinia said. "Oh, my. And the social security doesn't cover all it should."

"My sister, Rose, depends upon my contribution to the household," Petru said heavily.

Ron, Petru, and Lavinia stared at her in blank dismay. Sasha yawned and went back to sleep. Miles and Belli didn't move a muscle. But then, Sasha didn't get a salary, unless you counted his dog food, and Miles and Belli were guns hired by somebody else. So her clumsy proposal—not that it was a proposal—didn't affect *them* one little bit. But it clearly affected her human-styled staff.

"Of course Rose needs your help, Petru," Bree said hastily. "And of course social security is just this pitiful little amount, Lavinia. I didn't mean that I can't pay you. I just wondered if you needed . . ." she trailed off.

"If we spent our off-hours on some other plane of existence?" Ron said. "We don't."

"We have lives of our own, you see," Petru said.

Bree's head started to throb, and it wasn't due entirely to lack of sleep the night before.

"Sorry," Ron said, with very little sympathy. "So your little effort at reducing expenses by slashing payroll is not going to work. Unless you think we're not *worth* a paycheck."

"Of course you are! You're invaluable."

"My goodness," Ron said. "I should hope so. Two successful cases, and we've only been in business three months."

"We have not yet had performance reviews," Petru reminded Ron. "We do not actually know how invaluable we are. It seems not so much."

"I think you're splendid at your job, Petru," Ron said forcefully.

"And I, you, Ronald."

When it came to employee-management relations, it was clear that the two angels formed a temporary alliance. Bree wanted to clutch her hair and pull it, but she didn't. "I absolutely did not mean anything by my question about pay. You are all doing a terrific job. I wish I could pay you tons more. But I can't. I'm close to broke as it is."

"And there'll be the new hire, too," Ron said thoughtfully. "But any bank in town will give us a line of credit."

"The new hire?" Bree said. "For the Bay Street office, you mean? I thought we'd split our time between the two." This time she did clutch her hair. "I can't afford another employee."

"You essentially have two separate practices," Petru said kindly. "It is only practical to set them up that way. We cannot help you in any significant way on the strictly temporal cases."

"We'll run an ad in the newspaper for a part-time employee," Ron said. "And I'll ask around. Or better yet, I'll call the temp services place. They always have people looking for permanent employment. I'll take care of that right away. And I think a part-timer is best, don't you? We'll use a messaging service for the phones, at least until we can afford someone full-time over there. And that furniture. Ugh. Strictly awful. I've already scouted some much nicer stuff at Second Hand Rows. As soon as you get the lease squared away, I'll have it sent on over." He sat at his desk and reached for his phone. "Do you have time to meet with the facilities manager this morning?"

"Sure. Fine. Whatever." Bree got to her feet. She needed some downtime or she was going to go up like a rocket, right where she stood. "I'm going to go over those NYPD notes Eddie made on Russell O'Rourke's death. I'll be in my office." She took a breath. "And Ron? Hold my calls."

She shut the door to the small room that held her desk and her uncle's battered leather chair with a definitiveness just this short of a slam.

Then Sasha scratched imperatively at the outside. She reopened it to let him in and looked out into the living room. Petru had gone into the break room, where he had moved his desk after a spat with Ron. Ron was making phone calls. Lavinia had pulled the vacuum cleaner out and was preparing to do some cleaning. Miles and Belli were gone—which seemed to confirm everybody else's belief that the current crisis was over.

Sasha hopped up on the leather chair and looked at her with patient, affectionate eyes. Bree stuck one finger up in the air. "These are the problems: One. Monsters in the closet—or behind the office door at least." She raised her second finger. "Two. Not enough money in the checking account." And a third. "Three. And of course, the perennial problem of the Pendergasts, not to mention the thing that jumped me last night, which everyone else seems to think is a mere blip on the radar screen." She ran both hands over her face. "You want to run away with me, Sash? Maybe move to Detroit? Or to the Hundred Acre Wood? We could live under the name of Saunders."

You take yourself with you wherever you go.

"Oh, put it on a T-shirt," Bree said crossly. She sat down behind her desk and picked up the O'Rourke file. What she needed was some practical, real-time detective work. And that's what she was going to do.

She took a deep breath, counted backwards from ten, and settled down to work.

There was really only one question to answer:

If O'Rourke was murdered, who pulled the trigger?

Bree took out her yellow pad and a pen and went through the NYPD file carefully and methodically. She wasn't a great mystery reader, but she had gone through a Sherlock Holmes phase in her teens, and she remembered being struck by a point made over and over again by the first great fictional detective: after you've eliminated the impossible, you should focus on the improbable. And the only thing that made sense—as improbable as it seemed—was that Russell O'Rourke had sat in his office chair and stared down the barrel of a twelve-gauge shotgun until his wife opened his office door and walked in with a crowd of his friends. He pulled the trigger. The shot took off the top of his head and most of his brains with it.

The time of death was incontrovertible. Despite the horrific damage to his head, his heart had kept beating, and the official time of death occurred twenty-two minutes after the gunshot, as he was on his way to the emergency room.

And Eddie Chin hadn't been totally candid about how many people had come through the door with Tully and Barrie Fordham. Bree had written the names down as she read through the file, and she looked at them now.

Tully herself
Barrie Fordham
Fig O'Rourke
Buck Parsall
Harriet Parsall
Rutger VanHoughton

One of these five people—six, if you included Tully herself—must have set off the gun as the crowd had entered the room.

But how? O'Rourke just sat there, waiting for the gun to fire and take off his head? He hadn't been tied up.

Had Russell O'Rourke been drugged?

The toxology reports were as thorough as the autopsy had been: he'd had a Scotch or two several hours before his death—and there were traces of a mild antidepressant that had been prescribed for him some months before—but there were no sedatives, no narcotics, nothing. No bruising consistent with a blow that would have made him unconscious, either.

So either he just sat there with a shotgun pointed at his head or—what?

Somebody was hidden in the room with another gun

on him? Maybe the .22? And the six people who'd burst in hadn't noticed?

Bree didn't buy that for a minute.

All six people were conspiring to cover up the murder?

Bree didn't buy that, either. Why had Tully hired her if not to bring the murderer to justice?

Bree sat back with a sigh. "Well, Watson. It's a pretty little problem."

Sasha yawned, resettled himself, and went back to sleep.

Bree leaned forward and buzzed Ron on the phone intercom. "Can you track down Eddie Chin for me?"

"You bet."

"See if he'll let me buy him dinner. At B. Matthew's, about seven?"

"Will do. And I made an appointment for us with the facilities manager at the Bay Street office. Three o'clock this afternoon."

"Us?"

"We need to make some decorating decisions."

"We do?"

"We do."

"Okay. And thank you."

"And you had a couple of phone calls."

Bree waited a long moment, and then said, "Well?"

"Just seeing if you're ready to rejoin the universe. One from a Mr. Cullen Jameson. And two from Mrs. O'Rourke."

"Get Tully for me, please. I'll call Jameson later."

"And your mother called."

Bree suppressed a groan.

"And your sister."

"I'll call them back after lunch."

"Then hold for Mrs. O'Rourke. I'll put her on line two."

Bree sat with the receiver at her ear. To anyone on the outside looking in, it would seem as though she had a real law firm, with real clients and with professional, competent, normal employees. If she shut her eyes, she'd believe it herself.

"Bree?"

The strident, demanding voice was unmistakable. "Hello, Tully."

"Where in the world did you get that assistant?"

"Ron, you mean?"

"He has such a *pleasant* voice, Bree. Not pleasant, that's not the right word. It's rather lyrical."

"Angelic," Bree suggested dryly.

"Well, yes! You must bring him by sometime. Haddad would be enchanted."

"Ron's quite an asset," Bree agreed. "Is there something urgent, Tully?"

"They're all headed into town," she said flatly. "The suspects. Buck and Harriet will be coming in on the mid-morning flight today. They're booked at the Forsyth."

Bree wondered if Buck Parsall's brothers were footing the bill. The Forsyth was Savannah's only five-star hotel.

"And Cullen should have been in touch with you by now. He's at the Mulberry Inn. I told them all you're handling the new partnership agreements for the Shakespeare Players and I wanted them to review it with you."

"But I'm not."

"As of now you are. I gave you the contract copies when we last met."

They were in her briefcase. She hadn't read them over. She needed to read them over right now.

"Rutger's lawyers drew up those preliminary drafts and I need somebody representing my interests. It might as well be you."

"Rutger's lawyers?"

"Rutger's a sweetie, but he's investing a fair bit in this thing, and he wants his pound of flesh."

"But what does Cullen Jameson have to do with the Shakespeare Players?"

"I'm calling it reparations." Bree's silence must have communicated her bewilderment because Tully said impatiently, "I'm giving him a small share in the company. The Parsalls, too. Never mind why. But it ought to be crystal clear that I've given you a superb cover to find out if any of those three were the ones who killed my husband."

But Cullen Jameson was the only suspect who *hadn't* been present at the scene. Bree set her teeth, but managed to ask politely, "Have you set up the same cover story with the Parsalls? About the contract?"

"They're a pair of fools," Tully said dismissively. "I'm sure you can figure something out. And Harriet's dying to invest. We neeed to be consistent, here, don't you think?"

"A fool didn't commit this murder, Tully. If it was murder. I've just been reviewing the case evidence, and it seems so unlikely."

"I believe my husband," Tully said. "And I'm hiring you to believe him, too."

She dropped the phone into the cradle with a crash.

Bree listened to the dial tone for a moment and then hung up the receiver. Sasha raised his head and looked at her alertly.

"I just need a reality check, here. There is a logical, real-time solution to this case, right? Russell either killed himself or somebody else did it for him. Somebody human, I mean." Bree stood up and stretched. She was fidgety from sitting so long. "There's another thing to consider. Maybe Russell's visitations are a product of Tully's imagination, not from beyond—wherever beyond is—at all. What do you think, Sash?"

"He thinks we should work with what we've got. So do I," Ron said as he came into the room. "Mr. O'Rourke's death was either murder or suicide. Only temporal involved. Anything else is another department altogether, and nothing to do with us. Are you ready to go look at the Bay Street office space?"

Bree looked at her watch. "Is it three o'clock already? I've missed lunch."

"You did," Ron said, sympathetically. "So I picked up something at the Front Street deli. Lieutenant Chin won't be able to meet you until nine o'clock tonight, but you won't be eating dinner until late, late, late in any event."

Bree looked at him suspiciously. "How come?"

"Because Antonia's auditioning for Tony Haddad tonight at six and you absolutely have to be there and so do I."

"Oh, dear," Bree said guiltily, "I should have called her back."

"Well, I called her back on your behalf. We owe her moral support. I promised we'd be there. Both of us. And

I've set up an interview for our part-time help, right after you talk with the building manager. So you won't have time to eat before six. This chicken salad sandwich will have to do."

He dangled a paper bag with the familiar logo in front of her.

There was something blessedly normal about a chicken salad sandwich from the Front Street deli. It'd be her third or fourth one this week. She didn't care.

Bree ate all of it and was grateful.

Thirteen

**The mirror cracked from side to side—
"The curse is come upon me," cried
The Lady of Shalott.**
—Tennyson, "The Lady of Shalott"

"Billingsley," Bree said to the only applicant who had shown up for the position of part-time secretary to Beaufort & Company, Bay Street address. "Are you related to Danica?"

"My brother's girl," Emerald Billingsley said. "Yes." She was in her midforties and comfortably built. Her hands were work-roughened, but the nails were carefully tended. She held her purse in her lap. It was patent leather and, like her hands, worn, but well cared for. She wore a navy blue suit that strained a little at the seams, and a carefully ironed white blouse. "I'll be direct with you. I've been working down to the Hilton on Front Street. In the kitchen. Dani, she put me on to this online school? For secretarial work. I graduated last month."

She had a lovely speaking voice, a rich contralto. Bree liked it a lot. Clients would like it a lot, too.

They were in the newly leased premises. The office

looked perfectly ordinary in the afternoon light streaming in the window. The ceiling was eleven feet high. The room was twenty by twenty, which was spacious enough to put in a divider and make two work areas, one for the support staff and one for Bree herself. Nothing gruesome lurked underfoot except the indoor-outdoor carpeting, which was a glum gray color. The whole place smelled like fresh paint. The horrors of the night before might never have been.

Bree sat in the desk chair. Mrs. Billingsley sat on the straight-backed chair placed at the side of the desk. Ron stood at the window. Mrs. Billingsley hadn't registered his presence at all (and neither had the building manager who had asked Bree to sign the lease), which meant he was in angel mode. Mrs. Billingsley had acknowledged Sasha with a timid nod and a tentative pat, though.

The building manager had been willing to reduce the rent a little, to account for the removal of the existing office furniture that so offended Ron. Bree had flung a brief prayer to the Gods of Future Clients and signed a six-month lease.

"Dani said I should give you my particulars," Mrs. Billingsley said. She worked a manila envelope out of the purse and handed it to Bree, who opened it up. It contained a short résumé and a printed document from the Tucson College of Secretarial Science certifying that Emerald Billingsley was adept at word processing, bookkeeping, and appointment scheduling.

"I know this is a law firm," Emerald said, "and there are a lot of these specialized words, and all. But I'm a pretty good reader and I learn pretty quick. Quickly," she amended. "They had a grammar portion of this course I took online."

"We haven't established office hours yet," Bree said. "But it will probably be three mornings a week to start. You knew this was part-time work?"

"Can I afford to take part-time on, you mean? I ain't— haven't quit the Hilton yet, Miss Beaufort. Not yet. Dani, she thinks I need to work into the secretarial position by starting low on the ladder. No offense meant."

"No offense taken," Bree said cheerfully. "The pay's pretty awful. I'm sorry about that. We'll be able to afford more if things pick up.

"And we would want the secretary to start tomorrow morning. The new office furniture is coming, and the phones will be hooked up. We'll need someone here for that. I do have a small staff at the other office, but they aren't going to be available to help out here on any kind of routine basis."

"I suppose we'll meet up eventually, if you like me for the job," Mrs. Billingsley said. "I do like a happy office, where everybody gets along."

———✸———

"I like a happy office, too," Bree said to Ron as they waited to cross Broughton to get to Tully's house, some twenty minutes later. "And a happy office means everyone meets everyone else and then everyone gets along. You're visible, and then you're not. Is Mrs. Billingsley going to get to know you or not? With all these new expenses, I'm going to have to think about building a firm with real-time clients and a real-time bank account. That means more real-time employees. There has to be some organizing principle about when you guys show up and when you don't. What is it?"

Ron kept a hand on her shoulder. The traffic was slow, but heavy, and he seemed to feel she was going to dart out into the middle of it.

"Good point about building the firm to help with expenses," Ron said. "Franklin had his judge's salary. And of course, a bit of family money, too."

"You know very well I've got a bit of family money myself," Bree said.

"But you don't like to use it." The traffic slowed. Ron released her shoulder and they crossed the street. Sasha ranged ahead, sniffing at interesting bits of litter.

"It's not a huge amount. Enough to keep me in peanut butter sandwiches and living on an abandoned bus. I'll draw on it if I have to, of course, but darn it, Ron, I should be able to make my own way, without my family's help. And you're not answering my question."

Ron reached the brick pathway to Tully's house and turned around to look at her. It was close to six o'clock, and twilight cupped the sky, but his hair seemed filled with sunlight. "It's about energy, in a way. Every encounter leaves something behind. It's best to keep things to a minimum. For everyone's sake."

The breeze stirred his hair. "Loss and gain," he said. "Loss and gain."

Bree shivered and thought of Beazley and Caldecott and the changes in her own body. Ron's eyes were very blue. Very remote. There was compassion there, too, and that made Bree uneasiest of all.

After a long, silent moment, he gestured toward Tully's house and followed her in.

There seemed to be even more of a crowd than there had been the day before. Anthony Haddad stood by himself, scribbling intently on a clipboard. A mass of people about Bree's age chattered, gossiped, read scripts, drank coffee, and did stretches. Everyone seemed to be in sweats. There was no sign of Tully. A space had been cleared in front of the grand piano with folding chairs grouped around it. With a thump of excitement, she saw Ciaran Fordham, leaning against the floor-to-ceiling windows, his back to the street, his gaze impassive. Barrie Fordham stood at his side. She was dressed in a black cowl turtleneck and a long cotton skirt. Her hair was swept up in a knot, and soft brown tendrils drifted around her face. Bree hadn't read much poetry in school, but something about the way the Fordhams stood there jogged her memory. Barrie looked abandoned. Like the Lady of Shalott. Sir Ciaran looked— lost.

A familiar shriek made her jump.

"Thank God!" Antonia said. "I was afraid you weren't coming!" Her sister danced her way through the crowd. She was wildly excited. Like most everyone there, she wore sweats and a leotard. She looked gorgeous. "Where's Ron? He promised he'd be here, too, for a bit, he said. There he is. Keeping a low profile in the back. Is Sasha with him? Good. Sir Ciaran's allergic, you know." She waved energetically, and then shoved Bree into an armchair. Then she bent over and peered into Bree's face. "You're frowning. What's the matter? Do I look okay? Should I have worn something else?"

"You look great. I wasn't frowning at you." She glanced as discreetly as she could toward the Fordhams. "Neither one of them looks very happy."

Antonia rolled her eyes. "Yeah, well, I've been here a while, talking to people, and everybody's, like, totally amazed that Ciaran signed up for this, even though Tony's agreed to direct. It's awful, Bree. Everyone thinks that maybe Tony's got something on him. You know? Like a blackmail thing."

"Tony? Not Tully?"

"Sssht! Keep your voice down. Of course Tony. Tully doesn't know squat about Shakespeare. She never has. She's just in it for the prestige. All of the planning for this, it's Tony's bag, not hers."

"No kidding," Bree said. Somehow, she wasn't surprised. It was just like Tully to equate writing the check with creating the art. And Tully wasn't even writing the checks—she got other people's money to fund it. It was consummate gall, when you thought about it, but it had an epic sweep that Bree kind of admired.

Antonia perched on the chair's arm. "You know what else? I heard that Russell—Senior, not Fig—just hated the whole idea of the Players. And the person he hated most of all?" She tilted her head toward the Fordhams. "Couldn't stand either one of them, as a matter of fact. Thought they were phonies. Isn't it amazing, how some people think? I mean, the man's the greatest actor in the world!"

"Hang on a minute." Bree jerked upright. "Russell O'Rourke hated Sir Ciaran?"

"Sssht!" Antonia's whisper was so fierce she sputtered a bit, and Bree rubbed the spit off her cheek. "I told you to keep your voice down. Yes. He did. At least, that's the scuttlebutt. And now that O'Rourke Senior's out of the way . . . Tony's got the funds and the Fordhams, too."

"Whoa." Bree had a logical mind and she didn't like broadsides like this one. The addition of Anthony Haddad to the suspect list was unwelcome, for a whole bunch of reasons.

But he wasn't in the room when the gun went off. And that had to count for a lot.

And if he wasn't in the room when the gun went off, how could he have done it? She craned her neck, the better to see around Antonia. There he was, the clipboard tucked under his arm, a pair of sunglasses shoved to the top of his head, looking utterly gorgeous.

He clapped his hands together, and instantly the room fell silent. "Places, please. This is an audition, despite the fact that it's Tully's grand salon, so I want *quiet.*"

Bree was willing to bet that half the people in the room decided not to breathe until Tony gave the say-so.

"All right? We're good to go? We've got three actors here ready to knock my socks off, so settle down and enjoy, people. Andrea Colville? There you are, Andrea. I've asked everyone to prepare the same scene. Final scene of *The Winter's Tale.* Places, please. You're reading Paulina."

Bree didn't know much about *The Winter's Tale* (as a matter of fact, she knew very little about Shakespeare at all) but she did know it was the play with the infamous stage direction "exit, pursued by a bear" and that the not-very-well-regarded plot involved bringing a king's wife back from the dead.

Barrie Fordham stepped onto the stool in front of the piano, turned her palms upward, and somehow, through some magic alchemy of skin, bone, and imagination, became a grieving statue. Sir Ciaran placed himself beside her.

All of a sudden, he was a king. Regal. Imperious. Arrogant. Bree caught her breath in admiration.

"She's Hermione," Antonia said into her ear. "Hermione is King Leontes' wife, only she's in sort of, like, suspended animation, and Paulina comes and wakes her up."

Andrea was slim, pretty, and, to Bree's uncritical eye, very good as Paulina. But Antonia was better. Antonia, in Bree's opinion, was magnificent, and when she waved her arms and said, *Music, awake her! Strike! 'Tis time; descend and be stone no more!* and Barrie Fordham stirred and indeed was "stone no more," Bree wanted to burst into applause and cheer.

The third Paulina was a little older and not a patch on Antonia for beauty. Tony Haddad broke the auditions up with the casual, imperious authority that everyone else seemed to take for granted and thanked the crowd. People broke into little chattering groups and the brief magic was gone, as if it had never been.

He caught Bree's eye and beckoned her over to him.

"And you're here again, Miss Winston-Beaufort," he said pleasantly. "Another meeting with the dragon lady?"

"Tully? No. I just came to cheer Antonia on. I think she was very, very, very good. The best of the three, by far."

"She was the best of a bad lot," Tony agreed absently. "But I don't want any of them." He was looking past Bree, to the windows, where the Fordhams had resumed their places and Ron had disappeared. "And if Ciaran doesn't start shaping up some, I may not even want *him*." His dark eyes clouded, and for a moment, his good looks disappeared in a furious grimace. "After all the bullshit I went through to get him signed up, he ends up giving me mediocre performances at best."

"I thought he was wonderful," Bree said. "I mean, I'm no critic, but it was hard to take my eyes off him."

"No," Tony said bluntly, "you clearly aren't a critic. And he can't rely on his looks alone to get through. He's been phoning in his performances for the last year, and I'm not going to put up with it much longer, I can tell you that."

"How much bullshit *did* you go through to get them to sign up with the Players?"

He shrugged angrily. "It's Barrie mostly. Her demands are unbelievable. I thought we were in for clear sailing after Russell took the long ride home, but no such luck."

"You didn't care for Russell much?"

His eyes cleared, and he looked down at her with a smile. "Hey. Work's over for me. What if you and I get a head start on that glass of wine you promised and go out right now?"

Bree looked at her watch. She'd just have time to walk home with Tonia and then get to her dinner meeting with Eddie Chin. But she definitely wanted to talk to Tony Haddad, and soon. She'd just have to cancel the date with Hunter. "I've got an interview with a potential witness in a few minutes. Now, about Thursday?" She felt a touch at her sleeve and automatically moved aside.

"Mr. Haddad," Antonia said.

Bree recognized that determined tilt to her chin. Haddad frowned at her discouragingly. Bree grabbed at her sister, but Antonia shook her off. "I was just wondering when you were going to make the decision about the part."

"I have already made a decision about the part."

Antonia licked her lips nervously. "Okay, then, so what do you think?"

"I think I need an assistant tech director, and that you would do very well at that. If you are interested in the job, please let Danica Billingsley know. She's handling the payroll thing for us." He nodded pleasantly, then quirked his eyebrow at Bree. "You are not free at the moment?"

"Maybe later this week," Bree said pleasantly. She didn't look at her sister, but she could tell from the tension in the air that Antonia was on the brink of tears. And she didn't call Tony Haddad seven kinds of a jerk, but she wanted to.

"Thank you," Antonia said. "I appreciate the offer, sir. I'll have to make sure that I'm not leaving my current employer in the lurch. If they agree to let me go, I'll call Miss Billingsley first thing in the morning."

Haddad drifted away without a farewell. Bree put her arm around her sister and squeezed her, hard. "I am so proud of you. And you were the best of them up there. Including Lady Fordham herself."

"Yeah, well. Can you get me out of here? I'm just, like, barely holding it together." Antonia's eyes brimmed.

"Sure."

"And maybe pinch me, so I won't cry in front of all these people."

"Permission to pinch?" Bree said. "It's going to be hard

to resist that." She put her hand in the small of Antonia's back and began to steer her through the crowd. Ron had gone and Bree was sorry about that because he was terrific at cheering Antonia up. But by the time they reached the sidewalk, Antonia's volatile spirits had bounced back, and she spent the rest of the walk home devising ways to bring her acting talents back to Haddad's notice.

"What you said about being too young for the parts?" she said as Bree unlatched the small wrought-iron gate that led to their town house and waved absently as Sasha bounced toward them. "The very problem with Paulina. She's Hermione's maidservant, and even if you account for the fact that she was, like, fifteen when Hermione got turned to stone twenty years before the play opens . . . Ouch! What are you pinching me now for? I am so over being upset, it isn't even funny."

"Did you leave the lights on in the town house?" Bree stopped cold and fumbled for Sasha. She wasn't as recovered from last night's terrors as she thought. He stiffened under her cold fingers. A low growl started in his throat and died away.

"Me? I never leave the lights on," Antonia said indignantly. "Oh, my God. You know what?"

"What?" Bree asked tersely. The lights from the living room window cast a yellow glow onto the pathway. She could always call for Striker if she needed him. He hadn't failed her yet.

"I'll bet it's Mother and Dad. I forgot. They wanted to come down for some party of Aunt Cissy's. They said they were going to call you, too. Daddy heard about your involvement with the O'Rourke case."

"And who told him about that?" Bree asked.

Antonia's look of innocence didn't fool Bree for a second. "If you'd just get the battery on your cell fixed, Bree, you'd know all about this stuff."

"Damn it all," Bree said. She loved Francesca and Royal dearly. But they did have an annoying habit of popping up at the most inconvenient times. Like right now. "I've got to meet a witness in about ten seconds, Tonia. So you're going to have to handle them on your own."

"No way," Antonia said. "They're going to be all over me like a blanket, trying to get me to go back to school. I'm coming with you."

"No, you're not."

"Yes, I am."

"No, you're not!"

The door to the town house opened, and it wasn't the tall lean shape of their father that stepped out into the night. It was Sam Hunter. "Bree? Antonia?"

"What is it?" Bree demanded. "What's going on?"

"You had an appointment with Lieutenant Chin this evening?"

"At B. Matthew's." Bree turned and pointed to the restaurant, which was just across the street. "He's waiting for me right now. Why? Is anything wrong?"

Hunter stepped aside. Bree saw two uniformed cops in the small foyer and an ominous shape prone on the hall floor.

"Eddie's not waiting for anyone. Eddie's right here. Somebody shot him in the head. Probably a .22." Hunter's face was bleak. "He's dead."

Fourteen

Murder will out.
—Chaucer, "The Nun's Priest's Tale"

"There's no way Bree and I can stay in the house tonight."
Antonia stood in the kitchen, shivering. Bree had draped
a raincoat over her, but it didn't seem to help. "This is the
most horrible thing that's ever happened to my sister and
me, Lieutenant."

Bree thought about this for a moment. It was certainly
the worst thing that had happened to the two of them
together.

". . . And I know I should be braver about it, but I just . . ."
She bit her lip. "I just can't seem to stop shivering."

Hunter was unexpectedly gentle. "A little brandy might
help."

Bree had been leaning against the kitchen cabinet, her
arms folded across her chest. "There's some in the front in
the bookshelf. I'll get it."

The kitchen had two doors. The back door led directly
to the outside and a little stone porch with steps that
went down to River Street below. The other led straight

into the living room. The bookshelves were built into the wall directly across from the fireplace. Bree knelt down and got the brandy bottle from the lower shelf and looked to her left, through the small archway to the front door. Eddie lay facedown on the black and white tile. The back of his head didn't bear looking at, although the damage wasn't as horrific as Bree had expected. Two white-suited forensics guys were crowded into the small space. One had a video camera on her shoulder; the other bagged Eddie's left hand, and then his right. The front door was open, and the whap-whap-whap of the ambulance lights lit up the crowd gathered in the street.

Bree carried the bottle back into the kitchen and poured a small measure into a glass she took from the dish drainer by the sink. Tonia took a shaky sip, and then another. A little color came back into her cheeks. "I've never seen a dead body before," she said.

"Well, you shouldn't have looked at this one," Bree said in a practical way. Antonia had bolted to the front door, looked, screamed, and promptly been sick all over the brick stoop.

"And you don't need to spend the night here, or tomorrow night, for that matter. I called Aunt Cissy. She offered to come and get you, but Sam's going to have a patrol car take you over to her place."

"After we get your statement," Hunter said.

"Not you, Bree? You're going to stay *here*? Are you crazy?"

"This has to be part of the O'Rourke case. My case. I need to know what happened." Hunter made a noise. She shook her head apologetically. "It's true, Sam. Unless you think this was just a random shooting."

"I know damn well it wasn't a random shooting."

The back door opened a crack, and Hunter's red-haired sergeant stuck her head into the kitchen. Her name was Markham and she liked Bree about as well as a hound liked chiggers. She ignored Bree completely, cast a contemptuous glance at Antonia, and said, "Ready when you are, Lieutenant."

"Go put a few things into an overnight case, Tonia," Bree said. "We'll talk in the morning, okay?"

"Maybe I'll go home to Plessey," Tonia said. "Just for a little while."

"We'll talk about it in the morning," Bree repeated. "Sergeant Markham is going to take your statement and then you go straight to Cissy's."

"Can I take Sasha with me?"

Sasha butted his head against Bree's knees and the message came through clearly.

"How do you think Sweet Pea's going to feel about that?"

Antonia's woebegone face brightened. "I forgot about her. Sasha'd turn his nose up at all those pink ribbons Cissy uses, wouldn't you, Sash?"

"A poodle," Bree said to Hunter. "A very spoiled poodle."

"Okay," Antonia said. She blew her nose one more time into Hunter's handkerchief, then returned the wadded-up ball to him. "I'm off, then. And I'm sorry about your friend."

"So am I," Hunter said. His voice was grim.

Bree waited until Antonia had packed her overnight case and disappeared out the back door. The noises from the front told her Eddie's body was being wheeled out to the ambulance. A voice drifted back to them: "It's all over, folks. Time to go home."

"I'm surprised the media's not here yet," Bree said.

"Only a matter of time." Hunter drew a chair away from the kitchen table, sat down, and rubbed his hands over his face.

"Shall I make some coffee?"

"Good idea."

Bree liked good coffee, and she liked the whole process of making it. She ground the beans, boiled the water, and put both into the French press. She set cups out for both of them and then sat across the table from Hunter.

"You know this is related to the case."

Hunter nodded. "He thought he'd found something in the autopsy tapes."

"Really." Bree brought the coffee cup to her lips and then took it away again. She'd never be able to sleep if she had caffeine this late at night. It didn't seem to bother Hunter. "Did he tell you what?"

Hunter shook his head. "Just left me a message. Wanted me to join you at B. Matthew's tonight." He'd been staring into his hands. He lifted his head now and looked directly at her. His gray eyes were cold. "Then he left me another message. Said you wanted to change the meeting time."

"Nope," Bree said. "I didn't change a thing about the arrangements for tonight. And before you have to ask—I was with at least forty people from about six o'clock until eight thirty. Continuously."

Tully O'Rourke wasn't there. Jameson wasn't there. Fig and Danica weren't there.

Bree looked at Sasha and wondered if her suspect list had just gotten shorter.

"Did anyone hear a shot?" Bree blinked. "Wait a minute. There wasn't any blood on the tile on the front hall. He was *dumped* here?"

"That's my guess."

"Do we have an approximate time of death?"

"Not yet." He hesitated. "There were some obvious indicators. The body was fairly warm, and the clotting not too far advanced." His face darkened. "He was killed a couple of hours before we found him."

"Any sense of when someone dropped the poor soul in my front hall?"

"There's lot of traffic on Bay, especially during rush hour."

"And who did find him?"

"Your next-door neighbor. The antiques guy. He was locking up for the night about seven thirty and noticed your front door was slightly ajar."

"And he . . . ?"

Hunter spread both his hands wide. "We're getting a statement." He patted his pocket and took out his cell phone and spoke into it—"Right"—then got to his feet.

"You're leaving?"

"You know the drill, Bree. Eddie was on suspension, but he was still one of us. We'll put everything we have into nailing whoever did this."

"Of course," she murmured. "Whatever you have to

do." Then, as he was halfway out the back door: "The autopsy tapes. Do you have them?"

"Nope."

"But there are copies, surely?"

"Stay out of this, Bree."

"In New York, there must be copies. He wouldn't have been walking around with the originals."

"You heard what I said."

"I heard what you said."

"And that was?"

"Butt out, butt out, butt out." Bree sighed. "I'm so sorry, Hunter. You two must have gone back a long way."

He closed his eyes briefly. "I'll tell you about it sometime. After it's over."

"Maybe after another basketball game," she said. "You'll need a rain check on this one."

He nodded, sharply, and left.

The house was very quiet. Bree looked down at Sasha, who looked back at her and wagged his tail. "He didn't actually die here," she whispered. "But I suppose we can try." She put the coffee cups in the sink, smoothed her hair back, and went through the living room to the front door. There was crime scene tape in place, which wouldn't be removed until forensics had done a second sweep. The place where Eddie's body had lain was marked off with fluorescent tape. Bree waited. A siren sounded, a long way off. The grandfather clock in the corner of the living room ticked on. Sasha sighed, scratched at his side, and sighed again.

Nothing. No pale wraith rose from the black and white tiles to tell her a thing.

Suddenly she was exhausted.

She took a long shower, turned out the lights, and fell into bed, Sasha curled up next to her on the floor. "You know what, Sasha?" she said into the darkness. "We've got autopsy photos. Not the tape, but pictures. Petru collected a terrific file. And I know who can take a look at them for me, too."

Fifteen

O! That a man might know the end of this day's business, ere it come.

—Shakespeare, *Julius Caesar*

"Very interesting," Dr. Lowry said, "very, very interesting." She held a magnifying glass in her hand and bent over the photographs like an egret, slim neck extended, arms tucked into her sides like folded wings. "I don't suppose the actual body's available."

Bree knew her Company's limitations. "No, I'm afraid not."

"Hm." Dr. Lowry put the magnifying glass down and shuffled the photos into a neat stack. Then she perched on the round stool next to her examining table. "There should be a videotape of the autopsy itself. I'd like to see that before I commit myself."

"I don't know if I can obtain a copy for you or not," Bree said. The Company rules for collecting evidence were fairly clear to her by now. Any forensic evidence, files, interviews, or documents that would eventually be made available to the public were fair game for Petru and Ron. "But I'm not asking you to prepare testimony.

We just need a shove in the right direction. So commit away."

"Well." Dr. Lowry put her fingertips together and tapped her lips. "The twelve-gauge is a horrible weapon at . . . what was the distance again?" She flipped through the pages of the written autopsy report.

"Three feet, seven inches," Bree said, from memory.

"Yes. As is screamingly obvious to all, the damage to the cerebellum, the corpus callosum, and the parietal lobes is considerable."

"These are all parts of the brain," Bree said, who was struggling for accuracy.

"Correct. But the blast missed the medulla oblongata, or most of it. And that's what is so interesting." Dr. Lowry settled back onto the stool with a pleased air.

Bree made an encouraging face.

"Oh! Of course. You see this channel here? Right above C1. The C1 is the first vertebra in the spinal column. The medulla is at the base of the brain, just above it. It controls the autonomic nervous system. Breathing, heart rhythm, et cetera, et cetera."

The only time Bree had ever heard anyone actually pronounce "et cetera" was in a hugely old version of the musical *The King and I*.

"It looks like something was inserted between the medulla and C1."

"Something?"

"A different bullet, is my guess. A .22, maybe, from the size of the channel."

"You mean Russell O'Rourke was shot twice?"

"Maybe."

Bree's heart began to pound.

"Quadriplegics suffer damage to the spinal column right about here," Dr. Lowry said.

"You mean that bullet . . ."

"If it was a bullet. I'm going way out on a limb, here."

"That bullet would have paralyzed him."

"Oh, yes. Now, there's no damage up here. See? Lot of nice unaffected brain tissue between the mess up above and this channel down here."

"Paralyzed him. But not killed him."

"Nope. It was the massive trauma to the rest of the brain that did that."

Two separate shots.

Maybe hours apart.

And a killer that liked to move the bodies around.

"Good grief," Bree said. Then, "Lord."

"You did say you weren't preparing testimony. Because this is my best guess. Couldn't swear to it."

"Dr. Lowry . . ."

"Call me Megan."

"Megan. I may owe you the best dinner in town. I may owe you an entire European vacation."

"Well," Megan said, who was clearly pleased, "anytime, Bree. Anytime. I like Switzerland, by the way. And now . . ." She gave a regretful sigh and looked at her watch. "I've got a live patient waiting outside for me."

Bree gathered her file together and slipped it back into her briefcase. She resisted the urge to give Megan Lowry a big kiss on the cheek. But when she was outside the clinic, she did a victory dance, to the bemusement of two art students doing charcoal sketches on the sidewalk.

Sasha walked around in delighted circles, tail wagging furiously.

Bree hopped into her car and drove to Angelus Street. She wanted to bounce ideas for the next steps in the investigation off Ron and Petru. But when she let herself in the front door, the downstairs office was empty. No one was in the kitchen, where Petru's workstation sprawled messily next to the stove. No one was in the conference room, either.

Bree ran lightly up the stairs, with Sasha ticking along behind her. Lavinia's rooms occupied all of the second floor. Bree had only been in there once; she had a fuzzy recollection of her experience, of soft rain and large-eyed lemurs. She tapped softly on Lavinia's door. There were mutterings, whisperings, and the soft sounds of breezes. But no answer to her knock.

Out.

Bree looked down at her dog. "All of them? All at the same time? Who's answering the phones?" Rather crossly, Bree dialed her office number into her cell. She heard the phone downstairs shrilling away, and then her cell phone went dead and the ringer downstairs was cut off abruptly. "That bloody battery, Sasha." It was way past time for a new cell phone.

Bree stamped back downstairs. Ron was a neat and methodical worker, and his desktop was always precisely arranged. He'd set a note in the center of the blotter:

Out to buy you a new cell phone!

"Hm," Bree said. "The thing is, Sasha, it is totally unprofessional to leave the phones unattended. Answering machines are for the birds. Ron and Petru want a performance review? I'll give them a performance review." Rather crossly, she shoved her cell phone back into her purse. The phone lit up. The erratic battery was working again. She speed-dialed the office number. Either Petru or Ron would collect the messages when they wandered in, and in her current mood, she wanted to be very specific. Do. Not. Leave. The. Office. Phones. Unattended.

The phone on Ron's desk rang, and Bree took a breath. Short and sweet, that was the ticket. How's about: This is your boss. Never never never . . .

"Beaufort & Company," a vaguely familiar voice said. "May I help you?"

"Mrs. Billingsley?" Bree said. "Is that you, Mrs. Billingsley?" She looked around the empty room, expecting to see the contralto-voiced new hire hiding behind the couch, maybe.

"Miss Winston-Beaufort?"

"Yes." Bree stopped, then started again. "Where are you?"

There was a pause, then Mrs. Billingsley said politely, "Here in the office, ma'am. Answering the phone."

"*I'm* here in the office," Bree said. "I—oh. You're in the Bay Street office."

"Yes'm."

"I'm in the Angelus Street office," Bree said helpfully.

"Yes'm? You want I should switch the phone back there?"

"The phone rings here and you answer it there?"

"Yes'm." Was that a trace of impatience in Mrs. Billingsley's voice? Probably. Bree would have brained herself by now, if she'd been Mrs. Billingsley.

"You had the phone company set it up so both offices can ring either place."

"Seemed more efficient that way," Mrs. Billingsley said mildly. "You want phone coverage all the time, I expect. Except maybe not today. The newspapers and the TV people, they've been calling like a flood. No comment, is what I say to all of them. And sometimes I say: She's not available."

Bree had expected that. A corpse on the doorstep of a young lawyer practicing in a city as small as Savannah was bound to attract the newshounds. She was glad Antonia was safely out of the way, although it probably wouldn't be too long before they tracked down Aunt Cissy. Everyone knew who was related to everyone else in Savannah.

"Miss Winston-Beaufort? I've been handling things to your satisfaction so far?"

"Yes," Bree said. "Absolutely."

"Nobody knows you signed the lease on this place yet, so I don't expect they'll be hammering down the door here." She paused. "Now, then. The furniture man is at the door with the other desk and divider. If you'll wait on a minute, I'll be right back."

"You go ahead," Bree said. "I'll be there directly." Bree snapped her phone shut. "You know what I think, Sasha? I think we did a smart thing hiring Danica's auntie."

Parking at that end of Bay could be a problem during the workweek, so Bree walked the six blocks to the new office, thinking hard about Megan Lowry's theory of the second bullet.

The same security guard who'd retrieved her from Franklin's office two nights before was at the kiosk in the foyer. Bree waved at him in an absentminded way, punched the elevator button, stepped into the car when the doors swished open, and ran nose first into Payton the Rat.

"Ugh," she said coldly.

"And isn't *this* a surprise," Payton smirked. "I heard you were taking over the judge's old offices."

Bree stepped to the back of the car, ignoring him.

"Couple of guys brought in some used desks a little while ago," Payton said. "Headed for your place, were they?"

Bree punched the sixth-floor button in a pointed manner.

"Think there'll be enough room for all your clients up there?"

The doors began to close. Payton stuck his foot out to keep them open.

"Aren't you getting out?" Bree demanded. "Because if you aren't, I am."

"In a minute." Payton shot the cuff on his immaculate pinstriped shirt and looked at his watch. "I'm meeting a new client for lunch. He can wait. I'd much rather talk to you." For some reason—known only to the God of Irony—Payton got better looking each time she ran into him. He'd dropped the two-day-old-stubble look and the earring stud. He'd let his hair grow a little longer, and it curled around his ears in a repulsively adorable way.

"Like the new haircut," Bree said sweetly. "I'll bet it drives the sixteen-year-olds wild."

He smoothed his hair with both hands. "Yeah, well, screw you, too. Actually, running into you will save me some time. You know that our firm represents the interests of Cullen Jameson here in Savannah."

Bree addressed the air over Payton's head. "Why am I not surprised?" Then she looked at him. "Now, how did Mr. Jameson get the name of your firm? Oh! Of course. He called the 1-800 number you guys post on those infomercials. He's got an asbestos claim, maybe? Or he fell down in the Wal-Mart parking lot?"

Payton was a junior member in Savannah's most litigious law firm, Stubblefield, Marwick. John Stubblefield's smarmy smile was plastered all over the late night infomercials soliciting class action claims from the dying and the disabled.

"Yeah, well. We'd like to take a look at the contract between him and Mrs. O'Rourke, in the matter of the Shakespeare Players."

Bree addressed the ceiling again. "Fine."

"We need to take a meeting."

"Fine."

"Like, we need to take a meeting *now*. I have some serious questions about the indemnification portions of this alleged good deal."

Bree looked at him thoughtfully. She had the best lead of the entire case, and this bozo was wasting her time. And the know-it-all smirk drove her absolutely nuts. Her temper woke, stretched, and flexed. "Why don't you take a hike, instead." She put one hand against Payton's chest and shoved hard. He shouted, flew into the air, and thumped backwards into the foyer.

"Sacked. Just like the Miami Dolphins," Bree said to Sasha.

As the doors pulled closed, slowly, Payton glared at her from his position on the terrazzo floor. "You'll be hearing from me!"

"Can't wait!"

She did another little victory dance in the elevator, got off on the sixth floor, and walked down to 616 feeling almost smug.

"You look pleased with life this morning, Miss Beaufort."

"I am truly pleased with life this morning, Mrs. Billingsley." She looked around the small space with approval. "And this looks great."

Mrs. Billingsley wore the same carefully tended navy suit she'd worn for her interview. Her crisply ironed blouse was pink. She sat behind a massive old oak desk in the front half of the room, in an old but comfortable-looking leather chair. A pot of sweet potato vine and a framed photograph sat at one edge of the desk, in front of an old computer. An outdated telephone sat on the other side of the desk.

The back half of the room was separated off by a six-foot-high rattan folding screen.

"I told the delivery gentlemen to put your desk back here, Miss Beaufort." Mrs. Billingsley took a brand-new steno pad from the desk drawer, rose, and walked around the screen. The desk was made of battered mahogany and smelled slightly musty. It was smaller than the oak, and it was set facing the window. An old piecrust tea table was tucked into the far corner, next to a captain's chair made out of pine. The desk chair was a plain pine dining room chair with a gingham cushion.

Bree set her briefcase on the desk. Sasha sniffed at the carpeting, the desk legs, and Mrs. Billingsley. Then he pressed next to the secretary and allowed her to pet his ears.

"You think this is fancy enough for a law office?" Mrs. Billingsley asked dubiously.

"I think it's a miracle Ron got all this stuff on our budget." Bree sat down and contemplated her new offices with a feeling of satisfaction. "I've got some pictures stored away in a back closet in the town house. I can bring those in."

"I could spruce up things some with cushions and all."

Bree sat down in her pine chair. It was very uncomfortable. She nodded toward the captain's chair. "Try that one, Mrs. Billingsley."

She sat down cautiously and then settled back with a faint smile. "Now, this is not too bad."

"So here's what we do. Some clients get the good chair. Other clients get the bad chair."

"And how we going to decide that?"

"On how rude and obnoxious they are."

The smile was a little broader. "I can think of a few folks to put in the bad chair right now."

"Me, too." Bree abandoned the pine chair and perched on the edge of the desk. "Ron called you and told you to make a list of office supplies?"

"Yes'm." She shook her head. "That boy's got a voice on him. He black?"

"No," Bree said. "He's not black."

"Now, that's a shame. We could use a voice like that at the church choir. But he's going to stick out if he's not black."

"I wondered if you were a singer," Bree said. "You've got a lovely voice yourself."

"Thank you." She nodded gravely. "All for the good name of Jesus."

"Yes." Bree cleared her throat. "Now, Mrs. Billingsley, you know that I came to Savannah to take over my great-uncle Franklin's law practice."

"The gentleman that passed."

"Yes. He died. About four months ago."

"In this very office, I hear."

"That's true. There was some sort of freak accident with a fire."

"I'm sorry for your loss, Miss Beaufort."

"I wish I'd known him better. At any rate, he had a small number of regular clients—wills, estates, general family law. I sent them all a letter after his death, telling them that I would be happy to carry on where Franklin left off."

"Regular clients?" Mrs. Billingsley asked. "Are there other kinds of clients?"

"Well. Yes. The Angelus Street clients. You won't have to worry about those. They are mainly . . ." Bree paused, searching for an inspired word. "Out of state."

"This office is just for the Georgia clients, then." Mrs. Billingsley opened the steno pad and began to take notes.

"That's exactly right," Bree said. "Exactly. Anyhow, I'd like you to take the names and addresses and give each of these poor guys a courtesy call. Just let them know the office has been reopened, and that we're here if they need us."

"And a follow-up letter, too? In case they forget."

"Yes. A follow-up letter is an excellent idea." Bree pulled the Franklin Winston-Beaufort LLC bequest from her briefcase, where it'd sat unopened since her arrival in Savannah. "The original client files are in a vault at First Savannah Bank. I'll have them sent along directly. There'll be clients who've gone on to other firms, and we should forward any relevant information to them."

"Existing clients," Mrs. Billingsley murmured. "Now for the new clients."

"The new clients," Bree repeated. "The new temporal . . . I mean, the new Bay Street client is Tully O'Rourke."

"The lady with the husband that shot himself? I read about that in the papers. That our case?"

"That's our case." Bree's excitement at Dr. Lowry's postulate returned with a bang. "And it's a doozy, Mrs. Billingsley. Just wait until you hear what happened this morning."

⧫

"My, my, my." Mrs. Billingsley took an appreciative sip of her tea and swallowed the last of her oatmeal cookie. Bree's summary of the case had taken longer than she'd anticipated, and Mrs. Billingsley had insisted that Bree share her lunch. They split a tuna fish sandwich, a small bag of Cheetos, and a bag of celery sticks. They'd moved the captain's chair out to sit beside Mrs. Billingsley's leather office chair, so they could both be comfortable.

Fortunately, there'd been two home-baked oatmeal cookies.

Mrs. Billingsley frowned at the notes she'd made as

Bree listed the events of the past four days. "This is quite a confusing case, Miss Beaufort."

"You bet you is it. So, the big question is: what next?" Bree was talking more to herself than to her new secretary. "The weird thing about this murder is how long it took. The murderer paralyzed Russell with a shot to the spinal column and rigged up the shotgun to fire when the group of suspects came back into the room. And then Russell didn't actually die until he was on his way to the ER some twenty minutes later. Who was the last person to see Russell O'Rourke alive and whole? I'm going to have to work back from that."

Mrs. Billingsley dabbed at a bit of cookie. "Maybe the Eddie Chin case would get you there faster."

Bree looked at her. "You think so?"

"I do indeed think so. You've got yourself quite a list of suspects with this Russell. Do you think the same person killed Eddie Chin?"

"I'd be very surprised if it wasn't. The m.o. . . ."

"What's that mean? That m.o.? I hear that all the time on those TV police shows."

"*Modus operandi*. It's Latin for . . ." Bree stopped. Mrs. Billingsley, pen raised over her steno pad, looked at her expectantly. "I'm not exactly sure what the Latin is for. Operating method maybe." She looked inquiringly at Sasha, who gave her a doggy grin and started panting. Come to think of it, Sasha had never told her anything she didn't know already. "Well, whatever it means exactly, it refers to the murderer's signature method of committing a crime. Criminals tend to commit crimes the same way over and over again."

"Why is that?"

"I don't know that. Maybe they figure if it worked once, it'll work again."

"Now that makes a kind of sense." Mrs. Billingsley made a note. "Although I still think to do the same m.o. over again is the mark of a fool. Makes it easier to catch 'em. So the murder of Eddie Chin had the same modus operandi as the murder of Mr. O'Rourke?"

"The bullet straight to the head. And the body was moved. And, of course, Eddie told Hunter he'd finally come up with evidence to prove Russell's death was murder and not suicide. It's not totally convincing, I admit." Bree made a face. "Maybe Eddie's murderer is totally unconnected to O'Rourke's. He was a homicide policeman for a long time. He had to have made a lot of enemies."

Mrs. Billingsley snorted. "Coincidence? Two killers out there? Both in Savannah with a gun and they shoot the victim in the back of the head? Not likely. No, ma'am. We start with solving the murder of Eddie Chin, we come up with the killer of this Russell O'Rourke."

"I do believe you're right."

"You got an idea on how to start?"

"We need to trace Eddie's movements for the past twenty-four hours. We need his phone records, his laptop, and to interview anyone who saw him between Monday noon when I met him for lunch and the time of the shooting yesterday afternoon."

Mrs. Billingsley's pen flew across the page of her steno pad.

"And we need to stay out of the way of the police."

An odiously familiar voice jerked Bree upright and two figures appeared at her office door. "Now listen to that, Mr. Jameson. Savannah's most active Southern belle at work. From what I hear, you're spending more time with the police than a nice girl really should, Bree." Payton McAllister smirked at her from the doorway. "Getting to know Lieutenant Hunter a little better than most citizens, Miss Beaufort?"

Mrs. Billingsley looked at Bree.

"If we do offer Mr. McAllister a chair, we should bring in the one from my desk. But he's not staying." Bree turned and glared at Payton. "Are you." It wasn't a question.

She craned her neck to look behind him. A heavyset, dark-haired man lurked in the hallway. She'd seen that face in the case file. Ron was right. Cullen Jameson had a belligerent lower lip.

"Well, Payton," Bree said, "I'd say it's nice to see you again, but it's not. This is Payton McAllister, Mrs. Billingsley. You notice he's limping a trifle? He had an accident with a floor recently. I'd introduce you by saying that he's one of Savannah's gentlemen lawyers . . ."

"But he's no gentleman." Mrs. Billingsley was right on cue. She also was quite formidable when she stood up, folded her arms, and stuck out her chin. "And this man is?"

Payton stepped aside to let his client come into the office. "This is Cullen Jameson."

Jameson was the sort of man confusion made angry. He looked from Bree to her secretary and back again, a scowl distorting his heavy features. "You're the lawyer I'm supposed to see about these contracts from Tully?"

"Yes, I am."

"No one," said Mrs. Billingsley with considerable authority, "sees Miss Beaufort without an appointment."

"Oh, for Christ's sake," Payton said. "As if there's a line of clients outside."

"Sir," Mrs. Billingsley said, with even more authority, "you will not take the Lord's name in vain in this office."

Jameson gave him a disgusted glare. Not over Mrs. Billingsley's views on blasphemy, Bree was sure, but because Payton was in the middle of a scene.

"Ah, no, of course not," Payton said. "Sorry."

"Mrs. Billingsley," Bree said with a formal air, "do you think you could clear my two o'clock appointment? Mr. Jameson isn't in town for long, and I would like to get this chance to discuss the Savannah Players with him."

Her new secretary glowered at Payton. "The mayor's always been willing to adjust his schedule for you before, Miss Beaufort. I will see what I can do."

The mayor. This impressed Cullen Jameson. It made Payton cross. Bree bit her lip. She coughed. She waved her hand in the air, muttered a strangled "Be right back," and escaped behind the rattan screen. She covered her laughter with more coughing, collected her briefcase and suit jacket, and reemerged with a businesslike frown.

"We can go downstairs to the Stubblefield offices," Payton said. "Oh! If the mayor calls, Mrs. Billings, please give him my number." He extracted his business card from his suit jacket.

"It's Billingsley," she said firmly. "And I will pass along the number, if required."

Stubblefield, Marwick had a lavish set of main offices

in a modern office building near Abercorn, which was at the edge of Historic Savannah. The satellite office near the Savannah River was smaller but still occupied most of the second floor. The conservation rules laid down by the Historical Society had been flouted with aplomb, if not painful good taste. A set of huge hardwood double doors opened up into a large reception area. The wall-to-wall carpeting was thick, expensive, and a hard-to-maintain blush pink. A rosewood semicircular desk sat in the middle of the area. Rosewood paneling on the wall behind the desk carried the firm's name in foot-high brass letters. Fresh flower arrangements sat in the corners, on a coffee table in front of the pale leather couch, and in the center of the desk.

An expensively styled blonde sat behind the desk. She rose as they came through the front door and greeted them with a smile.

"Welcome to Stubblefield, Marwick. May I help you?"

"It's me, Kaylee," Payton said impatiently. "Put your glasses on, for Chri—for Pete's sake."

"Mr. McAllister!" Kaylee's smile got a little glossier. "And Mr. Jameson. And you are . . . ?" She waited. Payton looked everywhere but at Bree. Jameson clearly had forgotten her name. Bree stepped forward. "Brianna Winston-Beaufort."

"*You're* Bree Beaufort?" Kaylee took a pair of black-rimmed spectacles out of a desk drawer and fitted them over her perfect nose. "Gosh. I saw your place on Fox News this morning. Wasn't there a body in your living room or something?"

"The last client to get her bill," Payton said. "We'll

be in the small conference room," he added impatiently. "Cullen? Would you like coffee? Maybe something a little stronger?"

"Scotch'd do me."

"I'd like a coffee," Bree said. "Since you asked."

Bree followed Kaylee and the two men down a short carpeted hallway and into a conference room that was a design clone of the reception area, except there was a rose-wood table in the middle of it. Twelve chairs surrounded the table, and a phone, docking station, and cup holder sat at each place. The back wall held a huge TV screen. The only odd note in the room was the double-hung sash windows, looking out over Bay Street, exactly like the window in Franklin's office four floors above them. Bree waited until Jameson and Payton sat down and then seated herself two chairs away. Kaylee bustled for a moment at a built-in kitchen along the wall opposite the TV screen and brought over a tray with a decanter of Scotch, two glasses, and a cup of coffee. Then she bustled off, backing out of the room as she closed the doors.

"Is this your first time in Savannah, Mr. Jameson?" Bree took a cautious sip of coffee and smiled at him over the rim of the cup.

"Me? No, no. Tully and Russ used to have a big holiday party at the house in late December. Been here a couple of times before." He paused, then, in an apparent attempt to be sociable, said, "Nice town."

"We like it," Bree said. "You flew from New York yesterday morning?"

"Yeah."

"There's a ten A.M. from Kennedy."

"Yeah." He stared back at her. She'd read about the thousand-yard stare before; now she'd actually seen one.

Bree hadn't trained for criminal law, and it was only in her first couple of cases for Beaufort & Company that she was meeting villains on a more or less regular basis. But Cullen Jameson was a crook. She'd bet her JD on it. Whether he was a murderer was another thing altogether.

"I was sorry to hear of your troubles with the SEC," Bree said. Payton made a noise somewhere between a growl and a belch. "But glad to see that they didn't carry over into your relationship with Tully."

"Tully and I go back a long way."

"You were a friend of Russell's as well?"

"Not so much, toward the end." He shifted his bulk in the chair. "What 's this all about, anyway?"

"What do you know about Eddie Chin?"

He drew his eyebrows together. Bree recognized the look. He was puzzled. The name didn't ring a bell with him.

Payton jumped to his feet. "Bree, what the hell's going on here?"

Sasha growled softly at her feet.

Payton yelped. "Where'd that dog come from?!"

Bree bent over and patted Sasha on the head. "You remember Sasha."

"We don't allow animals in here. God damn it. Get him out!"

"Eddie Chin!" Jameson snapped his fingers. "That Chink detective, right? He was one of the investigators into Russell's suicide. Yeah. The guy still bugs me with phone calls once in a while. I tell him to fuck off. What about him? Somebody get wise and send him back to China?"

"Something like that," Bree said. "You haven't seen him since you arrived?"

He stared at her. "Why the hell should I?"

She got up, fighting the impulse to dump the rest of her coffee over Jameson's head. She wasn't going to get any further than swear words with this guy. She'd have to set Ron or Petru on his movements. "I'm finished here, gentlemen. If you have any questions about the contract, send me an e-mail."

Sixteen

Going to Hell is easy. It's the coming back that's hard.
                    —Virgil, *The Aeneid*

When Bree went back upstairs to 616, Mrs. Billingsley had gone for the day. A neatly lettered note informed her there'd been no calls and that the phones were forwarded to the Angelus Street office. Bree locked up and walked the six blocks back to find Petru, Ron, and Lavinia enjoying coffee in front of the fireplace. She slung her briefcase to the floor and sank into the only available armchair. Without any preamble, she said, "I learned something really interesting this morning. And I think it may lead us to the person who murdered Eddie Chin."

"It is a tragedy, this death of Lieutenant Chin," Petru said gravely.

"Yes." Bree glanced at the copy of the *Savannah Daily* on his knee. "Was there a lot of media coverage?"

"The death of a policeman in the middle of the tourist district?" Ron said. "You bet there was. Still is."

"And what you discovered?" Petru asked. "It is germane to this case of Russell O'Rourke?"

"I sure hope so." She summarized Megan Lowry's guess about the origin of the small wound at the base of the victim's neck.

"And how does Lieutenant Chin's murder figure into this?" Ron asked.

"That's just it. If we find out who killed Eddie, we'll find Russell's murderer."

"Very logical thinking, that," Petru said with approval.

"Mrs. Billingsley suggested it first."

"So she's working out?" Ron asked.

"I love her," Bree said frankly. "You should have seen how she handled Payton the Rat." She told them that story, too, and when she was finished, Lavinia chuckled into her teacup and said,"Well, I declare."

"Let's focus." Bree rapped her knuckles on the chest they used as a coffee table. "Eddie Chin. We need to track his every movement from Monday on. And we need to track our suspects, too. The Savannah police are on top of this, so we'll have to be careful not to step on any toes. Unusually careful, I mean."

"You will talk to Lieutenant Hunter about the progress of the police investigation?" Petru asked.

"I'm not going to get much joy from Hunter. Eddie was a good friend. And he was a member of the force. There's no hope that Hunter or anyone else in the police department is going to tolerate civilians in the investigation. So I'll move on to the suspects on our original list. The Parsalls, Rutger VanHoughton, Fig. Then Barrie Fordham and Sir Ciaran. I saw Cullen Jameson this afternoon, but the only way we're going to get information from him is if we tie him up and threaten him with agonizing pain. So somebody's got to track his movements since he came into town yesterday. He arrived on the ten A.M. from Kennedy, so he had enough time to do it. That'd be a good job for you, Ron.

"And you'll need to canvass Eddie's neighborhood and find out if anyone saw anything of significance—that will help us a lot. And Petru, can we somehow get hold of Eddie's phone records? Both cell and landline, if he had a landline. And of course the autopsy report . . ."

"We'll only be able to get that when it has been filed," Ron said. "We'll do our best."

"Yes," Bree said. "But there's one thing I want to concentrate on." She leaned forward and clenched her hands. "Eddie had been a policeman for a long time. And he knows what every cop knows: you can't make a case without hard evidence. Motive doesn't cut it. Circumstantial evidence doesn't cut it. Hard evidence is the only shot you've got at a successful conviction.

"Eddie was focused on three things. The suicide note. The surveillance cameras. The fragment of the .22 bullet found at the scene of the crime. I think once Eddie realized that O'Rourke had been shot and paralyzed maybe hours before he actually died, he knew there was one piece of evidence, and one piece only, that could link the killer to the crime.

"The other half of that bullet."

They sat for a moment in silence. Bree looked up at the *Rise of the Cormorant* over the fireplace. The shadowy traces of the beaked head in the fiery sky had darkened. The wind rose outside the little house, and the afternoon light was dim with oncoming rain. The excitement of the day's discoveries drained away.

Suddenly Bree was exhausted.

Lavinia brushed by her, the scent of lavender and thyme trailing her like a fragrant scarf. She bent and kissed Bree on the cheek. "You want some more coffee, child? Maybe some of my special tea?"

Bree clasped her hand affectionately. "No. Thank you, though. I'm off to 700 Drayton to beard the Parsalls in their den. They were supposed to come in yesterday. And Ron? Could you track down Rutger VanHoughton for me, and see if you can set up an appointment? He's back in town for Tully's party tomorrow, and he's not the sort of guy you can just drop in on."

Ron got up and went toward his desk. "I'm on it! And I got you a new cell phone, same number, better battery. I stuck it in your briefcase."

Bree collected her raincoat and briefcase. On her way out the door, she glanced at the frieze of angels treading up the stairs. The last angel had moved another quarter turn. You could almost see its face.

Outside, a heavy mist hung over the streets in a thick, gauzy swathe. The air was so damp and heavy, it took a conscious effort to breathe. Once in a while, a fog like this rose from the river to swaddle the city. It was a good time to light a fire, sit down with a book, and drink a few glasses of wine. Or take a nap. Bree had to stop herself from turning around and heading back to the couch. Instead, she went out to her car, willing her energy back with each reluctant step.

Sasha jumped into the backseat, and for a moment

she paused, with the driver's door ajar, so exhausted she could barely move. She could handle this. She was sure she could handle this. Every investigation had its jolts of adrenaline, followed by the slog, slog, slog of the patient accumulation of data.

Something glided by, on the other side of her car.

"Hello, Striker," she said. She glanced back at the Pendergast grave under the oak. The grave was almost totally obscured by the mist. This tall, battle-ready member of the Company only showed up when something serious threatened—or when Bree herself was a serious threat to somebody. Bree smiled at him. "If something's after me right now, they can have me. And I'm way too tired to whale on anybody."

"Maybe you should have had some of Lavinia's tea."

Bree raised her eyebrows. "Really? I didn't think magic potions were part of our arsenal."

He laughed. "No magic potions. Just a lot of caffeine." He turned and swept the mist with his gaze, and then he looked under the car. Bree bent and looked under it, too. He straightened up and slapped the car roof. "Everything looks okay. Get in."

"All this is waking me up, at least." Bree folded herself into the driver's seat and looked up at him. "Anything I should know about?"

"Guess not. But I'm puzzled. Everything's quiet."

"Too quiet?" Bree said cheekily.

"Yeah." His eyes looked steadily back at her. "Way too quiet."

"It's way past time that Tully did something for us," Harriet Parsall said. Her voice had a discontented whine. "This share of the Shakespeare Players better be just the start of what Tully's due us. And I'm assumin' that this time the deal's goin' to go through. It all collapsed when Russ kicked the bucket."

Bree looked around the suite on the fourth floor of the Mansion at Forsyth Park.

"And yes, she's payin' for this." Harriet gave a mean little smile. "Or rather, Rutger is."

Harriet was dressed in an expensive knit suit. St. John's, if Bree was any judge. She had a thick strand of pearls at her throat and big gold earrings. Big Buck fussed at the minibar and then thudded over with a drink in each hand. He gave one to his wife, took a large swallow of the other, and said, "Sure you won't change your mind?"

"Maybe later," Bree said. She tapped the edges of the contract together to make a neat stack. "You've had your own legal counsel take a look at this, is that right?"

"Yuh." Big Buck settled on the chintz-covered couch next to his wife. He wore a wrinkled white dress shirt, a bolo tie, jeans, and crocodile cowboy boots and he smelled of whiskey. Bree had a vague notion that his oversized silver belt buckle had something to do with cows.

"You're lookin' at last year's Barrel Racing World Championship," Buck said. He slapped the buckle in a satisfied way.

"My goodness," Bree said. "I wouldn't have guessed you were a barrel racer, Mr. Parsall. Bull riding, maybe."

"Oh, that's not his," Harriet said with a mean smile. "It's our foreman's."

Buck slewed around and glared at her. She ducked a little. Bree, who'd been predisposed to like—or at least understand Harriet—was rapidly changing her mind.

"Bought the horse, paid the foreman, and supervised the workouts myself, didn't I?" Buck demanded.

"Sure thing, honey." Harriet winked at Bree.

"I bought it, I own it."

"Sure thing, honey." This time, she rolled her eyes in a "get this!" gesture.

Buck drained his glass and got up again. "You sure about that drink, Miz Beaufort?"

"I'm sure." Bree offered her pen to Harriet. "The document requires both your signatures. I'll notarize it for you."

"I thought you were a lawyer," Harriet said sharply.

"Most lawyers are notaries, Mrs. Parsall. It saves time."

"And you sure we can sell our shares in this thing? What did you call it? An assignment?"

"Yes. You can assign your shares without the approval of the majority shareholders," Bree said.

She had, in fact, advised Tully against allowing this practice, but she'd waved Bree's objection aside impatiently. Seeing the Parsalls in action, Bree was beginning to understand why. There were a fair number of people anxious to break into Tully's circle, and they were undoubtedly willing to pay for the privilege. The Savannah Players was shaping up to be quite a little quid pro quo for its investors.

"Just put your John Hancock right there at the bottom, Harriet, and then plunk your initials where you're supposed to," Buck said from the bar. "And let that pretty girl notarize for you."

"I never know what that means." Harriet wrote her name on the last page of the contract and then began initialing as Bree turned the pages over. "John Hancock. Who the hell is he?"

"The first signer of the Declaration of Independence." Bree turned another page. "And right here, please."

"Was he a Texan?"

Bree bit her lip. Were these people for real? "No, ma'am. He wasn't a Texan." She put her notary stamp next to Harriet's signature and signed her own name. "And Mr. Parsall, you aren't a shareholder in this at all."

"No, ma'am." He wandered back toward them. This drink had a lot less water than the last one. And very little ice. "This little game is all Harriet's." He winked at her, too.

"I jus' don't know a thing about business," Harriet said. "But Tully's been so generous, at such a time in our lives, how could I pass it up?"

A sudden, very unwelcome (and highly probable) scenario flashed through Bree's mind. Harriet, selling three hundred percent of her shares in the Shakespeare Players for outrageous sums of money. Harriet, blinking those big, blue mascaraed eyes at a judge: *I jus' don' know a thang about bidness, Your Honor.*

"What?" Harriet asked sharply.

"Not a thing," Bree said easily. "Just checking to make sure all the *t*'s are crossed and the *i*'s dotted."

She had a theory about the murderer: whoever it was had to be smart, unscrupulous, and with nerves of steel.

And a planner. Her first reaction to the Parsalls had been to the comic-Texan act. They seemed too dumb, too greedy, and too impulsive to plan it. Now she wasn't so sure. And she admitted to an increased respect for Tully. If she'd planned to assure the suspects' presence at an investigation, the Shakespeare Players shares were a pretty nifty way to do it. And Bree was going to have to watch her own tendency to prejudge. She relaxed in her chair and crossed her legs. "Now that we've accomplished that, Mr. Parsall, I just might right rethink that drink."

"Don't like to be fuddled when doing business?" Buck said. "Your daddy raised a smart young woman."

'Thank you," Bree said demurely. She accepted the iced whiskey, took a swallow, and just managed not to choke. "Y'all have been in Savannah before."

"Sure thing," Buck said. "The Christmas parties, you know. When old Russ was alive and kicking."

"That was a terrible thing," Bree said. "I never met him. But Tully surely grieves his loss. I mean, this bee in her bonnet about his murder."

The Parsalls exchanged looks.

"Oh, sorry. I didn't mean to spill any beans." Bree waved the whiskey tumbler. "Not that used to having a little drink in the afternoon."

"Tully thinks somebody did for old Russ?" Buck rubbed his hand across his jaw.

"That Chinese cop," Harriet said sharply. "He was the one with all those accusations. He said Tully did it." Her lips thinned. "Wouldn't put it past her, either. I said so at the time, didn't I, darlin'?" She nudged Buck with her elbow.

"Yeah. You did."

Bree took a moment to marvel at Harriet's flexibility: from best friend to squealer in less than sixty seconds.

"And that Chinese cop turned up dead on *your* doorstep last night, didn't he, Miss Not-used-to-drinking-in-the-afternoon? I saw it on the news last night." Harriet's big blue eyes narrowed. "Tully do for him, too, do you think?"

"I think she thinks it was us." Buck grinned.

"Us!" Harriet shrieked. "Not likely, darlin'. Not likely at all. Not that Buck here didn't think about it."

Buck nodded heavily. "Got the Terminator out and waved it at him some, old Russ. But he ended up takin' care of it his ownself."

"Deserved it, too." Harriet's lips thinned to an even nastier line. "Was dead set against this whole Shakespeare Players thing from the git go, not to mention his turnin' poor old Buck down for a partnership in his stupid investment company. Anyways, about this Chinaman? Chin, his name is?"

"Was," Bree said quietly.

"Can't pin that one on us, either. We came straight from the airport yesterday. And we spent the rest of the afternoon and evening at the bar downstairs."

"At 700 Drayton?" It was a popular place. But it wouldn't have been that crowded on a Wednesday afternoon. And the charge slips would have been dated and timed.

"Nice bar," Buck said. "A lot of witnesses. The ball and chain is right on, as you youngsters say. Nope. We didn't do the Chinaman in."

"Sweet Jesus," Harriet muttered. "Ball and chain. You asshole."

"Now, missy, if you're about finished with the third degree, Tiger Woods is teein' up right about now. Not a bad player for a colored." Buck picked up the remote and clicked the wide screen on.

"Thanks. But I need to be moving on." Bree set her drink on the end table and collected the contracts.

"Don't let the door hit you on your way out," Harriet said. Then, to Buck: "How's about another little drink?"

"I don't think they did it," Bree said to Sasha as soon as she was downstairs, clear of the suite and away from the Parsalls. "Ugh!" She kicked at the bottom riser of the staircase. "Have you ever met a more obnoxious pair in your life? I want them to have done it. I want to call up Hunter and have them hauled off to the clink *right this minute*."

Sasha wagged his tail.

"And they didn't notice you. Why is that, do you suppose?"

Sasha shook himself, as if getting rid of muddy water.

"Right. Who needs attention from a female like that?" Her cell phone buzzed in her briefcase. She retrieved it and flipped it open.

RUTGER VH 4pm 700 DRYTN. RP

Bree texted back OK and looked at the time. She had an hour. Time for a quick lunch and a call to Hunter. She glanced up the staircase. With any luck, the two of them would pass out before the thirteenth hole. "So I'm not going to worry that they'll stumble into the bar and disrupt my interview with Rutger VanHoughton, Sasha. We'll eat right here. Maybe another chicken salad sandwich. See how this one stacks up against the Front Street deli."

Sasha sat down and scratched furiously at his ear, which Bree took as a sign of agreement.

Seven Hundred Drayton didn't have a single dining area, but rather a series of rooms that led directly into one another, without intervening hallways. The bar was in a long narrow room set between two square ones. Bree figured the decorator was fond of Frida Kahlo; the principal colors were gold, purple, and red with an accent of acid green.

She sat at a small table near the main bar and ordered a chicken salad sandwich. From her vantage point, she could see into both dining rooms and into the hall. She called Hunter's cell and left a message, telling him where she was and asking him to call back. She didn't have much hope of a response. She didn't have much hope that the Parsalls had been lying about how they'd spent the hours up to Eddie Chin's death, either. She was sure they had a decent alibi. She had to check it out, though, so when the waiter set down her lunch, she thanked him, and then said, "Is this your regular shift?"

"I get off at five thirty," he said, encouragingly. He sat down at the opposite side of the table and dared a quick glance behind him. "Can't sit here too long, before my manager comes out looking for me, but maybe long enough to exchange phone numbers?"

Bree realized her mouth was open. She closed it. Antonia was right. She was far, far too involved in her work.

She'd been out of things way too long if she couldn't recognize a pickup line when she heard it.

Not only that, now that she took a good look at him, this guy was really cute. Although definitely not much over twenty-three, which was pretty flattering. She smiled happily at him. "Sorry. I would be flirting with you like mad if I had the time, but I don't. I was just checking on a couple of friends of mine that may have been here yesterday."

"Oh. Huh. Too bad for us both, huh?" He bounced up cheerfully. "Let me know if you need anything. Ketchup?"

Bree poked dubiously at the sweet potato fries that accompanied the sandwich. "I think I'm fine for now. But I do want to know if you had an older couple here yesterday. The guy's about fifty, maybe sixty. Cowboy boots, string tie."

"The Texans," he said. He made a face. "Those are the friends you were looking for?"

Bree looked at him a little warily. "Not friends, especially. I'm actually trying to establish an alibi."

He leaned in a little closer. "For you or for them?"

"Them."

"So if I say they were here, they won't get dragged off and maybe water-boarded by the CIA?"

"'Fraid not."

"Didn't see 'em." He grinned. "Make the call. And I want to watch."

"Really," Bree said. "It's important."

He sighed. "They were here, all right. Guy knocked back five double Scotches."

"Five? Wow." Bree thought about that. If Parsall had actually drunk all that, would he have been sober enough to kill Eddie? Or maybe he drank all that to forget that he had killed Eddie? "You have a time frame for me?"

"They came in about two. By the time I got off at five thirty—I told you I get off at five thirty, didn't I?"

"You sure did," Bree said.

"By five thirty the guy was well into the bag. And the wife wasn't much better off." He cocked his head. "Didn't I see you on TV earlier today?"

"Me? I don't think so."

"Not you *live*. You on tape. It was some old footage they were running about that kid that swiped the money from the Girl Scout. But it was about some body found at your house."

"Lindsey Chandler?" Bree had endured more than a few press interviews in the middle of that particular case. The station must have kept the footage and rerun it when Eddie's body was discovered at her front door.

"You're Bree Beaufort!" He pointed his finger at her. A couple of the people sitting at the bar turned around and looked at them. "And you're the lawyer that has that dog with you all the time, right?" He leaned over and peered under the table. "Yep. There he is. Is this cool, or what? Hey, boy. How's it going?"

Sasha responded with a courteous "whuff."

"And they found that cop's body in your front hall yesterday night. That's who you are." His face brightened. "You think those Texans had something to do with the cop murder?"

"Not if they were here from two until five thirty."

"'Fraid so," he said sympathetically. "And they buzzed in straight from the airport. One of my friends works the front desk and he said they brought eight pieces of luggage for a weekend stay."

"They're planning on leaving soon?"

"Monday morning, or so I hear." He leaned forward and said in a near whisper, "They're already driving the staff nuts. Especially 'Big Buck.' We call him Big Pri—"

Bree cleared her throat.

"Yeah, well, you get my drift." He extended his hand. "Name's Brian. And I already know who you are and where to find you. But you don't have my phone number yet, although it's very, very available."

"Thanks, Brian. I'll think about asking you for it."

"You need me as a witness or anything, you just give me a call."

"I'll do that."

He glanced down at her uneaten sandwich. "Anything else I can get for you? Glass of wine, maybe?"

"Not right now." Parsall's whiskey was already sitting uncomfortably in her stomach. "I'm waiting for somebody. Very tall. Swedish blond—a guy," she added hastily, seeing his hopeful face. This guy must really need a date. "A Dutchman. If he comes in looking for me, please let him know I'm here."

She'd finished the sandwich and was seriously considering an order of bread pudding when Rutger VanHoughton walked into the bar.

VanHoughton had the kind of presence that made heads turn. He wore a double-breasted navy wool suit, a rep tie, and a striped shirt with white collar and cuffs. A gold watch so expensive even Bree didn't know the name of it was on one wrist. He caught sight of Bree almost immediately. By the time he'd made his way over to her table, Brian was at his elbow, menu in hand.

"No food," VanHoughton said. "A dark beer. Guinness will be fine." He leaned back in his chair, totally at ease. "Miss Beaufort? I am here, as you requested."

"Thank you."

"You look rather serious. Having a hard time of it, with Tully's little investigation?"

Bree didn't know a great deal about VanHoughton, but she read the financial papers, and she knew the basics. His father had made a respectable fortune in concrete right after World War II. Rutger had gone to Oxford, then the London School of Economics, and then returned to Holland to grow the respectable fortune into billions through a series of perfectly timed acquisitions and mergers. He wasn't married, but all of the tabloid press pictures of him showed him with two or three beautiful women at his side, and one or more beautiful men. Bree thought there was very little this man didn't know about human nature. The trouble was, she knew nothing at all about his.

Rather than answering his question directly she said, "Have you known Tully long?"

"I knew Russell before I knew Tully. But yes, I would say so. We first met over a deal I was doing in Brussels fifteen years ago." He moved his hands off the table when Brian set the stout in front of him. "Russell handled some of the financing." He smiled. His teeth were large and square. "We hit it off, Russell and I. And then I met Tully and the three of us hit it off extremely well."

Bree folded her napkin into a neat square, trying to size him up. "Do you think Russell was murdered?"

"Yes," he said. "I have always thought so."

"Do you have any concrete evidence, or is it just supposition?"

He cut her off before she finished. "Of course I have no evidence. If I had, I would have turned it over to that poor schmuck."

"And which schmuck would that be?" Bree asked.

"You are inferring that there are quite a few floating around this case?" He laughed. "You are correct of course. The so-awful Big Buck is a big schmuck, I believe. And the wife. Harriet." He shuddered delicately. "And there is poor Fig, of course."

Suddenly, she was dispirited. She wouldn't want to sit down to dinner with any of the people in this case. "Do you suppose any of them was once a nice little kid?"

"If that is a very indirect question about whether man is born bad or made bad, I can't answer that. On the whole, I believe genetics determines a great deal more of our character than we are ready to accept. As far as Fig? He was never a nice little boy. But you will find that out for yourself when you sit down and talk to him. As for the Parsalls? I think perhaps Buck has made a series of decisions that have had a bad effect on his character. The first of which was to marry the oh-so-repellent Harriet." VanHoughton gave a very European shrug. "Who is to say?"

Bree wasn't about to get into a discussion over free will

in a bar on Drayton Street, no matter how upscale the bar or the Dutchman. But she did appreciate the fact that Van-Houghton was as subtle as she'd guessed him to be.

VanHoughton's smile didn't quite reach his eyes, but he said, affably enough, "The schmuck I referred to in this case is the poor deceased policeman, Eddie 'the Ninja' Chin."

"Tully sued the NYPD to get him to stop investigating. I have an idea why, but I'd like your thoughts on the matter."

"Do you think Tully killed him?"

This startled her. "Good grief." She thought hard. "No. No, I don't. I may have at one time. But I don't think so now. I've been wrong before."

"I doubt that she did, myself. She is certainly capable of it. Tully, as you have already determined, is a woman who seeks her own vengeance. She wanted Eddie out of the way, and your legal system provided a tidy way to accomplish that. And you have to remember, too, that Chin's effort seriously impeded a pursuit of the real murderer. With all of the attention focused on Tully, there was none directed to finding out who actually did it."

"Had you seen or talked to Eddie Chin since he arrived in Savannah?"

"Our very own Oriental Don Quixote? No. I did not see him. He did leave a call for me on my cell phone. I rather suspect he left the same call on more phones than mine."

She stared at him. "You're not kidding, are you? He called you?" Then: "I don't suppose . . ."

"That I saved the message? Of course I did." He pulled

his cell phone from his suit jacket, tapped at the screen, and handed it to Bree.

Eddie's voice came through loud and clear. It was high, excited, and tense:

I know how you did it. And I'm coming to get it. Two o'clock at the visitors' center.

Seventeen

O what a tangled web we weave.
—Sir Walter Scott, *Marmion*

" 'I know how you did it. And I'm coming to get it.' " Petru repeated the message, then folded his hands on his cane and dropped into a broody silence.

"Did you manage to get the cell phone records?" Bree felt she'd been plugged into an electric socket. The recording of Eddie's phone call was a huge break in the case.

"I did." Petru held up a sheaf of paper. "The police have downloaded his cell phone. These are the numbers."

They were all in Bree's small office. Lavinia sat in the battered old recliner in the corner. Ron perched on her desk and peered over her shoulder. Petru stood in front of the desk, leaning on his cane. She spread the sheets across the desk. "We'll start with numbers from Tuesday on, shall we? With call durations of, say, thirty seconds or less." She started to read. Then, baffled, she looked up at Petru. "There have to be forty calls here, all within the space of an hour yesterday morning, and all lasting about thirty seconds! What's going on?" The penny dropped. She sat back and said, "Oh."

Petru nodded. "Yes. He called everyone possibly connected to the case. With precisely the same message. In the hope that this would flush out the actual perpetrator."

"Trolling," Lavinia said. "Like a fisherman with a big old net."

Bree bit her lip in frustration. "And you say Sam Hunter has this printout?"

"Of course. If not . . ."

"Right. We wouldn't have it. We're only allowed information that will pass into public record." She smacked the desk with her fist. "Hell!"

The ensuing silence was disapproving, but short.

"I mean, 'Nuts!' I guess."

"He's a smart killer, this one," Lavinia observed. "We catch him, there'll be a new grave all ready out back."

Bree put her hands over her eyes and leaned her elbows on her desk. "Let's think about this. Eddie set up a meet. At the visitors' center, which is smart, because it's right on the riverfront next to the Hyatt and it's always hugely busy. But the killer called him back, obviously, to reset the time and place, since the police weren't called to the scene of a shooting in broad daylight. Or we would have known about it."

"So there should be a return phone call, from the killer," Ron said. "Let's have a look." He ran his finger down the page of numbers.

Bree got up. "I don't think so. The killer wouldn't have wanted Eddie to set a trap, or alert somebody like Hunter. Eddie would have had half the Chatham County police force lurking in the bushes. No. I think Eddie got there and somebody handed him a note. Or somebody else met him and lured him away. Eddie was a smart cop, but it's pretty clear he was obsessed with this. He may have been so eager to move the case along that he abandoned the usual precautions. I've wondered all along why he didn't keep Hunter in the loop."

"No one really b'lieved him, though, did they?" Lavinia's voice was soft.

"That's very true," Bree said.

"So he gets, perhaps, this note from the killer. And it says something like: 'Go to the underpass at the electric company,'" Petru said. "Or, 'Come down to the docks by the river.' Yes. I can see that our clever killer would think in just this way. But how are we further along? We do not know what happened as a result of all these phone calls."

Bree realized, suddenly, that this promising lead had petered out. She got up. "We're almost back where we started." The room was too small and too crowded. She had to get out, to move. Then she sat back down again. She needed mental energy, not physical.

"At least I've made a good start on tracking his movements his last day," Ron said. "He's renting a room in a little house at the north end of Abercorn. It's on the second floor and the proprietor's bedroom is right under his and the insulation isn't all that good, so she knew when he was there and when he wasn't. She heard him making phone calls Wednesday morning, one right after the other, and now it turns out we know what that was all about. He went out about ten. I tracked him to the coffee shop on Broughton, and he had a couple of black coffees. The girl behind the counter remembers him because he was so restless. Up and down out of that big chair that sits under the window. Exactly like you're doing right now." He smiled at her. Ron saved that smile for occasions like this one, when she was wound up or overexcited, and it acted like a dose of Prozac, only quicker. Bree felt herself relax slightly. She sat back down. Ron patted her head. "And then I left the trail and came back here when you called this meeting. But I'll pick it up again in the morning. We may find out where he went and who he met, and solve this case after all. But I don't think we should try to do it all tonight."

"You're exhausted, child," Lavinia said reprovingly.

"We're getting very close," Bree said. "We can't stop now."

"It is time, perhaps, for all of us to take a break." Petru sighed. "Rose has promised pot roast for this evening's dinner. I am very fond of pot roast."

"Pot roast?" Bree demanded with some heat. "When we're inches away from tracking down someone who's killed two people, you're talking pot roast?"

Her cell phone rang. Impatiently, she flipped the cover. The little screen read: FRANCESCA. Bree put her head on her desk.

"Your parents, I think," Petru said kindly.

Bree put the phone to her ear. Her mother's light, pretty voice sounded anxious. "Bree, honey?"

"Hello, Mamma."

"Your father and I are here at the town house."

"Yes, Mamma."

"Did Antonia tell you we were coming?"

"I think so, Mamma."

"Are you working late, dear?"

Bree looked at Petru, Ron, and Lavinia. All three shook their heads and Ron mouthed, *Get some sleep.* "Not anymore, Mamma. I'll be right there."

She jogged back to the town house.

Francesca Winston-Beaufort was small, round, and the chief determiner of Antonia's red hair and blue eyes. Their father, Royal, was fond of saying that he fell in love with her hair the moment he saw her across the dining room at Duke University thirty years before, and that love for the rest of the woman came later.

By the time Bree and Sasha came through the back door and into the kitchen, her mother had set the dining room table for four and prepared a green salad, a fruit salad, and a basket of hot rolls. A welcome aroma drifted in the air. "You do smell Adelina's mushroom casserole in the oven. I brought it all the way down from Plessey. And she sent some of her cinnamon rolls, too." Her eyes darted to her daughter's too-slim frame, but she said merely, "And your father drove off to Cissy's to fetch Antonia."

"Then we'd better set a place for Cissy, too," Bree said practically. She kissed her mother and sat down at the kitchen table.

"You mean she'll want to know all about this horrible murder. You're right about that." Francesca bent and cuddled Sasha's face between her hands. "And you look pretty good for a dog recovering from a bullet wound." She smoothed his fur with her thumb. "My goodness, dear. It doesn't look like more than a scratch. From the way your sister talked about it, I thought poor Sasha'd be scarred for life."

"He's a good healer," Bree said. She also made a mental note to whale on her sister for blabbing.

"The poor pup certainly has been through a lot. First that steel trap and the broken leg. And then the bullet wound . . ." Her mother perched on the opposite chair and said, with an attempt at artlessness that didn't fool Bree for a minute, "Your life's taken on some excitement since you moved down here."

"That it has."

Francesca wore her favorite combination, a silk shirt and a pair of silk pants. This set was a deep cadet blue that matched her eyes. She set her jaw determinedly, which made her face pink and her eyes even bluer. "Bree, your father and I think that you've bitten off quite a lot here, with taking on Franklin's old practice and all."

Bree knew what was coming: *This job is too dangerous, Bree. We want you to come back to Raleigh and practice law with your father, Bree.* And her response? *Butt out, Mamma.* Or rather, since she was her adoptive mother, and Bree loved her dearly: *I can take care of myself, Mamma.*

She said merely, "I like the way you're doing your hair, Mamma."

Francesca bit her lip. Then she sighed heavily and gave it up. "You like this new style?" She touched the short red curls. "Your father, you know, likes it long. But what woman over fifty can get away with that? It's bad enough that I have to refresh the color every six weeks. I spend more time fussing with my hair than—Darling," she interrupted herself, "I'm so sorry. I just can't shut myself up. We're worried about you, your father and I. What in goodness' name is going on? You had a dead man in the front hall of this town house yesterday. Your father and I heard about it on the news."

There was an undercurrent of slight horror when she said the word "news." Her parents were firmly convinced the only time the family name should appear in the media was to announce a birth, a marriage, or a death.

"That I did, Mamma."

"And you look absolutely exhausted."

"Did I tell you I had a physical this week?"

"You did? You actually went and saw a doctor? Did he give you a tonic? Maybe that's what you need, a tonic." Her mother jumped up and took a bottle of wine from the rack next to the refrigerator. "We'll have a glass of wine. Red wine's good for strengthening the blood."

"What does Daddy say all the time? I'm finer than a frog hair. That's me. I'm in the best shape of my life, Mamma. The doctor says so."

Francesca looked doubtful. "What kind of doctor did you see, darling?"

A forensic pathologist, Mamma. Bree bit her lip. Her mother would totally flip at Megan's preference for corpses over people. "She's in practice with her brother, Megan Lowry is her name. I like her. She's very nice."

"Lowry." Francesca drew her eyebrow together. "The name's not familiar at all."

"Well, she practices here in Savannah, and you don't get down here all that much." Bree regretted *that* the minute she said it.

"We'd come down a lot more, darling, if you'd just say the word."

"You come down exactly the right amount," Bree said.

"We miss you girls, you know." Francesca cocked her head and smiled suddenly. "There's the back door. I think I hear your father."

Antonia burst through the back door first, hair flying. She shrieked and kissed her mother, and then she shrieked and kissed Bree. Royal followed her into the kitchen at a more sedate pace, Tonia's overnight bag in one hand. "Parking gets to be more problematic every time we visit, Chessie," he said to Bree's mother. He kissed Bree on the forehead. "Hello, daughter. You're looking well."

"She looks like hell," Antonia said frankly. "You're just glad to see her. I'm glad to see her, too, of course, but to me she looks like hell."

"Isn't anyone glad to see *me*?" Cissy walked through the kitchen and straight through into the living room without stopping. She wore a tracksuit, custom-made tennis shoes with her name emblazoned on the side in sequins, and heavy gold earrings.

"Where are you going, sister?" Francesca demanded. "You aren't going to stop to say hey, howdy?"

Cissy's voice floated back to them. "I'm taking a look at the scene of the crime, of course." Then: "Hey, howdy, sister."

"You're not going to mess with that scene if the police tape's still up," Royal grumbled. "Behave yourself, please." He followed Cissy into the front room. With a shrug, Bree got up and so did her mother. In a few moments they were all crowded together, looking at the little hall.

"Not a speck of difference that I can see," Cissy said in evident disappointment.

Francesca rolled her eyes. "My word, Cissy. Did you want blood and brains all over the place?"

"There weren't any," Bree said. "Just the head wound."

"Hm." Her father patted his sports coat pocket in an absentminded way. He'd quit smoking his pipe years before, but the reflexive habit died hard. "Killed somewhere else and dumped here?"

"That's the theory."

Cissy shuddered. "Thank the Lord he wasn't done in here. You might have had a ghost, Bree. Think of that."

"Think of that," Bree echoed.

"Well, *I'm* thinking of my dinner," Antonia said abruptly. "And I don't want to think about the way that poor man looked any more. I told y'all I upchucked like anything, didn't I?" She smiled sunnily at everyone. "That casserole just about warmed up, Mamma?"

"Now," Cissy said, as they were all seated at the dining room table a few moments later, "everyone's coming to Tully's party tomorrow night, I hope. I mean, that is why you came on down."

"We came on down to see the girls," Francesca said. "But we'd love to go to the party, wouldn't we, Royal? Ciaran Fordham! I had a crush on that man the first time I saw him in the first remake of *Wuthering Heights*. Gorgeous. Just gorgeous." She blushed prettily. "I have a copy of his biography with me. I was hoping I could ask him to sign it."

"Tony'll be there, too," Antonia said carelessly. "You know, the famous director? Anthony Haddad?"

"There's a chain of Haddad funeral homes," Francesca said doubtfully.

"Cousins, or brothers or something," Cissy said. "Honestly, Chessie, you need to get out of the house more. Tony Haddad is one of the most brilliant new stage directors around. He's won every theater award there is. It's just like you to bring up the funeral homes."

"I most certainly did not," Francesca said indignantly. "All I said was, isn't that the same family as the people who own the funeral homes, and you go off like a rocket."

"Ladies," Royal said. "Not at the dinner table, please."

Antonia and Bree looked at each other and started to giggle.

"Girls," Royal said.

"We know, Daddy," Tonia said. "We've heard it all our lives." Then she and Bree chimed in together, *"Not at the dinner table."*

"Tell us about Mr. Haddad and this new job," Royal said.

"Mamma doesn't keep up with the theater much," Antonia said. "If you did, Mamma, you'd be over the moon that I'm working for him."

"Tonia!" Cissy shrieked. "You got the part!"

"The part!" Antonia's eyes brimmed with sudden tears. "I should have gotten that part!"

Bree said hastily, "It's better than a part, Aunt Cissy. It's a continuing job with the stage management end of things. Much better than just a part. A part lasts as long as the play. A stage management job lasts as long as the company."

"My," Francesca said. "So this is more like regular employment?"

"You bet. A real career move." Bree reached over and

nudged her sister affectionately. "I take it John Allen Cavendish let you go without too much of a hoorah?"

"There was a hoorah, all right. But it wasn't over me. It was over the funding for the theater."

"Oh, dear," Francesca said. "Money troubles, I expect."

"Big time." Antonia took a huge bite of casserole and said through the mouthful, "I'd have lost the job there anyway. So it's a good thing this came along when it did."

"And the salary's adequate?" Royal asked.

Antonia smiled. "More fruit salad, Daddy?"

"You trying to divert my attention?"

"Is it working?"

Bree thought she heard a faint tap from the kitchen.

Sasha nudged Bree's foot.

Someone at the back door.

"Is that someone at the back door?" Cissy said. "You want me to get it?"

"I'll go." Bree tossed her napkin onto the table and wondered what would happen if she went on through the kitchen, out through the back door, and out into the night and didn't come back for the rest of the night. Her talkative family wouldn't miss her for hours. She could get some sleep on a park bench somewhere.

But the way out was blocked by Sam Hunter and her fantasy faded in the pleasure of seeing him again. Although he looked even more tired than she felt. His eyes were red-rimmed and there was faint stubble on his cheeks. She wanted to stroke the tiredness away. Instead, she smiled at him.

"Hey," he said.

"Hey, yourself," Bree said, pleased. "Are you returning my phone call?"

"We missed the basketball game, so I thought we might at least grab a bite of dinner." He caught sight of her mother, who'd come into the kitchen after her. "Sorry. I didn't realize you had company."

"Now, who is this?" Francesca said. "Bree, I don't think I've met this nice-looking man."

"Come in," Bree said. "You can join us for dinner."

"I thought we'd grab something at Huey's."

"This is Lieutenant Hunter, Mamma. He's with the Chatham County police."

"How nice to meet you, Lieutenant."

"And he hasn't eaten yet."

"You haven't eaten yet?" Francesca's eyes went wide. "My word, my word, man. It's well after nine o'clock. You'll be doing us a favor if you come and help us finish up all this food."

Hunter hesitated. Bree smiled encouragingly. "Thank you, ma'am. I'd like that."

Bree led him into the dining room. As Antonia set up a sixth place at the table, Bree introduced him. "Hunter? My father, Royal."

"Sir." The two men shook hands.

"And Cecilia Carmichael, my aunt."

Cissy gave him an appraising look. Then a flirtatious one. She patted the space next to her. Antonia set the extra chair next to Bree, instead, and Hunter sat down in a gingerly way.

"Hey, Hunter," Antonia said. "Grab the last of the casserole before my aunt does."

Cissy frowned at her as she put the serving spoon back into the dish. "Antonia, I eat like a bird. I always have."

"Some birds eat three times their own weight every twenty-four hours," Antonia said with an innocent air. "I saw that on a National Geographic special."

"Do you work with my daughter, Lieutenant Hunter?" Francesca ladled a large helping of fruit onto his plate and stacked two rolls next to them. "Have some butter with that. And your name isn't Hunter Hunter, is it? Like the character in that book? Major Major?"

"Sam," he said.

"Now, that's a name I've always liked." She passed the green salad to him. "You're the first of Bree's colleagues we've met so far. I've spoken on the phone with her secretary, Ron . . . that boy has the pleasantest voice I've ever heard! But we haven't seen hide nor hair of the others."

"Hunter and I aren't exactly colleagues, Mamma. He works for the police."

"You're on this current case, I take it?" Royal said.

"Yes, sir."

"Bad business, that."

"Yes, sir. He was a friend of mine."

"Things progressing well?"

"Well enough." Hunter nodded at Francesca. "Excellent casserole, ma'am."

"Do call me Francesca. And it's a wonderful casserole. It's one of Adelina's specialties. The girls have loved it since they were little."

Hunter cocked an eyebrow at Bree. "Adelina?"

"Our cook," Bree said shortly. She and Hunter didn't

see eye to eye on the advantages of her family background. He tended to resent it. She resented it, too. But she didn't like anyone else resenting it.

"About this case, Lieutenant." Cissy broke into the conversation with a determined air. "I'm just fascinated by the way y'all work in the police. You must know who committed this dreadful crime by now. Do you . . ."

"Cecilia." Royal's interruption was firm. "The lieutenant's not allowed to discuss current cases. Pass the fruit salad to me, would you? And tell me how things have been with you lately. Did your counsel—what's his name?"

"Dave Burbank?"

"That's the one. Did Burbank straighten out the quit-claim deed on the cabin for you?"

"I don't know."

"You don't want to let something like that drag on."

"Maybe Bree can handle it."

"Bree doesn't handle real estate law."

Bree cast her father a grateful look, both for the diversion in the conversation and for saving her from the irksome details of Cissy's muddled affairs.

"She could if she wanted to," Cissy said with sublime confidence. "Bree can handle anything. Besides, she'd never send me a bill."

Bree caught Hunter's eye and bit her lip so hard it hurt.

The conversation meandered on like the Savannah River on a hot afternoon, digressive and placid. When Bree got her relatives out the door at the end of the evening, she collapsed on the living room couch with a sigh of relief. Antonia bounced out the door to take Sasha for a last nighttime walk. Hunter leaned against the fireplace, arms crossed.

Bree batted her eyelashes and struck a pose. "Did Aunt Cissy manage to get your phone number?"

A look of alarm crossed his face.

"She's a force of nature, Cissy is."

"I like your mother."

Bree smiled. "Everyone likes Mamma."

"And your father, too. Your aunt's . . ."

"A caution," Bree agreed. "Mamma slipped up once and called her man-hungry. But she means well, Cissy does. She doesn't have a clue about what kind of law I actually practice, but she's always dragging prospective clients in to see me, no matter what the problem is."

"Like the O'Rourke case."

"Yes."

He came and sat next to her. He sat close, but they didn't touch. "We've got a few leads on Eddie's movements just before he met up with the killer."

"His cell phone records?"

Hunter's eyes narrowed. "What do you know about his cell phone records?"

"It makes sense, doesn't it? If he talked to you about what he discovered in the autopsy records he must have talked to a pathologist, right? Maybe even the killer. That's where I'd look first," she added disingenuously.

"We did run the cell phone records. He did talk to the police pathologist."

"What about?"

"Eddie had some notion that O'Rourke was shot twice."

"Twice?" Bree hadn't had time to think about how she'd present Lowry's theory to Hunter. She did know she faced a number of minefields. There would be a lot of questions about how she'd obtained the actual copies of the investigation from New York. She could fudge a little, maybe say that Eddie had let her have copies, but Hunter was too smart and too quick to swallow that whole. If she asked him leading questions, he was going to be furious if he found out later that she'd had information about the case that she hadn't turned promptly over to the police.

Finally, there was her duty to her clients—the live one and the dead one. The canon of ethics was quite clear: she had no obligation to turn information about past crimes over to the courts or the police.

"What did the police pathologist say about Eddie's idea?"

"Forester? He's a crusty old s.o.b. Told Eddie to get back on his meds. Not the kind of guy that likes to be proved wrong."

"Do you think he's wrong? The pathologist? That maybe O'Rourke was shot twice?"

Hunter shrugged. "Forester's the best we've got. When he gives an opinion, you can bet it's going to hold up under the toughest cross-examination."

"But?" Bree urged.

Hunter put his head back on the couch and stared up at the ceiling. "Evidence has to hold up in court. It's worthless unless it does. This second-bullet theory is a lead I'll follow up, of course. But I don't expect it to pan out. This case was so thoroughly covered the first time around, I'd be surprised if anything new came up at this point." He put his hand over hers. "You have any ideas?"

Bree got up and moved away from his warmth. It was dangerous, that warmth. And all that it represented.

"No," she said. "Not a one."

Eighteen

At the door of life, by the gate of breath,
There are worse things waiting for men than death.
—Swinburne, "The Triumph of Time"

"Auntie Em is having a wonderful time working for you," Danica Billingsley said. "I hope she's fitting in okay." She unlocked the door to Tully's den and stepped back so Bree and Sasha could go in.

"Auntie Em?" Bree paused in the doorway. Had she heard Dani correctly? She was on edge; in addition to talking to Fig O'Rourke this morning, Ron had arranged an interview with Sir Ciaran and Barrie Fordham. Bree had promised to get Francesca an autograph, if she could do it with aplomb. Or at the very least, without turning bright pink.

Danica winced. "I know. But we love *The Wizard of Oz*. We watch it every Easter, all of us squashed together in Aunt Emerald's trailer. And I mean squashed. My mamma's the same size as my aunt. It's a family tradition. Eating moon pies and singing our little hearts out. Ever since I was five and my little brother was three."

Bree laughed delightedly at the thought of the two small

children squashed on the couch between the "traditionally built" ladies. "She's great, your aunt Emerald. And quick. We hadn't been working together more than two hours before she pulverized a colleague I especially dislike. And talk about deft. The guy never knew what hit him."

Danica's smooth brown face sobered. "She didn't have the chances I did, Bree. If she had—she'd be governor by now! Never got beyond eighth grade and thought she'd be working in the Hyatt kitchen all her life, scrubbing pots. But she took that online secretarial course, and you gave her the first chance she's had to move on up. Things are going to get good for her. I can feel it."

"It's going to be a real pleasure working with her, I'll tell you that." Bree went into the office and sat down at the small conference table. Danica lingered in the doorway. Sasha sat in the corner, eyes alert. "I'm not so sure it's going to be a pleasure talking to Russell Junior, though." She glanced at her watch.

"He makes a point of being late," Danica said regretfully. "If he's in his Goth mode, you won't get much sense out of him at all. If he's in his Young Heir mode, he'll be insufferable. As for the Fordhams, whatever else they are, they're real professionals. If they said they'd be here at eleven, it'll be to the minute."

Danica lived with these people. She'd be a great source of information if Bree could get her to talk a bit. "Can you come in and sit down until Fig gets here?"

"I'd better not, as much as I'd love to. The house is in an uproar over the prep work for the party tonight."

"I noticed." When she'd walked in the front door, she'd dodged flower deliveries, professional cleaners, a caterer or two, and the liquor salesman. Anthony Haddad held court in the huge living room, surrounded by his acolytes. "How many guests do you expect?"

"Three hundred or so. Ah. Here he is. Hey, Fig."

Fig stopped just outside the door, hands shoved in his pockets. There were deep smudges under his eyes, his clothes were wrinkled, and he needed a shampoo. He yawned. "Somebody said I was supposed to come and see you. I see you. Now what."

Dani looked at Bree and mouthed: *Goth.*

"Why don't you come in and sit down?" Bree suggested.

"Yes, Fig. Miss Beaufort just has a few questions, and then you can go back to bed. I'll be around if you need me, Bree," Dani added. "Check with the kitchen. They'll track me down in nothing flat. Em's in there, and my mamma, too. Maybe you can meet them later. Oh. And be sure to lock the door when you've finished up, will you? Tully'll have a fit, otherwise." She turned and disappeared down the hallway.

As Fig slouched past the desk, he ran his hands over the top. Then he shouted, *"Dani!"*

Bree imagined that the short silence from the hall was an exasperated one. Danica's expressionless face appeared around the door a few seconds later. "Yes, Fig."

He pointed to the desk. "She's done it again. The pot, this time."

"Oh, for Pete's sake. Sorry, Bree, this will just take a minute. Okay, Fig. I'll let your mother know."

Fig sat down in the recliner and bumped the footrest up. "It's Her Highness, Lady Barrie," he explained, although Bree hadn't asked. "Tends to be light-fingered with small, valuable objects. Dani says it's because she grew up dirt-poor and is scared to be broke."

Bree had to admit she was shocked. Barrie, Lady Fordham, a petty thief? But it explained Dani's "whatever else they are" comment. And it did provide a good lead-in for one of the questions she had for Fig. "Is that why your father disliked the Fordhams? Because Barrie is a bit of a . . ."

"Crook?" Fig said. "How the heck should I know? Actually," he corrected himself, "I do know. He'd get all hot and bothered about missing petty cash, or some of Mother's jewelry, and then it'd blow over. She and Mother go way back, you know."

"I didn't know."

"You didn't know Mother Dear started out in the thee-ay-ter? Barrie went on to fame, if no fortune. Mother went on to Father. And to me."

Bree didn't deal well with adolescents. Lindsey Chandler had been as balky and rude as this kid, and she found herself wanting to give Fig a good smack up the side of the head, same as she had with Lindsey. At least Lindsey had washed her hair.

"Fig. You know that part of the reason your mother hired me was to look into your father's death."

He shrugged.

"Something very tragic has come up related to that."

"The Chinese guy. The cop. Somebody blew his head off, too." He grimaced. "Sweet."

"Yes. Tell me, how well did you know Eddie Chin?"

"Pretty well."

"Pretty well?" Bree stared at him, astonished.

"Sure. Eddie thought Father was murdered. I think so,

too. After it . . ." He paused, swallowed, and then went on. "After it happened, Eddie started to, like, cozy up to me, you know? Thinking maybe I'd spill some family secrets or whatever. But I said, like, Man! I'm down with this. I think somebody offed the old man, and I want to catch him just as much as you do."

"Did you see much of him when he was in Savannah?"

"Nah. After Mother Dear took him to court to stop harassing her, he kind of lost it, you know? Like maybe the wheels came off?" He whirled his forefinger around his ear in a rapid circle.

"So you didn't have any contact with him after that?"

"No. Well, there was that, like, totally off-the-wall phone call a couple of days ago. I was, like, 'Man, you're off your meds.'"

"What phone call was that?"

"Aah, let's see. I was awake, so it must have been after eleven. And the sun was out. And my cell rings and this voice says: 'I know you did it. I'm coming to get it.' And I go, like, 'Hey Eddie, is that you? It's Russell, man. What's going on?' And he goes, like, 'Russ? Is that you? Sorry, man, sorry.' Then he hangs up." His eyes shifted sideways. "That was it. Weird, huh?"

"What do you think he meant? 'I know you did it. I'm coming to get it.'"

"He knows I did what? Killed Father? No way. He's coming to get it? Get what?"

"He called you Russ, not Fig?"

"My friends call me Russ, yeah."

There was something about the story that didn't ring true. Bree looked at Sasha, still sitting patiently in the corner. Fig hadn't acknowledged the dog. It didn't mean he didn't see him. Sasha lifted a paw and set it down, which was not at all enlightening.

"Do you prefer to be called Fig, or Russ?"

"He's called Fig because he liked the cookie when he was little. You know, Fig Newtons?" Tully swept in. She held the silver inkstand in one hand and the little cloisonné jar in the other. She was wearing very well-cut jeans, a man's white shirt, and a small fortune in diamond earrings. "That damn Barrie," she said with a mock-tragic roll of her eyes. "Just one of her delightful failings. Where the hell should I put this? Not back on the desk, that's for sure. The credenza."

Fig got out of the recliner. "Here, Mother. I'll get it." He thought a minute. "Maybe you ought to put the earrings in there, too."

"Don't touch anything," Tully snapped. "And don't be more of an ass than you can help. And for God's sake, go clean up. We've got three hundred people showing up in a few hours and you look like an unmade bed." Tully slammed the credenza door closed and faced Bree. "Are you through with him?"

"Yes," Bree said mildly. "Thank you for your time, Russ."

"And do you think my son created this elaborate plot to kill my husband?"

"What the hell?" Fig said. "You think I had something to do with Father's death?"

Bree couldn't look at the expression on his face. She looked at her hands, instead. Then curled them into fists, so she wouldn't smack some sense into Tully.

"Go on, Fig, Make yourself useful for a change." Tully waited impatiently until the door closed behind her sullen son. "Well? Have you done anything significant yet? Other than pissing off most of my friends?"

"Really?" Bree said. "Which ones in particular? One of your friends, Tully, killed your husband. And a troubled cop. Not to mention the fact," she added with some heat, "that we drew up this list of suspects together."

Tully put her hands to her eyes and stood absolutely still. "Sorry." She sighed. "I'm sorry. This is the first big party I've given since Russ died, and I'm being a bitch. But that's what I do best. Be a bitch." Her eye fell on Sasha, who gazed somberly back at her. "And you have to go into the garden, kiddo. Unless you want Ciaran sneezing all over you."

"Oh, dear," Bree said. "I'd forgotten about that." She got up and beckoned Sasha into the hall. "Go find Emerald," she suggested. "She's in the kitchen. She might give you a nice bit of something." Sasha trotted outside obediently. Bree closed the door behind him.

"You'd think he understands you?" Tully asked sarcastically.

"I understand him. Works out to the same thing."

There was a light tap at the door. The clock on the credenza sounded eleven with a soft "ching."

"That'll be Miss Pickpocket and her husband," Tully said. Then, in one of those maddening swings of temperament, she said, "Do you need anything? Coffee? A drink?"

"I'd love a cup of coffee."

"I'll have it sent in." The door opened, and she said,

"Barrie, darling! And Ciaran. This is Miss Beaufort, whom you've met, and who is going to walk you through the contracts for your share in the Shakespeare Players."

Barrie floated in, followed by the magnificent figure of her husband. Neither Fordham was classically beautiful; Barrie's forehead was high, her pale face too long, her mouth a small curve too sweet for contemporary beauty. Ciaran was . . . Ciaran. It was hard not to look anywhere else when they were in the room.

Bree thought she did very well for a person interviewing a demigod of the theater and his possessive wife. She didn't stutter, she didn't blush, and she wasn't too shy to look the great actor right in the eye. Ciaran sat at his ease behind Tully's desk, graceful even in repose. The golden baritone was reduced to a languorous murmur. The late morning sunlight wasn't particularly kind to the lines around his eyes and his mouth, but that face! She'd seen that version of *Wuthering Heights* with Francesca and the image of Heathcliff gazing longingly through the windows at Catherine Earnshaw put the two of them in tears. And here he was, sitting right in front of her.

Sneezing.

"You had a dog in here," Barrie said accusingly. Up close, the great, tragic eyes took on a rather beady aspect. And the famous rose petal complexion was overlain with a skein of fine wrinkles. "I *told* you about Sir Ciaran's allergies."

Sir Ciaran sneezed again.

Tully shook her head. "I'll get you some tissue, Ciaran."

"Quite all right," the great man said. The sneezing made him so approachable, Bree was sure she could get him to sign an autograph for her mother.

Bree began the interview with the ploy provided by Tully. "You've had your own attorney look at the contracts giving you shares in the Players?" she asked.

"We can't afford a lawyer," Barrie said. She smiled tightly. "Only if you screw us over. Then, of course, we can sue you. I understand that solicitors here in the United States operate on what's called a contingency fee?"

"That's what it's called," Bree said agreeably. "The agreement offers you ten percent of the Players in return for Sir Ciaran's performance as leading man in the company for a period of three years. It also provides for your contribution as a member of the troupe for the same period of time."

"I do believe Tully meant to give us fifteen percent."

"No, she was quite clear about the division, Lady Fordham."

"Well." She sighed, and for just a moment, she seemed old, vulnerable, and very, very tired. "You know, Miss Winston-Beaufort, there aren't many secure positions for people like us. We've never been in those dreadful, moneymaking shows like *The Producers* or *The Lion King* that bring in lots of lovely lolly. Although Ciaran here is my lion king." She smiled at her husband. "Yes, we'll sign, and be grateful, too. Won't we, darling?" The look she cast at Sir Ciaran was so full of love, and longing, that Bree's heart contracted.

She looked away, fumbling a bit with the contract. Then she put each page in front of Barrie, who signed and passed it on to Sir Ciaran. After the very last page, Bree took out Sir Ciaran's biography, *A Rogue and Peasant Slave: An Actor's Life*, and offered it to him. "My mother

Francesca and I would be so pleased if you'd sign this, Sir Ciaran."

He'd been gazing out the window in an absentminded way, but turned and looked at her. The brilliant turquoise eyes narrowed, focused, and searched her face. ("He looked at me, Mamma," she was later to say to Francesca, "just like he looked at Cathy on the heath. I practically melted in my chair.") "I'd be delighted. To Bree? And Francesca? Lovely ladies of my acquaintance." He signed with a flourish and large, open strokes of his pen.

"Thank you." Bree tucked the book back into her briefcase.

"Where," Barrie asked, in her vague, demanding way, "are the elevenses?"

There was a knock at the door. Emerald Billingsley opened the door with one hand and held a tray of coffee and tea in the other. A box of tissues sat next to the sugar and creamer.

"Ah," Sir Ciaran said. "Excellent timing, fair maid."

"I'm not a maid, sir," Mrs. Billingsley said politely. "I'm Miss Winston-Beaufort's secretary. I'm just helping my niece out, who is shorthanded today."

"I used 'maid' in the sense of 'fair lady.'" Sir Ciaran rose, relieved her of the tray, and set it on the desk. Then he took her hand and kissed it.

"Well," Mrs. Billingsley said. "That was very nice of you, sir." She bit her lip and made an astonished face at Bree.

"Thank you, Mrs. Billingsley. If you could drop back after Sir Ciaran and Lady Fordham leave, I'd appreciate it. I'd like you to get these contracts back to the office."

"Surely." She left with as much dignity as she had coming in, which was considerable.

"I'll be Mother, shall I?" Barrie drifted to the tray and began to pour the coffee.

"There are just a few other questions I have, before we finish up here." Barrie raised an inquiring eyebrow and set a cup of coffee in front of Bree. "Tully's asked me to look into some of the consequences of Mr. O'Rourke's death."

"That fellow," Sir Ciaran said with distaste. "Tully and Barrie have been friends for years, and we tolerated the man for her sake, but truly." He broke off, took a sip of coffee, and set it down. "Philistine."

"We would have tolerated him for more than that," Barrie said. "My friendship with Tully, that is. May I speak frankly, Miss Beaufort?"

"Sure."

"We were between a rock and a hard place after Russell killed himself."

"Scylla and Charybdis," Ciaran said.

"The theater doesn't have the patrons it used to."

"And we're getting older." Ciaran returned his wife's indignant glance with an apologetic look. "Sorry, my dear."

"And the last thing we wanted was Russell's death. It was disastrous for us. Financially, I mean. The great parts have been drying up. The theater itself is in dreadful shape. The Players was the first offer to come along that would provide a true venue for Ciaran's talents." She lifted the tea ball out of the pot and poured the liquid into her cup with the elegance of a queen. "I understand from some of the investors in the Players that you are looking into the circumstances surrounding Russell's suicide." She placed a thin slice of lemon into the cup and took a delicate sip. "As well as the murder of this unfortunate man from the New York Police Department." She raised her great eyes to Bree's. "Is this true?"

"After a fashion," Bree said cautiously. "I have no official standing, of course."

"Of course. Unofficially, it would be good for you to know we had nothing to do with either problem."

"I see," Bree said. Then: "Did either of you know the detective in charge of the case in New York?"

"Eddie Chin?" Barrie said. She moved suddenly—and Bree never did figure out how she accomplished it—and poor Eddie seemed to sit there, bitten nails, twitchy nerves, and all. She gave a faint, pleased smile at Bree's look of surprise. "Actors collect idiosyncrasies."

"Have you heard from him at all, since you were in Savannah?"

"I don't think so," Barrie said doubtfully.

"A cell phone message, perhaps?"

"We don't have a cell phone," Ciaran said. "Can't stand the things."

Barrie looked rueful. Bree was willing to bet that as soon as the income from the Players kicked in, Ciaran's prejudice would disappear. "We have an answering service, of course," Barrie said. "We could check with them to see if Lieutenant Chin left us a message there."

"If you wouldn't mind leaving me the number, I'll take care of that for you," Bree said.

"My card." Ciaran withdrew his calling card from his vest pocket. It was on heavy stock, with raised press letterhead. It listed their names and a phone number.

Barrie looked at her watch. "The Act Two run-through, darling. Tony will be furious if we're at all behind time."

"Thank you," Bree said. "Thank you both very much. If there's anything I can do for either of you, please let me know. Here, sir, is my card."

Sir Ciaran's eyes sought hers again. ("Honestly, Tonia," Bree said to her sister, much later, "the man's face ought to be illegal.") "Thank you. But I already have one, my dear."

"It's time, darling," Barrie said.

As if on cue, the small clock on the credenza chimed twelve, and the Fordhams swept out the door, leaving it slightly ajar.

Bree sat at the conference table. Fine. Good. Nobody had killed Eddie Chin. Or Russell O'Rourke. They were all as pure as the driven snow.

She walked over to the desk and addressed the empty air. "Mr. O'Rourke?"

Nothing.

She swept her hand over the surface.

"Mr. O'Rourke? I could use a little assistance here."

Still nothing.

Bree's temper stirred. In both her previous cases, her clients had managed to send her tangible clues from beyond their graves, and she could use a few tangible clues right now.

"Beazley? Caldecott? I'm entitled to a conference with my client."

Still nothing.

Frustrated, Bree walked behind the desk with the fuddled idea that a different angle might work. Right now, it looked as if nobody had done it, and she was furious at the thought of having to interview everyone over again. She must have missed something. Some cue. Some lie someone had told her with a perfectly straight face. She thought of that look of puzzlement in Cullen Jameson's eyes; the mockery in VanHoughton's; the confusion in poor old Fig's; the artful innocence in Barrie's; the malicious glee in Harriet's.

And, of course, the erratic behavior of Tully herself.

A curious humming filled the room. Like a top spinning. The air grew very hot. The door pushed wide open, and Miles and Belli walked in, their eyes a fierce red.

Bree whirled.

The humming came from behind her. From the credenza. The doors flew open and the entire cabinet vibrated with a weird, desert wind keening.

The cloisonné jar.

Miles shouldered her aside and caught the jar with a snap of his jaws.

The air cooled.

The humming died away.

Miles dropped the jar on the floor in front of her, where it bounced and lay still.

The heat had softened the wax around the lip. Bree peeled it carefully away and shook out the contents.

Among the bits and pieces that lay there was a coiled wad of fishing line.

<hr />

"Fishing line." Bree settled the jar on the chest that served as a coffee table in the living room of the office at Angelus Street. She'd replaced the line and the dried bits and pieces that had fallen out of the jar, put them back, and resealed it.

"We can see from your expression that you think it's a clue," Ron said.

"I'm sure it's a clue."

"If it is, you have broken the chain of evidence, perhaps," Petru said.

"I hope not." Bree bit her lip and held up her new cell phone. "This has all kinds of extra features. One of them is a video function. So I called in Mrs. Billingsley, and we did a sort of discovery. I resealed the jar and she witnessed my opening it." She lowered the cell phone. "It's better than nothing."

"Of course it is," Ron said. "But what does it have to do with the case?"

"You've thought about how the murder was accomplished, haven't you? There's only one theory that makes any kind of sense. The murderer shot O'Rourke in the neck several hours before the shotgun blast that eventually killed him went off. It was a clever shot, and it could have killed him, but it didn't. It paralyzed him, though. We won't know if the crime was actually planned this way, or whether the murderer was an opportunist who decided that a death later in the day would provide an alibi. The point's moot, anyway, because what happened, happened." Bree sat a moment, marshaling her thoughts. "The murderer rigged up the shotgun and attached fishing line to the trigger. When the crowd of people burst into the room several hours later, the gun went off. In the shock and confusion that followed, the murderer rolled up the fishing line and dropped it into the jar on O'Rourke's desk, knowing that the police would search everyone in the room as a matter of course."

Everyone looked at the jar. The enameled colors glowed sapphire, ruby, and emerald.

"But how do you find out who rolled the fishing line up and hid it? How do we prove who bought it and rigged the rifle?" Ron asked.

"The twelve-gauge is a shotgun, not a rifle," Petru said.

Ron scowled a little. "Whatever. You know what I mean, though. How do we prove it? In a temporal court, I mean."

"You can't, of course. Not with this evidence. Even if we find the fragment of the .22 in the murderer's pocket, it's going to be hard to prove it." Bree looked at the assembled members of her Company in turn. "Have you guys ever wondered why we exist, as a company, I mean? Once in a while I think it's because we have a chance to do justice when it isn't possible, otherwise."

"I don't get the business about the bullet fragment," Ron said.

"He dug it out of the poor man's neck," Lavinia said. "To confuse the time of the murder."

"I don't see that this gets us any further forward, however," Petru said heavily.

"That's because we haven't collected all the data," Bree said firmly. "We've got the fishing line, right?"

"Which helps confirm your postulate," Petru said.

"Exactly. And the suspect list. I've finished with the first round of interviews, and at the moment, it looks like none of them did it." She tapped the lid of the jar with the fishing line in it. "One of the people who burst into that room triggered the blast, rolled up the fishing line that had been attached to the door or whatever, and hid it in that." She pointed to the jar. "We're going to find him. Or her. So we have to start checking alibis. Ron? I need you to find out what flight the Parsalls were on. Did they really get into town when they said they did? Same with Jameson, although since he wasn't in the room when the shot was fired, I've put him at the bottom of the list. Petru? We need a complete financial history for everybody involved: the Parsalls, Jameson, and the Fordhams. And one final thing: I need to see copies of Russell O'Rourke's correspondence for the two months preceding his death."

"And Herr VanHoughton?" Petru asked.

Bree hesitated. "I don't see any possible motive there. He's cold-blooded enough to have done it, but he doesn't seem to have any reason." Petru drew breath, and Bree held up her hand to forestall his objection. "I know. Motive's almost useless as far as temporal indictments go. It's not illegal to hate somebody. It can be illegal to act on that hate, of course. But you need proof of the act. Intent's a loser. Besides," she added, "if Rutger Van-Houghton wanted you dead, he'd just run you over with a tank. Or ruin you financially. It's just not his kind of crime."

"Well, I'm on it," Ron said.

"And I." Petru put his hands on his knees and shoved himself off the couch.

"You're forgettin' that . . ." Lavinia said quietly.

Bree looked at her with some surprise. "That what?"

"You haven't notice the change around here? There's something Dark movin' around, and I don't like it at all. And it only started when you began looking into the demise of this Mr. O'Rourke." She pointed to the painting on the mantel. "I'm talking about *that*."

They looked at the *Rise of the Cormorant*.

The new image in the sky had blackened, and darkened to a curious letter shape. Petru stumped closer and peered up at it. "Oh, dear. This is not good. Not good at all. It appears to me to be the letter peh."

"The letter peh?" Bree frowned in puzzlement.

"From the ancient Hebrew alphabet. It means . . ."

An imperative knock sounded at the front door. It froze them all with surprise. Sasha rose from his seat by the fireplace and growled.

The knock sounded again.

"Nobody comes here, now that we're up and runnin' the Company," Lavinia said. "What is it?"

Bree found herself short of breath—Lavinia hadn't said "who" but "what." "The Pendergasts?" she asked, with a fair semblance of calm.

Lavinia shook her head, wondering.

"One way to find out, I guess." Bree moved quickly across the room to their small hallway.

The knock sounded a third time.

Bree glanced at the angel at the foot of the stairs. She stared up at Bree. Her eyes were green, like Bree's own. She looked angry. She looked scared.

The latch rattled. The door opened.

Ciaran Fordham stepped into the office at Angelus Street.

Nineteen

Justice delayed is justice denied.
—The Honorable Chief Justice Learned Hand

Ciaran held Bree's card in one hand. "Miss Beaufort?" He inclined his head in greeting. "I've come to see how my case is progressing."

Outside, the mist was back. It wrapped around the actor like a shroud. Bree opened her mouth, but no sound at all came out.

"Your case?" Bree said, finally.

"Is this an inconvenient time?" Ciaran asked.

"You can't be here," Bree said. "You can't just walk in here!"

"I can't?" He closed his eyes and swayed a little. "But you gave me your card."

"Well, yes, but . . ."

"May I come in?"

"Of course you can come *in*. It's just . . ." She fought for a word. ". . . unexpected."

He looked at her. She opened the door all the way. He stepped into the hall.

Then he said, "You said you would help me. Please. Help me. I looked back. I want to go home. You have to help me go home."

He drew away from her and just stood there, his face a mask of appeal.

"Go home?" Bree said. None of this made any sense.

"My goodness," Lavinia said. She trotted into the little hall, Sasha at her heels. She peered up at Ciaran Fordham's face. She stared for a long moment. Then she turned and stared at Bree. "This man is dead."

"Dead?" Bree echoed, stupidly. She reached out and clasped his hand. It was light, cold, and dry.

The hand of a corpse.

Bree looked down at her dog. How had he missed this? Shouldn't he have warned her about this?

Lavinia tsked. "Russell O'Rourke didn't ask for you, child. This man did." She stood on her tiptoes and touched his face. "He's been gone a long while. A long while."

"You mean I've been representing the wrong client?" Bree was so astounded, she couldn't move.

"You have, yes." Lavinia shook her head somberly. "My, oh, my. And look here." She bent down and patted the silver-haired angel on the frieze. The angel's eyes were closed and her wings were folded tightly against her body. "He's illegal, too, this poor soul. He's outside our Heaven and Hell."

"He's what?" Bree, like the angel, wanted to close her eyes. If she did, maybe this would go away.

"For Heaven's sake," Ron said, as he came up to them. "You can't just leave the poor fellow here standing on the doorstep. Here." Ron fussed around the actor and led him into the living room, with Bree and Lavinia trailing behind. "Please come in, sir. Have a seat here. No, no, not the couch. There's a broken spring under that one cushion. Sit here in the chair."

Sir Ciaran sat down in the armchair facing the fireplace. He looked up at the *Rise of the Cormorant* and everyone in the room followed his gaze. Bree stiffened. The letter in the sky now glowed as if it were made of banked coals. It looked like a left-facing fishhook, or a question mark with an up-curled tail, except that the smooth curves of the arc were broken into sharp angles.

Ciaran put his hands on his knees and dropped his gaze.

Nobody said anything. Lavinia sat on the couch and pulled her shawl around her shoulders. Sasha crowded close to her, watching Ciaran, his head tilted first one way and then the other.

"I think we could all use some coffee," Ron said.

"I'll get it," Bree offered. She needed some time to think.

"You make terrible coffee. It's worse than Petru's," Ron said. "You'd better let me do it."

Bree, Petru, and Ron went into the kitchen.

"Well," Bree said. "This is a stunner. What's going on? Lavinia said he's an illegal. An illegal what? And why have we been blindsided like this?"

"This is my fault, I think." Petru sat down heavily at his desk. He looked very unhappy. "This is a dybbuk, perhaps. Or a golem. I'm not certain of which. But yes, soulless bodies are outside the jurisdiction of the Celestial Courts. He is therefore an illegal. T'cha!" He bit his lip. "And the peh in front of me all the while. I am stupid, stupid."

271

Bree took a moment to line up her questions in an orderly way. She took a firm grip on her confusion. A trial lawyer that could be knocked off her feet by an un-expected development was no kind of trial lawyer at all. "Okay. What's the peh?"

"It's a letter. No. That is the wrong translation. It is a symbol of transformation, of change. It is a word, when used, which speaks directly to the Godhead and transforms a temporal being into a being less vulnerable to time."

"Less vulnerable to time," Bree repeated. "You mean Ciaran Fordham is an immortal?" The tag "immortal of the stage" had followed Ciaran around most of his life. Except he wasn't alive; he was dead. So Bree was pretty sure the critics had been engaging in hyperbole. Ha. She bit her lip. "Hang on a minute, guys." She took three deep breaths. "Okay. I'm on it. I'm focused. Except I think I'm getting a headache."

"He is not an immortal," Petru said impatiently. "His body is proceeding toward death, but very slowly. It will take hundreds of temporal years for the body to die, per-haps. His soul has already gone beyond him. Somebody used the peh just as Ciaran was passing from this life to the next. His body stayed here. His soul did not." He frowned. "Which is why he must be a dybbuk and not a golem. A dybbuk is animated by a malicious spirit. A golem is a creature of clay animated by such."

"A malicious spirit," Bree said. She was beginning to feel like Archie, with his annoying tendency to echo phrases.

"Yes. This is from the traditions of the Kabbalah, which is not used so often, now. The Kabbalah is one step further along the Path from its predecessors, the Egyptians. The Egyptians of Osiris, Set, Hathor, and Isis, that is. Not Mr. Sadat and his ilk. The dybbuk is a very old creature of the Sphere. Its animating spirit is not so much Dark as it is unenlightened."

Bree peeked out into the living room. Ciaran and Lavinia were talking. Sasha looked from one to the other, his tail wagging anxiously. "Are you saying that whatever makes Ciaran's body function is like a poltergeist?"

Petru's gloomy face lightened. "That is a very good expression for the inexpressible. This poltergeist has no mind or knowledge of its own, you see. It is an animator, merely. Like yeast."

"Yeast," Bree said and pinched herself hard. Pain helped you focus better than anything.

"When we free Sir Ciaran's body to die as it should have died, the spirit will dissolve away."

Bree took a deep breath and let it out slowly. "Are we supposed to do things like that?"

"Not us, personally, no. We are advocates, not judges. We must represent his case to the proper authorities."

"But if he's outside the Celestial legal system, what can we do?" At some level, Bree was aware that she was keeping her mind busy with questions about process. Process was a secure thing in a world that was becoming increasingly insecure. Process was important. She couldn't take on a client for whom there was no possible remedy in law.

But it appeared that she had. She had left her card on the desk at the auction house, five days ago. Of course Ciaran had her card. He'd gotten it then.

"I will have to research this, perhaps." Petru sat down at his desk.

"Good grief," Bree said. "Not now!"

"When should I do it, then? He believes we are his counsel. We must have an answer for him."

"You're right. Of course. Please. Look something up. Anything. Maybe we should call Goldstein."

"Goldstein is a clerk of court," Petru said. "Not a scholar. The professor will be able to help us, if I am at a standstill. But I am rarely at a standstill."

"Sure. Fine. Whatever." Bree wanted to tell him to stop being such a pedant, but she didn't. If he'd been more of a pedant about the strange symbol in the painting, she might have had a little more forewarning. So she said, "Thank you. I appreciate your efforts."

Ron fussed with the coffee grounds and shook his head disapprovingly. "So where does this leave us with the O'Rourke murder? Not to mention Lieutenant Chin's murder? Can you believe it? We're representing the wrong client!" He gasped. "What if the murders and the client aren't related at all? All this work, right down the tubes!"

"Shh," Bree said crossly. "Sir Ciaran might hear you. And Tully hired me to solve the murder of her husband, so we haven't wasted a thing."

"I suppose we could look on this as a totally new case," Ron said.

"Of course it's a new case!"

"Shall I start a file?"

"You can start by not bugging me," Bree snapped. She held her hand up in quick apology. "I'm sorry. I'm feeling foolish. And when I feel foolish, I get crabby. Let's take this one thing at a time. You bring the coffee out, Ron. Petru, for Pete's sake, if you have any ideas about what to do next, come into the living room right away."

Lavinia rose from the couch as Bree came back in. Sir Ciaran sat quietly, his face in repose. Bree recalled seeing him with Barrie in Tully's living room the day before. Then, as now, the sense of absence was strong.

And I was outside.

Bree looked at Sasha.

I met him just now, for the first time.

This was new, too. This direct communication from her dog.

Bree made herself relax. "Can you tell us what brought you to this, Sir Ciaran?"

"He doesn't remember much," Lavinia said. "But his heart went bad on him, oh, maybe a year ago."

"He had a heart attack," Bree said. "I remember reading about it."

"He went toward the Light, like a lamb. And he says something big and cold snatched him up before he could get to the end. Something with a voice like concrete, he says."

Bree recalled the huge, chilling thing in Franklin's office. "What was it?"

Lavinia pulled her woolly sweater a little closer. The fog that swirled outside the windows darkened the room. "I don't know. This poor creature"—she patted Ciaran's knee—"he's stuck at the beginning of his journey home. All this talking and walking around? He's got some kind of knowing that it's going on. But mostly, he jus' waiting."

"For what?" Bree asked, although she was afraid she knew.

Lavinia's voice was filled with pity. "He wants to go back. To go home. To finish the trip to the Light. He asks her all the time, his wife, What happened to me? And she says, I couldn't let you go."

"Yes," Bree said. "Tully told me that Barrie had dabbled in the Kabbalah." She looked at Ciaran with something like awe. "Some dabbling."

Ciaran stirred. "Can you help me? Can you help me go home?"

"I think perhaps we can." Petru stumped solemnly into the room. He had a computer printout in one hand. "The rule of law is quite clear. If I had not been so distracted by my own failure to address the omen of the *Cormorant*, I should have known immediately what to do." He addressed Sir Ciaran. "You are a Displaced Person, sir."

Ciaran sighed, a long, slow exhalation that was like a dank breeze from a tomb.

"We can file the necessary briefs, but it will take some time. Perhaps you will agree to wait? I am sorry for the delay."

"How long?" Ciaran asked. "It's pleasant here in this room, I admit. But I do need to go on."

"Not long." Then Petru added kindly, "We will move as fast as we possibly can. But you cannot, I think, wait here."

"I see." He got up slowly. "You will let me know, as soon as you hear anything?"

"We will, indeed. You may, in point of fact, need to appear with counsel to answer any inquiries into your case. But the resolution should be ke-vite rapid after that."

"I do hope so." The actor got to his feet.

"One moment." Petru reached up and retrieved the cloisonné jar from the mantel. "You will need this, I think."

"Thank you. I cannot, as you perceive, be very far from it." He slipped the jar into his coat pocket. And then, whatever was left of Sir Ciaran Fordham bowed gracefully to them and walked out of the offices on Angelus Street.

"That's the only evidence we have," Bree said to Petru. "The fishing line's in there."

"So is his heart," Petru said dryly. "Dybbuks are created by . . ."

Bree held a hand up. "You know what? I don't think I want to know right now. Maybe later. But I take it that whatever means Barrie used to create the dybbuk involved a sort of mummification."

"Yes."

"It was Barrie that did this to him? His own wife?" Ron set the coffee tray down on the table and put his hands on his hips.

"I think so," Bree said. "And I think that Tully knew about it. As a matter of fact, I'd bet a month's pay on that. Tully was really anxious to get the jar back. And when she did, she made sure that the jar was kept locked up in the office. And you remember how surprised everyone was that the great Sir Ciaran Fordham would sign on to a company like the Shakespeare Players? Antonia thought it was because his heart attack made him feel vulnerable, that the Players would be a safe haven for him. I think it was because Tully and Russell got hold of the cloisonné jar and wouldn't let Ciaran go. Tully said she and Barrie dabbled in the Kabbalah together. Tully would have seen the change in Ciaran's acting right away. And Tully's no fool. You remember the crime scene photos? That jar was right there on the desk where Russell could keep an eye on it."

"That is quite awful," Petru said.

"She loved him too hard," Lavinia said. "Wouldn't let the poor man go."

Ron's lips thinned with disgust. "Well, boss. I'm certainly glad I don't have a partner like Barrie Fordham! The man's in agony! Talk about the tortures of the damned!"

"There's love that's so selfish, it doesn't care," Lavinia said. "You can see that, Ronald. I see it, too."

"Well, if she's our murderer, and Bree catches her, it serves her right." Ron picked up a cup of coffee and set it down again. "I'm so upset I don't even want this coffee. Anybody else? No? Then I'm going to dump this out in the sink. Right along with my good opinion of Barrie, Lady Fordham."

Bree smiled at him. "Except that Barrie's not our killer. The jar was at hand and the killer dumped the fishing line in it because there was nowhere else to put it. I may have had the wrong client all this time, but I have the right case. Barrie didn't kill either one of the victims. But I know who did."

Twenty

> There needs no ghost, my lord, come from the grave to
> tell us this.
>
> —Shakespeare, *Hamlet*

The house on the square blazed with light. Tiny white
garden lights glittered in the trees and hedges. At the
windows, the curtains were drawn back so that the yellow
warmth of the chandeliers spilled into the street. A couple
of kids in black pants and white dress shirts parked the
cars as guest after guest arrived.

Bree wore her red velvet dress. It was tea-length and
swirled just above her ankles. It had a cowl neckline and
no sleeves. The fabric was tissue-thin and the color was
the soft sheen of a sunset. The only jewelry she wore was
a pair of gold Scales of Justice earrings left to her by her
birth mother, Leah. Her silver-gilt hair was swept up and
out of the way on the top of her head.

She'd walked from the town house, and she was late.
If she hadn't had the kind of employees who could work
minor miracles, she would have been later still. But if the
information existed in a public record somewhere, it didn't
take Ron and Petru long to come up with it. The biggest

time waster had come about due to the very quality she valued so much in Petru: his stubborn insistence on understanding and following the rules.

The Beaufort & Company charter, Petru argued, did not allow the angels to work on temporal cases unless the case was related directly to the needs of a client. Russell O'Rourke was apparently grateful to be assigned to Purgatory and not any of the circles of Hell to which an unkind Providence might have assigned him to. ("And so he should be," Ron had sniffed. "How many widows and orphans did the crash of O'Rourke Investment Bank leave in the lurch, anyway?") So what did Ciaran Fordham's plight have to do with the murders? He, Petru, could not in good conscience use his unique talents to produce the data Bree needed by the time of Tully's party.

Bree pointed out that the cloisonné jar would be held in evidence for as long as it took to convict the murderer— and given that the wheels of temporal justice ground exceeding slow—it was in Ciaran's best interests to get the murderer convicted as quickly as possible. And Ciaran *was* their client.

So Ron and Petru had come up the circumstantial evidence in excellent time. And if all went well, Bree would have her murderer, and she could finally wrap up the Case of the Mistaken Client.

The party filled the living room and the dining room and spilled out of the French doors into the garden courtyard at the rear of the house. Waiters circled the crowd with trays of drinks and food. Someone at the piano played show tunes. A few of the young actresses from Haddad's group linked arms and started to sing "There's No Business Like Show Business." Haddad stood out with his black jeans, black T-shirt, and handsome face. He waved at her. Bree nodded back.

Bree caught a glimpse of her mother's bright head in one corner, and Antonia's in another. As usual, Antonia was mobbed with men: older businessmen, young actors, a stockbroker or two, and poor Fig, who stood with his hands stuffed into the pockets of his gray flannel trousers at the edge of the crowd. As Bree watched, Antonia's slim arm emerged from the group and pulled Fig in a little closer.

"You're pretty fond of your sister," Hunter said. "You ought to see your own smile when you look at her."

"There you are. I hoped you'd gotten my message." Bree slipped her hand into the crook of his arm. "And yes, I am fond of Antonia, at that. She'll drive me to the screaming point, and then she'll do something really sweet, like make sure that poor old clueless Fig isn't left out of a good time. But if you tell her that, I'll have to pull your hair out. I can't explain it. It's a girl thing."

"You were right about the rental car," he said abruptly. "We found Eddie's blood and hair in the trunk."

"Thank God."

He narrowed his eyes at her. "I thought this was a lead pipe cinch. That's what you said on the phone—it's a lead pipe cinch."

"I was darn sure of the motive—the financial records Petru unearthed leave no doubt about that. And I was darn sure about the means. But you said it yourself—you can never be certain. Poor Eddie. But that ought to clinch the case, for sure." She nudged him. "Over there."

Hunter scanned the crowd. "Got it."

"You're going to make the arrest?"

"Markham's ready when I am."

"Can you wait two seconds? I want to ask the piano player to do something for me."

He cocked an eyebrow at her. Bree held up two fingers. "Two seconds. I'll meet you there."

Bree made her request, and as the pianist broke into the obnoxiously jaunty theme from *The Producers* Sam Hunter arrested Harriet and Big Buck Parsall for the murder of Edward Chin, formerly a sergeant in the Homicide Division of the New York Police Department.

"You sure know how to break up a party," Aunt Cissy grumbled. "Of all the things, Buck and Harriet doing for Russell O'Rourke."

"They weren't arrested for that murder, Cissy," Francesca said. "Although our Bree said they did that, too. They're going to be convicted of Lieutenant Chin's death."

"I sure hope so." Bree tucked her feet under her. They were all seated at the dining room table, Royal, Francesca, Cissy, Antonia, and Bree herself, eating crab cakes and sweet potato fries from Huey's. The arrest of Harriet and Buck might have gone unnoticed by most of the partygoers, but for the fact that Harriet threw a spectacular fit of hysterics and attacked Tully O'Rourke with a party skewer before Markham could get the handcuffs on her. Tully, with a notable scratch down one cheek, had thrown everyone out. The last Bree had seen of her temporal client was a rueful look and a shrug: *Sorry about that,* the look said, and then, *who knew it'd turn out like this?*

"But you're pretty sure they committed both crimes?" Royal patted his blazer jacket for his absent pipe and sighed.

"Almost certain," Bree said. "But Hunter doesn't think there's enough hard evidence to get them on the first one."

"Why kill anyone in the first place?" Cissy said. "It's just stupid, that kind of thing."

"Buck and Harriet couldn't handle losing all their money," Bree said. "And they blamed Russell O'Rourke for it. They started raising some funds by selling off their shares in the Shakespeare Players over and over again. Just like that silly plot in *The Producers.*"

Cissy looked blank.

"Never mind, Aunt," Antonia said kindly. "I just think it's totally cool my sister solved a murder with a theater clue."

"That isn't exactly true, Tonia, but thanks all the same. Anyway," Bree sighed, "Russell discovered the scam and threatened them with exposure. So Harriet set up the very elaborate murder scheme, and it worked."

"You're fairly sure they can't be convicted of that crime, too?" her father asked.

"The suicide note was torn from a letter Russell sent to Buck accusing him of fraud with the Players' stock. Petru unearthed the original letter. It starts with accusing the Parsalls of selling the shares over and over again, and ends with O'Rourke's apology for losing all the Parsalls' money in the crash. 'I very much regret the collapse of the

O'Rourke Investment Bank, a regret that I will carry to my grave. My apologies to all. Good-bye.' That's where all the language about guilt over the collapse of Russell's own business venture came. He was greedy, Russell was, but Tully was right. He was within his rights to run his company the way he did. And VanHoughton did step in with an offer to put things right. But then O'Rourke died.

"And the Players started up again. And Harriet went right back to her old tricks. She was selling the same ten percent of the company to at least five different prospects that we've turned up so far.

"They got Eddie's phone call, of course, and decided he was too much of a threat to live. They booked an early flight into Savannah, rented a car, and met Eddie at the visitors' center much earlier than the two o'clock time Eddie requested. They shot him, put his body in the trunk, and checked into the Mansion at Forsyth Park. It takes five minutes or less to get from Forsyth Park to here on Factor's Walk, by car. And whatever Buck is, he's got the balls of a buffalo. Sorry, Daddy. Eddie was wrapped in canvas. Buck and Harriet sat in the bar all afternoon, then Buck excused himself for a bit, drove over here, dropped him into my hallway with some fuzzy idea of implicating me in the murder, and scooted on back to the bar at 700 Drayton in the time it'd take some folks to go to the bathroom and back."

"Why you?" Francesca asked anxiously.

"When they called Eddie back to arrange an earlier meeting time, he told them he was about to turn all the evidence over to me and Hunter." Bree shrugged. "It must have seemed like a good idea at the time,. My guess is if they'd laid off the whiskey they might have come up with a better way of disposing of the body—but they didn't have much time. And it's hard to get rid of a corpse."

"Some nerve," Antonia said.

"That's what it took," Bree agreed. "Some nerve. And a half bottle of Jameson's whiskey, They were due to leave here tomorrow, so we had to act fast."

"This is the third time you've had to deal with a body in as many months," Francesca said. "I hope you aren't considering criminal law as a career, Bree, darlin'."

Bree reached down and scratched Sasha's ears. "Not in this life, Mamma."

Epilogue

Ron adjusted Bree's courtroom robes over her shoulders, fixed the collar that rose behind her head, and smoothed the lapels. "Very nice," he said. "Did you notice what Lavinia embroidered on the hem?"

Bree shook out the folds of the heavy red velvet. Tiny, elegantly shaped letters had been added under the gold spheres: *Beaufort & Company.* Lavinia did beautiful work. She could stand here and look at it all night. Especially in preference to pleading this case before the Celestial Court.

Ciaran Fordham stood with them on the seventh floor of the Chatham County Courthouse. He held the cloisonné bowl in one hand.

At least the red velvet robes made her *look* competent. "Are you ready, Sir Ciaran?"

"Are you taking me home?"

"I hope so," she said gently. "We're applying for a Writ of Sanctuary. If the judge grants it . . ." She paused. She wasn't sure what would happen after that. The case precedents Petru found were based on a small, almost forgotten Christian sect that believed all the bits and pieces of a person had to be in place for a correct and proper burial. Barrie and Tully had removed Ciaran's heart and kept it in the cloisonné jar. It wasn't a decorative piece at all, but a canopic jar, made especially for the purpose. Ciaran's spirit was bound to a spirit so old, Petru had been unable to find any written references to it. "There are hieroglyphs, which perhaps allude to its presence. But we truly know not much, dear Bree. All we know is that it is hungry."

The Celestial Courts were ecumenical in their application of the legal code. As long as the petitioner hadn't committed a variant on one of the Seven Deadly Felonies (and especially if the defendant had—and Bree was sure the Being, whatever it was, was guilty of an attempted murder of Ciaran's spirit), all temporal beliefs were worthy of consideration.

So they had a shot. If she could convince the Judicial Presence that Ciaran should be offered sanctuary, he could indeed go home to the Light that called him. If Beazley and Caldecott prevailed, the case would be thrown out of court for lack of jurisdiction.

And Ciaran's terrible half-life would go on.

Ron pushed the door to Superior Court open and stepped aside to let them enter.

Bree had been in Superior Court once before, and she breathed a faint sigh of relief to see that the venue hadn't changed. A long elevator led from the entrance platform to the vast courtroom below. Scenes from the current case were painted on the walls, colorful murals that flickered with movement. Bree paused in front of the one that showed Ciaran in the hands of those who had removed his heart. She hoped the Judicial Presence took a long time looking at that one.

The judge's platform held the scales of justice, made of gold and, for now, evenly balanced.

Bree took a seat on the bench provided for the plaintiff on the right. Ciaran sat down beside her. First Beazley, then Caldecott appeared on the bench at her left.

All rise.

Bree got to her feet again, as did the others. She didn't know the source of the voice. It was everywhere and nowhere.

A soft gold light shone behind the scales. There was no shape to it. It was a presence without form. The Judicial Presence.

Be seated.

And then a soft, glorious voice, stern and beautiful all at once:

"Plaintiff's counsel may present her case."

Bree stepped forward and began her plea for the death of Ciaran Fordham.

"Displaced Persons, indeed," Caldecott sniped when the verdict had been rendered. "Sanctuary offered and received. Phooey!" The four of them rode up the escalator back to the seventh floor. "Crock of baloney. We should have been granted that Motion for Dismissal. This case is *not* part of our jurisdiction."

"Caldecott hates to lose," Beazley said. He smiled at Bree. It wasn't a nice smile. "On the other hand, Caldecott, she has to deliver the Writ of Sanctuary to whatever it is that holds her client's soul. Bad luck to you, Miss Beaufort."

They exited into the seventh floor. Bree and Ciaran turned right. Beazley and Caldecott turned left. When Bree looked back over her shoulder, both lawyers had disappeared.

"I'm to go home?" Ciaran asked. He held the canopic jar in one hand and the Writ of Sanctuary in the other.

"I hope so." Bree shepherded him into the elevator. "It'll be just a little longer."

Ron was waiting for them in the lobby. It was very late at night. It had taken Petru all weekend to track down the case precedents to make the argument that Ciaran's soul had been stolen and his true death desired. The security guard touched his cap in a wry salute as he unlocked the front door and let her out.

"You sure you don't want an escort home, ma'am? Kind of late for the two of you to be out on the streets all by yourself."

Bree ran her hand over Sasha's ears and smiled at Ron. "We'll be fine, Officer. Thank you."

The security guard at the Bay Street office building was new, and wasn't anywhere near as solicitous as the other one had been, merely bored. He unlocked the doors with a yawn and waved Bree and Ciaran toward the elevators with indifference.

Sasha and Ron rode up with them.

They rode to the sixth floor in silence. As the elevator doors opened, Bree was in the middle of recalling a particularly apt objection she'd made to one of Caldecott's snide objections. She was totally unprepared for the shrieking figure that jumped at her.

"You!" Barrie Fordham screamed. She swung out wildly, and her nails raked down Bree's face. "You leave my husband alone!"

"Barrie," Ciaran said. He glanced at her but continued to walk down the hall. Barrie ran after him. Bree dropped her briefcase and touched the blood on her cheek.

"Ciaran! Ciaran! What are you doing?" Barrie clutched at his waist. He walked on. Barrie fell to her knees and scrambled to her feet again.

"Oh, my," Ron said. "We'll have to stop her. He has to get through the door."

Bree ran down the hall. Ciaran reached 616 and stopped, his hand on the door. Barrie grabbed at him again, tugging at his coat. She was a small woman, and frail, but her strength was rooted in utter panic. Ciaran swayed backwards. Bree caught Barrie's wrist and pulled her away from her husband. Barrie turned and beat at Bree's face with her fists. "Let me go! Let me go!"

Ciaran opened the door into the deep, cold black that had greeted Bree once before. He stepped in and closed the door behind him. Barrie screamed, a long anguished shriek of despair.

A great white light flared behind the door.

Then silence.

From the Savannah Daily, Tuesday

FAMED ACTOR DEAD

Family friend and noted stage director Anthony Haddad announced the death of Shakespearean great Sir Ciaran Fordham, due to a sudden heart attack. The body has been cremated, in accordance with the actor's wishes. Barrie, Lady Fordham, is in seclusion.

Bree folded the newspaper carefully and set it on the fireplace mantel, just under the gilded mirror left to her by Uncle Franklin. She tilted her head back slightly. The mottled glass reflected the living room behind her: the worn, comfortable couch; Sasha fast asleep under the coffee table; a glimpse of the foyer where Eddie Chin's body had lain less than a week ago.

Where Bree herself stood, the mirror showed only a column of faint silver light, encasing a tall, slim shadow with a cascade of hair.

Bree closed her eyes and fought off the clutch of fear inside her heart.

"You taking today off, or what?"

"I'm thinking about it."

Antonia slipped an arm around her waist and gave her a quick hug. "Awful about Sir Ciaran, isn't it?"

Bree opened her eyes and stared up at the mirror. For a horrible, heart-stopping moment, Antonia stood there alone, with the couch, the coffee table, the dog, all reflected behind her, as if Bree herself didn't exist.

"That is *so* weird," Antonia said. "Look! If the angle's wrong, you can't see yourself at all! Just me!" She placed both palms under the bottom of the frame and shoved it straight. "There you are!' she said cheerfully. "You're back in the picture!"

Bree stood with her arm tucked into Antonia's, her own silvery blonde hair next to her sister's deep red curls. She reached up and touched the cold glass. "You remember that time I got caught in that undertow at Tybee Beach?"

Antonia frowned. "What in the world made you think of that?"

"I got myself out, didn't I?"

"You would have gotten out faster if you'd thought to yell for help," Antonia said. "But as usual, you figured on doing it yourself."

"But I got myself out," Bree said. She stared defiantly into the mirror. "And I can do it again, if I have to."

"Whatever," Antonia said. "You going to give me a ride downtown or not?"

ALSO FROM
MARY STANTON

ANGEL'S
Advocate

Money's been tight ever since Brianna Winston-Beaufort inherited Savannah's haunted law firm Beaufort & Company—along with its less-than-angelic staff. But she's finally going to tackle a case that pays the bills, representing a spoiled girl who robbed a Girl Scout. But soon enough Bree finds that her client's departed millionaire father needs help, too. Can she help an unsavory father/daughter duo and make a living off of the living?